I0557593

Twisted Reprisals

L. A. BURCH

Books by L.A. Burch

This is a work of fiction. Names, characters, places, and incidents are either the product of the author's imagination or are used fictitiously. Any resemblance to actual persons, living or dead, business establishments, events, or locales is entirely coincidental.

Lyrics From:
"Shot Clock" By Ella Mai
"Girls Need Love Too" By Summer Walker
Kindle Direct Publishing
Cover Design: Michelle D. Josey

All rights reserved. This publication has been copywritten
by the Copyright Law of the United States and Related
Laws Contained in Title 17 of the United States Code. No
part of this publication may be reproduced, transmitted in
any way or by any means, electronic, mechanical, data
mining, photocopying, recording or otherwise, without
the prior written permission of the author.

ISBN: 9798990247246

Dedication

This book is for everyone who keeps me sane. The people who encourage me to push forward, no matter how challenging life gets. My family and friends, people who love me and will forever be by my side. Thank you for all the support. Nothing is as hard as it seems when you have people to lean on through any situation.

Twisted

Reprisals

Prologue

Fear of the unknown.

Doubt of self.

Death was a constant companion which could claim you at any second.

Bravery was the only thing pushing you forward.

Excitement was like a drug flooding your system.

Confidence was built and cultivated to present yourself in the best light.

Adrenaline making your heart pound 120 beats a minute.

Laser sharp focus is a must; one meniscal mistake could lead to a catastrophic result.

But these feelings were nothing new. This was the norm when you strapped yourself inside of a rocket and launched yourself down a bumpy road going upwards of 200 mph. These races weren't for the faint of heart. Ambulances and Coroner vans made weekly stops at The Strip. Competition would pause until the investigation was complete, then it was next two up.

The day had started with an astonishing 50 cars, and a sun broiling everything in its reach. Hour after torturous hour, match after grueling match, had seen a lot of money changing hands, and a lot of cars eliminated from contention. This wasn't Street Outlaws or Dunk Masters. The guys who showed up at The Strip either won, or they might not be able to feed their families. More than once in the past, shots had rung out over accusations of cheating. Fights were pretty much an everyday occurrence.

Now, darkness had taken over. There was no moon to illuminate the night, nor stars shining to guide your way. 50 feet in any direction away from the stadium lights coverage, and the obsidian night would swallow you whole. That's why the 500 or so fans were packed tight towards the front of the stands, eyes focused with rapt attention to see who would win the Championship race.

This was it. No one could have picked a more suitable pair to duke it out for the $100,000 reward. It was anyone's guess why the two men hated each other so much, but their beef spanned farther back than the race track. Some people thought it involved a girl, others thought it was over money. No matter where the animosity originated, when these two raced, the air filled with tension and anticipation.

For as long as anyone could remember, The Golden Boy ruled The Strip. It had only been up and running in the city of Rockwell, North Carolina, for three years. Since its inception, The Golden Boy had won all but two of the sponsored tournaments. If he wasn't already a millionaire, he surely would have been after the purses he'd accumulated over his reign.

Everyone loved him, and when he raced, the crowds screamed his name. But, while the fans celebrated him, his competitors hated him with a passion. None more than The Black Sheep.

Where The Golden Boy was rich and loved, The Black Sheep was poor and reviled. The fans booed when they heard his name. At first, he couldn't understand why. He was the underdog. He never bragged when he won a race. Then the answer came to him when he won his first tournament: He was the only threat to the people's beloved hero.

The burnouts were completed and the two cars were lined up and set to go. The Golden Boy revving the engine of his gold 1800hp Hennessey Venom F5, with its 300 plus top speed, and its $2 Million price tag. The Black Sheep, sitting silently in his $2.3 Million electric 1973hp, aqua and white Lotus Evija. Normally, he would be in some half broken down, fixer upper, but he'd picked up a sponsor for this tournament to even the odds a little. No one could doubt that The Black Sheep was the better driver, but The Golden Boy, with all his money, usually had the better car. Tonight, that wasn't the case.

No more talking. No more posturing. No more predictions. It was finally time to see which one of these juggernauts was the GOAT.

The tree lit up red!

The roar from the crowd almost drowning out the revving engine of the Hennessey. Both drivers tensed as they prepared to launch their futuristic vehicles down the quarter mile track.

The light turned yellow!

The rivals sucked in a breath as their hands clutched the sensitive brakes.

The light turned green!

The Black Sheep, in his Lotus, was faster with his reflexes and coordination by a fraction of a second. This translated to the near silent supercar gaining a half car length lead a fraction of a second after the start. But, the Hennessey Venom, with its twin-turbo V8 wouldn't be defeated that easily. Within the span of a second, The Golden Boy took a full car length lead on his opponent.

For about three seconds, the drivers seesawed back and forth. Both of these cars were whistle quick, so the full race would be over in about eight seconds. Five seconds in, the cars were neck to neck, bumper to bumper, as the crowd surged to its feet to try and see the finish. This was one for the ages. The cameraman, at the finish line with his iPhone, would have a story to tell his kids when he got home. The best two drivers in the area, in two supercars, battling to a photo finish. It made the brutal heat of the all-day event worthwhile. Then…. Disaster.

With a second to go, The Black Sheep heard a clink. The car jerked to the left towards the far wall, and it took all of his skill to hold control of the vehicle. Smoke billowed from the front, driver's side tire. Blinded, he was forced to slam on his brakes or risk crashing the super-expensive car. The Golden Boy rocketed ahead and claimed yet another Championship.

The Hennessey turned around and zoomed back down the track, never once stopping to check on The Black Sheep as he climbed out of the smoking car. He walked back slowly, arriving just in time to witness the tournament sponsor hand over the $100,000 in cash. What happened next was the reason all the hungry drivers hated the bastard and the fans loved him. The Golden Boy threw $10,000 of the prize money into his car, took the bands off the remaining $90,000, and tossed it all into the stands.

The spectators went wild. Some of the silly ones actually tried catching the money as it floated on the air. The serious money grubbers scrambled on the ground for their take. Most of the drivers had left long ago so they wouldn't have to witness this spectacle. But the ones who stayed, felt the humiliation down to their bones. Mumbling and grumbling, one by one, the remaining drivers left.

The Black Sheep didn't go anywhere. He let the chanting crowd add fuel to the hatred running through his body. He vowed, right then and there, one day soon, he was gonna do whatever it took to knock the King of The Strip off his throne. With envy in his heart, and vengeance on his mind, he turned and made his way back to the broken down, borrowed car that he would probably have to spend his last to fix.

Part One

Chapter 1

James smiled as he watched his girlfriend's younger sister handle the infatuated boys with the grace of a seasoned vet. Her beautiful smile held the three youths captive while, at the same time, her words encouraged them to go home. Anyone watching could see two things clearly: 1) Amia was enjoying the attention all attractive women had to put up with. 2) The young guys didn't have a chance in hell of capturing the newly minted 18-year-old.

He tilted his head back, tossing his hair out of the way, and stared at the full moon floating low over the city. The June night had to be about 80 degrees, and the humidity made it feel hotter. James inhaled deeply as he yearned for a cool breeze to come and touch his overheated skin.

As Amia attempted to extract herself from the clutches of her admirers, James turned his head to the left as the blackberry vanilla fragrance announced the arrival of his mesmerizing girlfriend, Alanah Knight. She smiled, revealing perfect white teeth, as she snaked her arms around his neck and leaned in for a quick kiss. He didn't want to take things pass PG since they still had an audience, so after the one kiss, he pulled her to his side so they could both watch Amia work her magic.

"You know, it's your fault she's being held hostage. I still can't believe you bought her that outfit." She really was livid about his birthday present to Amia, but she leaned her head on his shoulder to take the bite out of the reprimand.

They'd already had it out over his gift, so he just smiled and watched as Amia finally convinced the boys to let her go. As she strutted in their direction, the Louboutin's he'd bought her clipped and clopped on the asphalt. Her curvaceous hips swung back and forth in the hot pink Givenchy bodysuit as she clutched her new Chanel bag.

With her short, spiky, blond hair, and easy, carefree smile, it wasn't hard to see why the young boys were so enchanted. At 5-foot 8-inches, her young, supple body filled the bodysuit to the max. As she got closer, he could see the sparkle in her magnetic, dark blue eyes that predicted the full life she had ahead of her.

James peeled his tall, 200-pound body away from Alanah and met Amia with open arms. "Did you have fun, Birthday Girl?"

She wrapped her arms around his neck and gave him a big kiss on the cheek. "Yes, I did! And I want to thank you for going through all the trouble to put this together."

He kissed her forehead and said, "No trouble at all. It was definitely my pleasure." With a teasing smile, he asked, "How many boys did you give your number to?"

Blushing prettily, and trying to hide her face, the Italian and Black beauty said, "None! I don't want any of these little boys!"

Alanah joined in with, "Look at you! Barely 18 years old and already too grown and glamorous for normal boys."

James turned and hooked his arm around Amia's waist as he studied the woman who had stolen his heart at 14 years old. Amia and Alanah were trading insults as only sisters could, but his eyes tracked up and down the delectable shape of Alanah with the intensity of a starving man seeing his first meal.

At 20 years old, Alanah Knight was truly his one and only love. Her tanned skin hinted at her Italian and African heritage. Her teal-colored eyes, and mid-back length, dark blond hair lit a fire in his gut that only her touch could extinguish. At 5-foot 9-inches, her body, with measurements similar to J-Lo's, could make him weak in the knees. Even though her beauty was unmatched in his eyes, it was her spirit and mind that drew him to her like a moth to a flame.

He was so engrossed in the sight of Alanah, Amia had to pull his shoulder-length dreads to get his attention. "Oh, huh? You say something?"

The sisters shared a look and laughed as Amia said, "Just Alanah talking trash about you spoiling me."

James said, "You notice she never says a word when I buy her clothes. I mean, this Ali Karoui minidress she's wearing set me back..."

"Alright, alright, alright," Alanah interrupted, putting her hand over his mouth. "She doesn't need to know all of our business." Alanah loved to wear skimpy, expensive clothes. All three of them knew he would pay any amount of money to watch her parade around in her sexy outfits. Looking around, she said, "Everyone's gone. Let's get Amia home so we can all get some sleep."

Amia sucked her teeth and rolled her eyes as she walked to the passenger door of the car. "Yeah right. Sleep."

Alanah pinched her arm and, with mock sternness, said, "Hey! You're not too old for me to put you over my knee." All James could do was laugh and shake his head as he made his way over to the driver's side of the sports car.

It was 2:00am and James could honestly say he'd just had one of the best days of his life. He'd gone over to the Knight residence around 3:00 the previous afternoon and surprised Amia with her birthday gifts. He knew their family didn't have the money to throw her a big, extravagant party, so secretly he'd put together a plan. After celebrating with her family for a few hours, he'd told her to put on her outfit because he and Alanah were taking her out for her first adult night on the town.

There wasn't a lot to do in their hometown of Concord, North Carolina, so he suggested they spend the day in Charlotte. Amia said she wanted to go to a game room and experience gambling on the fish tables. When they arrived, and Alanah turned her back, he slipped Amia $1,000 and told her to have fun.

Amia had joyously celebrated every penny she won, and shrugged indifferently whenever she loss. By the time he pulled her away from the table, she had tripled the money and deemed the day a huge success. A couple of guys had tried to push up on her as they left, but Amia, like her sister and mother, had been hit on her whole life. She was well equipped to let them down easy, and each of the men walked off with smiles on their faces after the rejections.

When they got to the car this time, James walked to the passenger side of the 2-door car. The sisters looked at him speculatively until he handed the keys to Amia and told her she was driving. She screamed with joy as she snatched the keys to the $300,000 sports car before he could change his mind.

He climbed in the backseat as the sisters excitedly chatted back and forth in the front. He reached between the seats, activated the navigation, and told Amia to follow the directions to their next destination. She knew the car was one he routinely raced, so she initially revved the engine loudly, but took it easy when she pulled off.

The liquid silver, metallic paint on the Nissan GT-R50, and the red Nismo accents, demanded the attention of every passerby they encountered. The 3.8L, V6 engine that came standard, had been swapped out for a V10 beast that made the heart pump anytime you touched the gas. No one but him had ever been behind the wheel, so he knew Amia would appreciate the gift he was giving her.

They arrived at the club and James directed her to park in a reserved spot right at the door. The sisters exited and Amia looked around the empty parking lot in confusion. James climbed out wearing his Louis Vuitton jeans and t-shirt and smiled as he led the two lovely women over to the door.

When they entered the dark area, Amia said, "Uh, I think we're either too early, or too late." As soon as she finished the statement, the lights turned on and all her family and her friends from school yelled, "SURPRISE!" She screamed as she turned to him, wrapped her arms around his neck, and cried tears of joy for the first five minutes of her party. Not a lot of eyes stayed dry during her emotional display of gratitude.

Alanah eventually led her to the bathroom and fixed her makeup. When they returned, the party kicked off and went hard until about 1:00am, when things finally started to wind down.

James had hired a van to take all the gifts Amia received at the party to her house in Concord. Now, all that was left was to drop Amia off and then James and Alanah could spend some quality time together. He had set up a surprise or two for her, also.

At 2:00am on a Friday, there wasn't a lot of traffic on the streets. By the time he reached the backroad that would take them home, he noticed a pair of headlights that seemed to be following them at every turn. He kept his eyes on the rearview mirror as the girls teased each other about their dance moves at the party. He'd only been on the road for about two minutes when the car swung next to him and threateningly swerved close to his door.

The passenger window of the other car came down, and the driver motioned for him to lower his window. By now, the girls were aware of what was going on and began taunting the other driver. James said, "Yo! Chill! We've had a beautiful day. I'm not letting this clown mess it up for us." After they ignored the other driver for about a mile, the guy raised his window, honked his horn belligerently, and roared off into the night.

After five minutes of silence, Alanah, trying to regain the party atmosphere, turned the music on. She turned it to the local Hip-Hop and R&B station and James gritted his teeth when the notes of the song playing filled the car. He wondered what God was punishing him for as Alanah's new favorite song started to play.

Singing along with the artist, both sisters sang, "24 seconds, yeah you better not step. You got 24 seconds; can you beat the shot clock? What you waiting on Lil Daddy, I aint got that much time? You seem anxious, you seem adamant, but you aint press my line." The girls went along singing as Ella Mai put the pressure on every man alive to stop procrastinating and pop the question.

As she did every time the second verse started, Alanah got just a little bit louder. "Five years of dating, tired of being patient. What the fuck you waiting for?" This was her way of telling him to stop playing with her heart and ask her to marry him. They had both spoke of an eternity together, but he didn't see the point in rushing into anything. They were perfect for each other. He didn't need some minister or ceremony to tell him God had blessed their union, but he was very much aware that she did.

After the women's mantra went off, the opening cords to Alisha Keys, *Diary*, came on, and their eyes connected in the darkened interior of the car. Their hands laced together as they sought a physical touch to go along with the invisible bond between them. They were lost in their own memories that accompanied the first song they'd made love to, when Amia yelled from the back seat.

"James! Look out!" He snapped back to reality just in time to slam on the brakes and avoid hitting the car parked across the road. Thank God Amia had been awake and paying attention. A perfect day could have turned into tragedy all because of an asshole who was also a sore loser.

After making sure both ladies were okay, he tore his seatbelt off and jumped out of the car. It registered that his grill was mere feet from the other vehicle, but his anger made him focus on the man arrogantly leaning on the passenger side of his own car.

James stopped about a foot from the slightly older, slightly smaller man, and just stared into his almost black eyes. The man had this mocking smile etched across his face that made James want to knock all his teeth out. The thought actually calmed him down as he realized how close to the edge he actually was.

Getting control of himself, James sent his agitator a mocking smile of his own. As James turned to walk away from the idiot, he saw all the amusement fade from his face. James took two steps before the man demanded, "Race me, you coward! All your precious money can buy you these fancy cars, but it can't buy you courage. Come on chump! Race me!"

James kept walking as he wondered when these games would stop. There was no doubt the other man was the best driver around, but he couldn't afford to spend $300,000 on a real race car. His reputation for BS was so bad, most people wouldn't even let him participate in their paid tournaments. His problem with James was that, in a race the man had been winning, car troubles had led to James being the victor. Now, he pestered him all the time for a rematch.

Getting back in the car, James put his seatbelt back on, preparing to drive off, but Alanah put her hand on his to stop him. Looking at him with sadness in her eyes, she said, "This is never going to stop. On top of that, it will continue to get

14

worse as long as he's under the illusion he's better than you. Baby, just race him again, kick his ass, then he'll leave you alone."

He stared at her for a while, then turned to look at the man still standing in the road. Turning back to Alanah, he nodded and said, "Alright, I'll get with him…"

She was shaking her head. "No, not later. Do it now."

James looked at her like she'd lost her mind. "Are you crazy? Hell no! There's no telling what that psycho will do. I'm not risking the two of you just to settle a petty beef."

She wrapped her hands around his. "That's the thing. I think with us in the car, he won't try anything stupid. If you're in the car by yourself, I think he'll try to kill you for embarrassing him." They argued back and forth for a minute with Amia joining in on her sister's side. Eventually they all fell silent.

Shaking his head, he leaned out his window and said, "Let's go. Meet me at the light." Now that his mind was clear, he should have known the bastard would try something around this area. Less than half a mile away was the light where they did most of their illegal street races. The distance to the next light after that one was exactly the quarter of a mile needed to classify it as a real race.

The other driver peeled rubber in his haste to get to the spot. Probably thought, if he delayed, James would back out of the race. Amia and Alanah were giving him encouragement as he slowly followed the path the other car had already taken.

Before pulling all the way up to the light where the other car waited, James made sure both ladies were secured and quiet. He said, "I have to be able to hear the engine and the tires on the road. I need you both to stay quiet until we pass the other light. Don't move around because any shift can throw the balance off and I'll have to correct, which can be very dangerous at the speeds we'll be traveling." Both girls nodded their understanding, so he pulled up next to the other vehicle and lowered his window again.

The man said, "I don't want to hear any excuses after I beat you. I have my camera on, so any disputes, we'll be able to play it back. Go on green." The man raised his window and prepared his car for launch. James followed suit with his own preparations.

The light changed from green to yellow to red, which signified the 15 second countdown until green again. With one push on his touchscreen, the V10 beast revved up to its full capacity. The foreign motor deceptively sounded like a toy. Its high-pitched whine made car enthusiast from all over the world understand how much money and power was packed under the hood. The uninformed would be oblivious to the monster they would have to contend with. The GT-R50 outwardly appeared street legal, just as long as the police didn't take too close a look under the hood.

His internal countdown reached three and his mind locked in. At two, all the muscles in his body tensed. At one, his whole being focused in on the unlit green light. When the faintest illumination flickered, his brain fired, his hand released the brake, and the car shot forward like a rocket. The extra 200 plus pounds of female flesh didn't even register as the torque glued them to their seats. A quick glance told him he was already three car lengths ahead of his adversary.

During the acceleration process, extra weight could make a big difference. In a normal car, 200 pounds could add seconds to a timed run. In racing, you normally tried to get your car as light as possible. But, with enough power and torque, you could overcome pretty much anything. Although, having too much of either came with problems of its own.

In the Silver Bullet he was driving now, the pressure from the torque could force an untrained man to slam on the brakes to stop the feeling of suffocation. As both ladies had been in cars with him on the practice tracks, they knew what to expect. So, he kept his foot on the gas and smoked his competition.

It really wasn't even a fair race. His Nissan was a six second street car, while his opponents Mustang Shelby GT was an eight second track car at best. With over two seconds of play, there really wasn't a lot of skill involved. All James had to do was press the gas and hold the car straight to win the race. At most tracks, they wouldn't have even allowed the race because it was so one sided.

When the speedometer hit 180 mph, James eased up because there was no way the man could catch him. He blasted through the finish line and both Amia and Alanah screamed in victory. He had just slowed the car down to about 90 mph when he felt the purposeful push on his driver's side rear panel.

James had been 15-years-old when he started racing, and the first thing his dad taught him was defensive driving. If he had thought for one moment his opponent would do this, he wouldn't have given him the chance to. James knew the man was a sore loser, but never in a million years would he have thought he'd go this far.

Immediately, the car jerked to the left. Now, the screams turned to shouts of terror instead of expressions of joy. The second the tires started to skid, James knew it was over. The first flip was high enough that his side didn't make impact with the ground. Everything slowed down and he could see things so clearly. Arms and heads were tossed and jerked around the interior of the car. Then, his side finally made contact with the ground, and nothingness descended.

He came to for a few seconds, hanging upside down and hearing the sounds of alarms and OnStar telling him that help was on the way. All the glass was busted and he could smell the heat pooling around the vehicle. Through all of that, the only thing he could really comprehend was that the taillights belonging to the Mustang never glowed to show the driver even tried to slow down. He just kept going down the road, trying his best to get away from the destruction he'd caused. James thought he heard approaching sirens, but couldn't be sure, as darkness once again crept up and swallowed him whole.

· ·

The first thing James became aware of was the pain. His body ached in places he didn't even know could ache. The pain left him gasping for breath, but it also reassured him he was alive.

"That's it, Sir. Take deep breaths and open your eyes if you can." The voice was calm and smooth and seemed to cast a spell over him. Almost immediately after the words registered, his breathing evened out and his eyes peeled open. The paramedic leaning over him said, "Good, good. That's it. Just focus on me."

A disarrayed James stared up into bright blue eyes as the man calmed and comforted him. Once he was calm, he was able to start thinking clearly. The next thing that registered was the hard ground under his back. He wasn't even aware of trying to get up until the man placed a hand on his chest and eased him back down. "Easy there, buddy. Try not to move around. You might have some internal bleeding that your movements could make worse."

Laying back down, the realization of what really happened hit him all at once. The sounds of the emergency vehicles and personnel moving about, along with the strobing red and blue lights, confirmed what his brain was already telling him. His head whipped from side to side as his eyes darted about trying to catch sight of Alanah and Amia.

"Sir! You have to stay still! You're okay buddy. You've just been involved in a bad car accident." The paramedic was trying his hardest to keep him calm, but James was heading towards a full-blown panic attack.

"Where's Alanah and Amia?" he asked, clutching the man's arm. "They were in the car with me! Where are they?"

James was once again trying to sit up, and the man was struggling, trying in vain to keep him on the ground.

In the process of looking around the scene, James suddenly went still when he saw the white sheet draped over something in the middle of the road. "No," he whispered to himself. "NO!" he roared as he dislodged the man trying to hold him down.

"Help! Somebody, help!" screamed the paramedic.

James scrambled to his feet and took off in the direction of the sheet-draped figure. "Alanah! Alanah!" he screamed as he pushed past the officers and medical personnel attempting to stop him.

"Sir, you need to step back! This is an active crime scene!" yelled one of the officers. James tried to dodge his arms as more people formed a barrier between him and his objective. Figuring avoidance wasn't working too well, he launched his stout body at the obstacle, knocking people out of the way who didn't move fast enough.

Once he broke through, and he had a clear view of the area, he again froze in horror. There wasn't just one sheet-draped form, there were two. "Oh God! No! No!" he yelled as tears cascaded down his face and stole his vision. He persisted in stumbling towards their direction, until one of the police officers tackled him to the ground.

"Mr. Jordan! Stop! We don't want to hurt you!" He could feel the officers trying to drag his hands behind his back, but James had to see what was under the sheets. He continued to use his knees and elbows to power his body over to the forms that were now only feet away.

He carried on his screaming. "Alanah! Please God! Don't do this! Alanah! Amia!" The police were now doing some real damage. One of them was trying to get him in a chokehold. Another one was beating at his legs with a baton. Distantly, he could feel the pain, but he had to see what was under the sheets, even though he was sure what he would encounter.

With the last of his strength, he moved the pile of men the last few inches he needed for his hands to reach the two sheets blocking his view. Once his fingers curled into them, he tightened his grip and finally allowed the police to pull his arms behind his back.

They were trying to pull the sheets out of his grip, but his muscles petrified with the visions on either side of his face. First, he turned to the left, and all the blood drained from his head. Amia, in her bright, pink bodysuit, lay with the stillness of death, eyes staring straight up to heaven. Whatever had killed her, he couldn't tell because her face didn't have a mark on it.

"Amia! I'm so sorry. Wake up sweetie. Please! Amia! Get up!" He knew she was dead, but deep down, he was praying that all this was a nightmare he'd soon wake from. He squeezed his eyes closed, and kept them that way as he slowly turned his head to the right.

He started pleading before he even opened his eyes. "Alanah, sweetheart, I need you to be okay. You know I can't do this without you. Please God! Don't take her away from me." But when he opened his eyes, he was greeted with the dead eyes of Alanah staring right back at him. Unlike with Amia, he could clearly see Alanah's neck was twisted in an unnatural way.

Blinking deeply, he continued to talk to his best friend in the world. "I love you, Alanah. Please don't leave me. I need you. You want to get married? Fine, we'll get married. Just don't leave me." The officers jerked him to his feet, but he kept his gaze on the two young women. Finally, someone came with two new sheets and recovered the bodies of the two young ladies he loved with his whole heart.

One of the officers leading him said, "They didn't leave you, you piece of shit. You sent them away when you decided to race with them in the car."

James cocked his head and delivered a brutal head butt right to the officer's face. The beating he received in response was one he deserved for more than one reason. The cop was right: No matter what caused the wreck, Alanah and Amia should never have been in the car with him.

With that thought running through his mind, he didn't even attempt to dodge the baton coming right at his head. Instead, he welcomed the pain as his punishment, and embraced the darkness that followed the massive blow.

Chapter 2

When James regained consciousness, the pain he was feeling was so tremendous, tears instantly rained down his face. But it wasn't physical pain. It was pain born from a deep despair he was certain he would feel forever. He knew he would never see the inviting, radiant faces of Alanah and Amia ever again. He would never be greeted by one of their joyful smiles or one of their playful taunts. The sad part was, he deserved the depression that was eating him up on the inside.

As far as physical pain, his boxers and smock clad body wasn't feeling too much of anything. Whatever drug the hospital was pumping into his veins, it was working like a charm. About three years ago, he'd stupidly taken a pill at a party that he hadn't known the origins of. It had put him in a state where his body went numb and a floating sensation had overtaken his mind. Whatever he was on now gave him the numb feeling, but left his mind clear. For what he was going through, he thought it was more a curse than blessing.

With his eyes still closed, he mourned the two lives cut short by his own stupidity. Something had been telling him not to go through with the race. Seeing the excitement pumping through the bodies of the two women had led him to making the worst decision of his life. He had not wanted to let them down, but he ended up doing more damage than some petty disappointment. He just wondered why he was still alive. He couldn't see the purpose in that outcome.

He would honestly give his life to bring back either girl. The memory of the first time he'd met them drifted into his mind. The memory created mixed feelings as a smile crossed his face, but his sorrow intensified.

James had not gone to the same middle school as Alanah. So, when he saw her walking the hallways of Northwest Cabarrus High School, his jaw had hit the floor. She was actually in the process of being escorted to the Principal's office because her skirt was too short.

His 14-year-old hormones had taken over his system and he'd pretty much stalked her for the next week. Too shy to approach what he considered the most glamorous girl alive, he was content with glimpses of her in between classes. Sometimes he'd even get brave and follow her so he could smell her intoxicating perfume on the air.

One of his friends had talked him into going to a Varsity girls basketball game and he'd been pleasantly surprised when she entered and went through warmups with the team. Knowing she was a freshman, it shocked him to learn she was the starting point guard.

He got a seat as close to their bench as he could and cheered and rooted for every amazing play she made. James had yelled to his friend, "Now that's wifey material right there. The girl Alanah is a beast!" He noticed the young girl's shocked expression sitting below him, but he didn't think anything of it at the time.

Alanah ended up with 32 points, 8 assists, and 5 rebounds. The home town Trojans wiped the floor with the visiting Rowan County school by a score of 75 to 32. James was so busy celebrating the win, he didn't notice the two girls approaching him until the younger one yelled, "That's him! He's the one who said you were wifey material and a beast!"

The whole area had fallen silent as Alanah walked up in his face. She was still sweaty, still in her uniform and sneakers, but his heart accelerated just from being so close to her. He wanted to run away so bad, but he would become the laughing stock of the school. So instead, he put forth a confidence that was as thin as the layer of nervous sweat breaking out all over his body.

"What else can I say?" he asked on a shrug. "You're absolutely gorgeous, you always smell amazing, you wear the best clothes, and you're the best baller I've ever seen. Sounds like a wifey and a beast to me." He smiled and tried to keep his cool, even though he was quaking on the inside.

Alanah stepped even closer and said, "I've been sweating hard for the last two hours. Do I still smell good to you?" This question brought a few chuckles from the gathered crowd. But, when she moved her dark blond ponytail to the side and extended her neck, he wasn't gonna pass up the opportunity she was offering.

He stepped up so that their bodies brushed as he bent his head and inhaled deeply the blackberry vanilla scent that had been driving him crazy since the first day of school. In her ear, he whispered, "You smell absolutely delicious. Blackberry vanilla is now my favorite fragrance in the whole world."

He could tell his words affected her as she jerked back with a surprised expression. She asked, "Do you have a pen?" He was handed one by his friend and he handed it to her, trying not to get his hopes up. She grabbed his hand and wrote her number down, saying, "Call me tonight. I'll stay up and wait for your call." She had sent him one last smile, grabbed her sister's hand, and hurried out the door to a waiting car.

After that night, they'd become inseparable. A lot of people had doubted their young love, but it blossomed and morphed into the real deal. Laying in the hospital bed now, he moaned in misery at the loss of his soulmate. He hadn't known anyone was in the room with him until his mother whispered, "James?"

His eyes snapped open and focused on his mother's delightful face as she looked down at him with understanding. "Mom," he said, softly. Just like mothers all over the world, she knew exactly what her son needed.

Brianna Jordan's face crumpled as she climbed onto the bed and wrapper her small, compact body around his. Her long, jet-black hair created a shield around them as she planted kiss after kiss all over his face. Her tears mixed with his as they held each other in mourning.

She kept repeating, "Let it out, baby. We're gonna get pass this. It's gonna be okay." His mother had never lied to him before, but he didn't see how anything would ever be okay. Eventually, they stopped crying and he just stared into the dark chocolate, soulful eyes of his mother that she'd passed onto her only child.

Pulling her curtain of hair out of the way, Brianna revealed her high cheekbones, full, pink lips, and slightly slanted eyes. The eyes, hair, and bronze complexion told the world of her Asian ancestry. But her overall look came from her South African father.

His 41-year-old, soft spoken, intelligent mother said, "We tried to get them to wait for you, but their family wasn't trying to hear it. I'm sorry, but they had the funeral yesterday."

He jerked back in confusion. "Yesterday? What's today?"

Sadly, she said, "It's June 18ᵗʰ. You've been out of it for eight days. Amanda tried to convince Alex to hold off until Monday, but he's not in the right state of mind to accommodate anyone." Amanda and Alex Knight were the parents of Alanah and Amia.

"Eight days?" he murmured. "After the crash, I felt fine. I mean, there was some pain, but how did I wake up and then end up unconscious for eight days?"

"Um, you don't remember the fight with the police?" He scrunched his face in thought. He remembered trying to get to the bodies of Alanah and Amia, but nothing after that. She frowned and said, "We were told you attacked a bunch of police and paramedics. They said, during the fight, one of the officers hit you with a baton. Corey is trying to get the officer's body cam footage. In the meantime, they have an officer posted outside the room."

He opened his mouth to ask why, but then it registered what she'd said earlier. "Wait a minute! They had the

27

funeral? You mean, I won't even get to say goodbye?" The tears started falling again and he turned away to signify his need for privacy. Brianna patted his chest and stood up, understanding that this pain was too raw to share.

"Your father is down in the cafeteria. I'll give you some time alone while I go get him." She hesitated for a few seconds, and then left him alone.

He cried for a couple more minutes, then the anger started to take over. He couldn't believe that bastard Alex had done this to him. To bury the love of his life and not give him a chance to say bye! The ungrateful piece of shit. And to think, all his family had done for theirs.

It had been another sign from fate that, when he met Alanah, her dad had been a mechanic at his father's body shop. In fact, he'd been the very first worker his dad had hired. James had been ten years old when the shop opened, but he never paid a visit until racing had led to a fascination with cars. In later years, when his dad found out Alex was Alanah's father, he'd hired Alex's son, AJ, and promoted Alex to manager.

Samuel, James' father, had saw the Knights as family. The love between James and Alanah had been so deep and real, it had turned the two families into one. For Alex to do something like this, in the eyes of James, was unforgivable. He understood the man was hurting, but Alex had to know he was hurting, too.

The door opened again, and James expected his father to come barreling in. Instead, it was a young, dark skinned nurse whose eyes lit up when she saw him looking at her.

"Well hello there, Mr. Jordan! It's so nice to see you awake." She hustled over to him with a cheery smile on her pretty face, as she did her best to ignore the tears on his. "Are you hurting anywhere physically?"

He shook his head no, but the wording of the question let him know she knew what had happened with him. She checked some things and asked a few more questions, then said, "Let me alert your doctor that you're up and he'll be right in, okay?" He nodded as she patted his hand and bustled back out the door.

Within minutes, an older white guy with thick grey hair came in and started dictating. "How are you today, Mr. Jordan? I'm glad you're back in the world of the living. You gave everyone quite the scare. Nothing too serious. You actually came out of the wreck relatively unscathed, just a minor concussion. It was the baton to the head that put you out of commission.

"Two concussions that close together, had all of us worried. The baton hits to your legs and back didn't cause too much damage. We'll keep you for a few more days to evaluate your progress, then we'll see about cutting you loose. Glad to have you back. Hit the button for the nurse if you start feeling any pain. I'll be back through after a while." Then he turned on his heels and was out the door.

James stared at the door with open-mouth astonishment. The doctor had never even given him time to say anything. He'd talked while checking the machines and then peeled out. On a normal day, the doctor's actions would have been hilarious to James. Today, all he could do was shake his head in disbelief.

Still getting over the shock of the doctor's visit, he got another shock when he heard his father yelling in the hallway.

"I already told you, you're not talking to my son! He hasn't been awake for ten minutes! How the hell did you even find out he was up? I bet it was that little nurse running around here!" A muffled voice tried to reason with him, but he wasn't in the mood to be reasonable. "I said NO!" he screamed. "I don't give a rat's ass about your investigation!"

The next voice he heard was his mother's. "Sammy! Calm down! Just let him ask his questions and he can be on his way." They all went quiet for a minute, but he was staring at the door when the three people finally entered the room.

His mother entered first in her tan colored jeans, orange t-shirt, and white AirMax tennis shoes. At some point since leaving the room, she'd braided her waist-length hair, so the worried expression was clearly visible on her face. She came right over to the bed and parked her 5-foot 7-inch body on the edge. With arms crossed over her chest, she looked the part of a scared mama bear willing to do anything to protect her cub.

Next, his father, Samuel Jordan Jr., stepped in, but he paused at the door to take in the sight of his son. Sammy was 6-foot 3-inches, 220-pounds of ripped muscle. His coffee-black skin tone, and deeply packed waves in his low-cut hair, caused women to stare at him wherever he went. Most of the time, when father and son went out together, women thought he was his older brother instead of his dad. It didn't help that he dressed like a far younger man than he was.

Today, to go with the scowl on his face, he had on an all-black, Versace sweat suit, a pair of Balenciaga boots, and Gucci shades covering his eyes. He finished off the expensive, but thuggish, look with a Patek Philippe watch worth about $400,000. No one seeing him would guess he was 41 years old, but they would believe he was worth north of $150 Million.

He stepped to the side and a man that James had never seen before walked into the room. He had his 5-foot 8-inch, slim body conservatively covered with a pair of khakis and a white button up. His light-brown skin and eyes, along with his buzzcut, made him look serious and solemn. Then he smiled and you could almost forget he was a cop, which he announced to the world with the badge clipped to his belt.

Marching right up to the bed, with his arm extended, he said in a melodic tenor, "Hi, Mr. Jordan. It's a pleasure to finally meet you. My name is Detective Maxwell Hall and, if it's okay with you, I'd like to ask you some questions about the deaths of Alanah and Amia Knight." James shook the detective's hand, but glanced over his shoulder at his father, who was shaking his head and making the classic signal to be quiet.

After the shake, Det. Hall said, "Since I'll be asking questions about an on-going case, I have to read you your rights before we proceed. Is that alright?" James nodded and Det. Hall pulled out a card, read him his rights, then gave James the card and a pen to sign it. After he signed, the smile faded away and the detective started his interrogation.

"Our Crash Scene Investigator finished her analysis two days ago and she reported some very interesting things.

31

Things that could mean big trouble for you if you decide not to cooperate with this investigation."

"Hey man! I done told you…"

"Dad!" James yelled, putting his hand up to stop his dad's advance. "Hold on a minute." Turning to the detective, he asked, "What do you mean by big trouble?"

Detective Hall walked around the hospital bed so Sammy was no longer at his back. Only after a brief stare down with Sammy did he focus back on James. "Let me fill you in on the report before we get into that."

Glancing at his parents, the detective took a deep breath before going on. "First off, the report on the car came back as being not street legal. Pretty much, you were driving around a track only car on the street. Also, by measurements and markings on the road, the investigator concluded you were going somewhere around 100mph when you started to flip."

"Oh my God!" his mother exclaimed, dropping her face in her hands. His father hurried over and wrapped her in his arms. While doing so, he shot James a look filled with anger and disappointment.

"Now, everyone present," the detective continued, "knows this isn't your first brush with the law. It doesn't look good that you have a record for street racing."

"He was 17-years-old for God's sake!" his dad exploded.

The detective nodded and said, "I understand, but it means everyone involved will view this as a street race that resulted in a crash. I'm sure all of you are familiar with the Felony Murder rule."

"Man, what in the hell you talking about murder? This was an accident. Nothing more." Sammy still clung to his wife of 22 years, but he looked ready to jump over the bed and strangle the cop.

"Well, if it's proven that this was an illegal street race, it could mean murder charges for all involved. Which leads up to the other piece of information passed on in the report. I won't lie and say I understand it all, but the CSI has this computer that can create a reenactment of a crash based on crash scene information, and a 3-D scan of the car."

The man pulled out his phone, tapped the screen a few times, then turned the phone so it was facing James. Sammy and Brianna also jumped up so they could see what the officer had.

The first picture showed his crunched up and totally destroyed GT-R50 from the front. The next few pictures showed the damaged car from several different angles. The next one showed a view of the driver's side rear panel. There was clearly a well-defined dent that hadn't come from a flat surface, like the ground. The last picture showed a close up of the area with a ruler marking the dent. You could also clearly see a smudge of something black.

The officer turned the phone back around and started jabbing at the screen once again. "Now, I'm gonna show you a simulation." He turned the phone so they could all see it, then hit play on the screen.

The simulator had Atari level graphic at best, but it clearly showed his silver car speeding down the road from an overhead view. All of a sudden, the car seemed to make a left turn towards nowhere and flip a dozen or more times. A reading on the side of the screen said the car flipped 14 times at a speed of 102mph.

You could hear a pen drop in the room as the detective pulled the phone back and started typing. "Alright, that was the reenactment when you take out the dent and black mark on the panel." Turning the phone back around, he said, "This is what the simulator came up with when we put all the data in."

It started out the same way as the first one, his silver GT-R50 speeding down the road. Then it changed. A black car slowly gained on him and then performed a perfect PIT maneuver to turn his car sideways. James watched as the black car faded from the video and his own car flipped over and over again. The reading on the screen changed slightly this time around. It now read 12 flips at a speed of 99mph.

James wasn't even aware he was crying until he heard his mother's soft, "Oh baby," then she wrapped his head in her chest. While they held each other, his dad asked, "So, what does all this mean?"

"It means that, when we load all the data into the program, it is 70% sure that the second video is how this crash went down. It also means that, whoever was driving the second car is gonna get away with murder if James here doesn't tell us who it was."

"I'm not a lawyer," said Sammy, "but I know enough to know, you can't step into court with a 70% probability on a simulator that no one knows a thing about."

"But we're not in court yet," answered the detective. "With his past record, and the fact that he had an illegal racing car on the road travelling 100mph, I definitely have enough to charge him. Only out of respect and compassion for his loss am I even allowing him to be here instead of sitting in jail charged with double murder. Now, I came here to get his version of events and offer him a chance to help himself."

"You mean incriminate himself," his mother said, sitting up.

Shaking his head, Det. Hall said, "I'm just trying to help..."

"NO!" interrupted Brianna. "What you're trying to do is convince my son to help your case. You see, all these videos and pictures mean nothing. That dent and black mark could have happened weeks ago. Maybe in a parking lot somewhere and James never even noticed it.

"Now, you show up seconds after my son regains consciousness, and offer him a perfect story to ease his pain and guilt. 'The other person is responsible' theory sounds good on the surface. Except, it means James would have to admit he was racing someone. Which in turn would make him guilty of Felony murder."

Det. Hall said, "Brianna, I'm just offering your son..."

"What?" she interrupted again. "A life sentence? An opportunity to be another notch under your belt? You get the hell out of here and you communicate through his lawyer from now on!"

"Mrs. Jordan…"

"You heard what my wife said," his father growled ominously. "Get your ass out of here while you still have the option of walking." His dad reached out and moved his mom behind him as he gestured for the cop to leave.

Det. Hall turned to James and said, "I understand your parents' need to protect you, but really, they're making this worse for you. You're still looking at four charges of assault on an officer, and three additional charges of assault on a first responder. So far, all I've done is place an officer at your door. If you want to play hardball, I can always have you placed in the hospital wing of the county jail."

"HA!" barked his dad. "You put him there and he'll be out on bond within the hour. Don't forget who you're talking to."

The detective looked like he was about to start arguing with his dad once again. To stop the exchange, James said, "I'm sorry I can't be more helpful to you, but there wasn't another car because it wasn't a race. As far as the car being illegal, ask your technicians to take a closer look at the engine. I had it specially built to have two settings, one of which is street legal as long as I have street tires on the car. When they check them, they'll see that the tires are street legal.

"In regards to what happened after the wreck, I remember trying to get to Alanah and Amia, but I don't remember a fight or anything like that. It's like I have flashes of scenes in my mind, but nothing like an assault. If I hurt someone while I was out of my mind, I am truly sorry. But, like I said, I can't remember anything right now."

The detective was looking at him speculatively when his dad said, "Alright man, you done came up in here with your stupid ass questions. The boy answered you, even though he didn't have to say anything at all. Now, I asked you to leave once already. If I have to ask you again…"

"What you gonna do, Big Sammy? We're not in high school anymore. I'm a cop now. You keep throwing these threats around, you're gonna find yourself in a jail cell." The detective tried swelling up to look more intimidating, but he still looked pitiful next to his muscular dad.

Sammy snatched his shades off and said, "Boy! I will bust your head to the…"

"Hey! Hey! Hey!" yelled the doctor, storming back into the room. "What the hell is going on in here?" Looking around, he said, "I need to examine my patient. All of you need to leave, now!" When nobody moved, he yelled, "NOW, DAMMIT!"

His mother turned back to him and kissed his cheek before saying, "Your jewelry, wallet, and money are in the drawer right here," she explained, pointing to the side table. "We had to get your replacement phone from your house because the other one was destroyed in the crash. Me and your father have been here since they brought you in. Now

37

that you're awake, we'll go home and get some rest. We'll be back tomorrow. Love you, Sweetie."

Being dragged to the door by his wife, Sammy said, "Love you boy. I'll see you tomorrow." He was still staring daggers at the cop until Brianna tugged him out the door.

"That means you too, detective," the doctor demanded.

Detective Hall turned back at the door and said, "James, I'm truly sorry for your loss, but you have to be a man and accept responsibility for your actions. Those two young ladies you care so much about deserve justice." With that said, he gave a little wave, and walked out of the room.

The doctor took the next 20 minutes doing his examination. This one was way more thorough than the last and it left James exhausted. When the doctor left, he just laid there staring at the ceiling, replaying memories of Alanah and Amia in his mind. He smiled some, he even barked out a few laughs at some of their past antics. But, when he drifted off to sleep, his face and ears were wet from a waterfall of guilty tears.

Chapter 3

The sun was shining bright in the Carolina blue sky, making everyone who felt it's rays smile. It was almost 2:00pm and the temperature was dangerously close to 100 degrees. But the birds were still chirping, and people were out in droves enjoying the southern summer heat.

Slamming the door of his white Range Rover Sport, Samuel Jordan Jr. didn't give a damn about the weather. All he wanted to do was get away from Northeast Medical Center before he was the one in cuffs for committing murder. Detective Maxwell Hall was a year younger than his own 41 years of age. And the little bastard was still holding a grudge over decades old high school antics. One thing was for sure, if Sammy concluded the man was coming at his son because of their old beef, cop or not, old Max would get more than some sweaty drawers in his mouth this time around.

He started the Range Rover and glanced over at his wife of 22 years. A ray of sunshine penetrated the windshield making her bronze skin and long, jet-black hair glow. His breath caught a little like it did every time he looked at his better half. Some of his anger receded because he knew it upset her to see him so mad. This is what Sammy had wished for James and Alanah. When you are so deeply connected to your spouse, both of your emotions merge. That's when you know you had something real.

Smiling a little, he put the SUV in gear and drove them out the maze the hospital called a parking lot. On a whim, he decided to take the route that would take them pass the body shop he'd had built ten years ago. Alanah's father, Alex, was now the manager, so Sammy really just dropped in from time to time to help out. Brianna, as the book keeper, still had to be on-site a few times a week. Neither one of them had been since the accident involving James, so a trip to see how things were going was in order.

Even though neither of them had spoken a word since leaving their son's room, through their connection, Sammy could tell something was on his wife's mind. Before she worried herself into a migraine, he said, "Since when can't you talk to me? Spit it out, Brianna."

Steadfastly keeping her gaze towards the road, she asked, "Do you believe him?"

"Who? Max? Hell no, I don't believe him! Those simulations look like he did them on a Gameboy."

Shaking her head, she said, "Not Max, Sammy." After a pause, she said, "I'm talking about James."

Once again, they were thinking along the same path. Truth be told, that had been the source of Sammy's anger the whole time. That's why he'd told his son to stay quiet when he entered with the detective. After his trip out to the crash site, it had only taken him seconds to conclude what had happened.

Sammy was by no means an expert, but as a teenager, he'd enjoyed a street race or two. At 16-years-old, he thought it was romantic to load his girlfriend Brianna into a car, and race his friends on back roads. During the weekends, they would enjoy the weather and camaraderie of three other young couples, while indulging in some friendly races.

All of that came to a stop after one of the girlfriends cheated and the boys had mercilessly teased the kid who loss his girl. A fist fight erupted, but it was short lived and everyone thought it was over.

The next weekend, the two boys had decided to race for a little cash. The kid with his girlfriend in the car with him had been in the lead. But, when it became apparent the lone boy was about to lose, he bumped the rear panel on the passenger side of the lead car. Being a relatively inexperienced driver, the kid overcorrected, causing the car to flip nine times. Both occupants died on the scene. At only 16-years-old, the boy who caused the wreck received two consecutive life sentences for murdering the two teens.

When Sammy had cruised the road at his son's crash scene, the marks on the road had been nearly identical to the ones from back then. Knowing his son was an excellent driver, he didn't believe for a minute he'd just lost control for no reason, no matter how fast he was going. No. Someone had performed a PIT maneuver on him during an illegal street race.

Driving down the road now, he reached over and took his wife's hand. "At this point babe, it doesn't matter what we believe because it doesn't matter what he did. Our job is just to make sure he doesn't go to prison. We both know how this ends. If he is convicted for the deaths of Alanah and Amia, he'll spend the rest of his life in prison. This isn't a time to try and teach him any lessons. We can't allow this to mess up his life more than it already has."

Finally looking over at Sammy, Brianna said, "Yeah, I got that. But equally important is our son's mental health. I

41

mean, if he really just lost control of the car, he would feel bad, but he understands mistakes happen. On the other hand, if he was racing with them in the car, he has to be devastated for making that decision."

Sammy felt his wife's pain because it was the same pain he was feeling. He was about to fill her in on his thoughts when his body shop came into view. Confusion erased the thoughts right out of his head. "What the hell?" he whispered, turning into the lot.

Sammy's Body Shop had been open for the past ten years. One of the reasons it was so successful was, the 8-Bay garage was open 24 hours a day, seven days a week. Sammy had three shifts of mechanics working, as well as a shuttle service to accommodate anyone's time table. So, the parking lot being empty, and the roll-up doors being closed, was a complete shock to him.

Well, the parking lot wasn't completely empty. Cars waiting for their turn to be serviced sat on the side of the building. And the truck of his manager sat in front of the office door. Pulling up next to the Ford F150, he said, "Hold tight for a minute, Babe. Let me go see what Alex has going on." He patted her leg, and exited the SUV, making his way to the office in search of answers.

When he entered the structure, the 45-year-old Alexander Knight Sr. was sitting in his office at his desk, rubbing his bald head, and talking on the phone. Seeing movement at the door, Alex finished up his call, stood up, and walked purposely toward his boss.

Sammy eyed the 6-foot 1-inch, 190-pound, muscular man from behind his shades. He knew the man was about to start some trouble. The former Duke cornerback had this aggressive look on his face like he was ready for war. The two men knew each other well, so if war was what Alex wanted, he knew Sammy was willing and able to bring it.

Slamming into the lobby area, Alex said, "I sent everyone home for the day so you'd have enough time to find another manager."

Smiling, Sammy asked, "Why would I need another manager? My manager is standing right in front of me."

"I can't work for you anymore. I took another manager position at a shop in North Charlotte."

Slowly nodding, Sammy said, "Look Alex, I know you're going through a lot of shit right now, but this isn't the time to make rash decisions. You're in pain, and the rest of us are hurting, too. But, we're family. I loved your daughters like they were my own. This is a time for us to pull together, not push each other away."

In outrage, Alex said, "Are you kidding me! You think I want to be close to your family after your son just murdered my little girls. Fuck you! You aint no family of mine!"

Removing his glasses in an attempt to calm himself, Sammy took a deep breath before speaking. "In respect for what your family is going through right now, I'm gonna let that slide. I'm also going to let it slide that you closed my shop down for the first time in ten years without consulting me. But, don't take my patience for weakness. My son didn't murder anyone, and you saying otherwise could cause your mouth to write a check your ass can't cash."

Taking a step closer, Alex said, "Fuck you! Fuck your son, your family, your shop, and your patience. You people kill me thinking, because you're rich, people are supposed to fear you. News flash Sammy: I'm. Not. Scared. Of. You!"

With a dead serious expression on his face, Sammy said, "Say something else about my family!" When Alex remained silent, Sammy said, "You want to take it there? Fine, let's take it there. Say something else about my family and I'll knock your teeth down your throat."

From the left, a voice asked, "Pops? You alright?"

Briefly glancing in that direction, Sammy eyed the tall, slim form of Alex Jr. His slicked back, shoulder-length, dark hair added substance to the mean stare coming out of his intense, black eyes. The 22-year-old thought he was a tough guy. Sammy didn't mind proving to the kid he wasn't as tough as he thought.

"I'm good," Alex Sr. responded. "Did you get all our stuff out the lockers?"

Stepping farther into the room from the garage entrance, AJ said, "Yeah. We're all set to go. That's as long as we don't have a problem."

Chuckling, but still staring at Alex, Sammy said, "And what if we do have a problem, Jr? You think you and your father stand a chance against a real man?"

"I think a family member for a family member might be in order," AJ responded, setting the box down. "Your son killed my sisters, maybe we can settle the score by killing you now, and then going after him when we're done."

Sammy dropped his head on a laugh. Then, striking like a 220-pound Cobra, unleashed a vicious right hook that lifted Alex off his feet. He spun just in time to duck under the haymaker thrown by AJ and grabbed the young man around his waist. While he was lifting AJ over his head, Alex took a diving leap at his legs, effectively knocking all of them to the ground.

Two against one weren't the greatest odds for a fight under any circumstances, but you were definitely asking for a whipping if you were on the ground. They wouldn't let Sammy get to his feet as Alex held on to his legs, while AJ attempted to knock his head off. A shot being fired caused all of them to freeze in place.

Alex and AJ had a better view, and their hands raised to the sky as they jumped up and backpedaled. Sammy regained his feet and smiled at the vision of his magnificent and classy wife standing at the front door holding the gun. She said, "I don't know what the hell is happening in here, but if either of you moves, I promise I'll blow your head clean off your shoulders."

Sammy dusted off his outfit, then threw a massive overhand right that connected flush with AJ's chin. His lights instantly turned off and he fell face first to the concrete floor. Alex flinched like he wanted some more action but, remembering the gun, raised his hands back over his head.

Sammy said, "Go ahead and get your son, and get your shit. You try to come at my family again, verbally or

45

physically, I'll make you glad your daughters aren't around to see what I do to you." He instructed Brianna to hold the door open while Alex hustled his son and belongings out to his truck.

Standing at the front of the Range Rover, Sammy took control of the gun until Alex roared out of the parking lot. When he was sure Alex wasn't coming back, he tucked the gun behind his back and then turned to his wife with a huge smile on his face. "You were gonna blow their heads clean off their shoulders?" he teased her with a laugh.

"You should be thanking me instead of mocking me!" she said in fake indignation. "I saved you from getting your ass kicked."

Wrapping his arms around her waist, he said, "I had them exactly where I wanted them." He leaned in and the couple shared a few lingering kisses.

When they finally separated, she said, "Tell me what happened. Why'd they take all their stuff?"

He told her how aggressive the two men had been and how Alex kept accusing James of murdering Alanah and Amia. After telling her what AJ said about evening up the score, he said, "That was the tipping point for me. I don't know how serious he was about that, but we all need to be on point from now on."

They jumped into the SUV and Brianna asked, "What are you gonna do about the shop?"

He started the vehicle and pulled off before saying, "I'll call everyone once we get home and make sure the next shift comes in. Tomorrow I'll come back and manage the place until I can make up my mind who to promote. But right now, I really just want to focus on James. Later tonight, I'll call the attorney so we can really see where he stands. I think it's a good thing they haven't charged him with anything, but I don't like the cop guarding his room."

Corey McCann, the lawyer, was a light-brown skinned, bald head, Harvard Law School graduate. He had expensive taste, so he made sure he kept his 5-foot 9-inch body encased in designer suits. His fees were very high, but the energy he put into every case made him worth every penny.

Brianna nodded her head, agreeing with the itinerary for the night. Then they fell into an uneasy silence while they continued their trek home. One thing Sammy never wanted to do was lie to his wife. Mostly because he knew that she'd never lie to him. They had definitely been through some tough times during their 22-year marriage, but nothing as serious as this. Sammy felt a wave of resentment towards his son. He and his wife normally shared everything with each other, but now they were forced to choose silence. Because, to put voice to what they felt about their son's situation, could bring to fruition a reality that neither of them wanted to face.

· · · · · · · · · · ·

· · · · · · · · · · · · · · · · · · ·

Detective Maxwell Hall fumed as he watched Sammy's Range Rover leave the hospital after their confrontation. As a cop, he knew it was his job to protect and serve the citizens in his jurisdiction. But ever since he'd been 12-years-old, he's had visions of putting Samuel Jordan in his place. He would settle for seeing him broke and broken, but where he really wanted to see him was in the morgue.

Sammy and Brianna were both a year older than him, but when he was a 12-year-old 7th grader, he'd been pushed up to the 8th grade because his scores were so high. Knowing he'd finally been singled out, and his genius recognized, his confidence level had gone through the roof. He'd known exactly who the power couple was, but he didn't run in their circle. So, after witnessing a fight between the two longtime sweethearts, he thought it was high time someone else stepped up and showed the Queen what she deserved.

Putting his unmarked police car in gear, he still remembered the cool March night like it was yesterday. Pulling out into traffic, he pictured his young, naive self, making one of the worst decisions of his life.

The epic fight had been over Brianna talking and laughing with another boy. They were all at the movie theater at Carolina Mall, and Sammy had walked over to the counter to buy popcorn and candy. When he turned around with his purchases, he was greeted with the sight of Brianna joking around with a boy from another school. Sammy had been all set to pummel the kid into the ground, until four of his friends arrived on the scene. When he realized it would be stupid to take on five guys, he threw the snacks in the trash and stormed out of the lobby, ignoring Brianna's hurried explanation.

At that point, Max hadn't had any interactions with Sammy. He was just a fly on the wall watching the lives of the rich and famous. But, watching Sammy hop in the taxi and leave Brianna standing at the curb, had been too cruel for Max to let slide.

After watching all the other kids enter the screening rooms, and noticing Brianna sitting out in the cold, he decided it was time to make his move. He ran out the door, shedding his jacket on the way, and told Brianna she could sit on it instead of the concrete bench she was perched on. Smiling graciously, she folded it up and thanked him for the padding.

He was relishing his time alone with the charming girl, and her looks and intelligence were driving him wild. During one of their comfortable silences, he pushed his luck and leaned in for a quick kiss. Her body jerked back and she jumped up and smacked the shit out of him. Walking off, she called him a pervert and demanded he stay away from her.

In his young mind he couldn't understand what had happened. She was being so nice to him and they were having such a glorious time. It baffled him to see her respond that way over a little kiss.

The following Monday, in the locker room after gym class, he found out that the encounter had more repercussions than just the single smack. Max heard his name being called and, when he looked up at the demented grin on Sammy's face, he knew he was in for a world of trouble.

It started with daily beatings. Soon, it progressed to minute-by-minute psychological torture. The problem was, Max wasn't scared of the bigger boy, so Sammy took personal joy in trying to break him. Max always fought back, but the other kid would just laugh and continue doing whatever he wanted to do.

The torture went on all the way up until Max was 15-years-old and Sammy's two friends had died. Matter of fact, it had been a wreck eerily similar to the one James had just been in. Sammy had still sent him hateful looks whenever their paths crossed, but it seemed he became bored with the whole thing. Brianna, for her part, had pulled him over one day during their senior year and apologized for all the trouble she'd caused him. At the time, the hormone fueled Max had thought the hug and peck on the cheek she'd given him more than made up for the years of torture he endured.

Now, heading back to the department to catch up on some of his other cases, his phone vibrated on his hip. Using the cars Bluetooth, he answered it after seeing the call was from the Crash Investigator that was working the James Jordan case.

He answered with, "What do you have for me?"

The 20-year vet huffed out a breath, which Max knew meant this was not a good news call. "We have absolutely nothing. We even have less than we did this morning after the techs took a deeper dive into the car. Seems the engine was modified in a way to qualify it as street legal. The tires were also approved for road use. So, the only thing we have is my testimony that the car had to be traveling over 90mph when it started to flip. But, 90 in a 70mph zone won't get our guy convicted of murder."

Kimberly Gibson was a wiz when it came to traffic accidents. Her knowledge had even garnered national attention after an interview on CNN. No one would ever second guess her conclusion of the facts, but Max thought there had to be something they could do. Two women had lost their lives. No way was he comfortable with just letting the perp walk.

He asked, "What about the fact he was going 20mph over the speed limit? Can't we get him for that?"

Kim sighed again. "The 20 is only an estimation. We can't use the simulations in court because the programming is still questionable. And the truth is, even though it's highly unlikely, Mr. Jordan could have been going 80mph and achieved the same results. As of now, the only thing we can charge him with, and likely get a favorable outcome, is speeding."

"What about reckless driving? If we can get him on that, at least we can change him with a lesser crime for the deaths."

"The problem with that is, we've never charged someone with reckless driving for going 10mph over the speed limit. I know because I looked it up. His lawyer would yell as loud as possible about discriminatory actions against his client, and he'd be right. Bottom line, Max, without more evidence, or a confession, this case will end with Mr. Jordan paying a $200 ticket, and that will be that."

"Shit!" cursed Det. Hall. "You get anything on the black paint?"

"Yeah. It came from an after-market paint shop because it's not standard on any car in the national database. So, pretty much a dead end unless we can find a particular car to test."

Feeling dejected, Max thanked his colleague and disconnected the call. He felt the hopelessness flowing through his veins, but he used it to fuel his determination. Quitting was never an option for him. There was no way in hell James Jordan was gonna use his family's money and power to get away with murder. Max just needed to find that one piece of evidence to hang his ass with.

Max was well aware he was on edge about this case. He tried to convince himself that his view of the son was not clouded by his hatred of the father. But, no matter how many times he repeated the thought in his mind, he knew the truth. He would use any means necessary to bring the smirking bastard down to his knees. Even if he had to sacrifice James to achieve his goal.

Chapter 4

The Jordan family lawyer, Mr. Corey McCann, was clearly getting frustrated with the story James was adamantly sticking to. He was damn near vibrating with energy as he interrogated James more thoroughly than the detective had. As far as lawyers went, Mr. McCann was very trustworthy, but if he thought James was about to bare his soul to him, he had another thing coming.

In his Armani suit, bouncing from one Dior Homme shoe to the other, he said, "James, I can't help you if you won't tell me the truth. Your tire didn't blow out. You weren't trying to avoid something in the road. Your steering didn't malfunction. Come on man, tell me the truth! It's the only way I can be prepared if anything comes out later in the process."

James was sitting on his hospital bed with his legs dangling off the side, just staring at the man. It was early Tuesday morning and James was wearing a pair of athletic shorts and a t-shirt as he'd been working out when the lawyer arrived. He was sick of the hospital and ready to go home, but the doctor was talking about keeping him for at least another three days.

After a quick swig of water, James said, "I don't know what else I can tell you, Mr. McCann. Like I said before, I was driving back from the party. There was no alcohol at the event, so none of us had been drinking. We were just cruising along, listening to some music, then I woke up on the ground. The police say I attacked some people trying to

53

get to Alanah and Amia, but I don't remember that. I have no idea what happened to cause the wreck. I can't even tell you if I was speeding or not. We were just riding the high of Amia turning 18."

Corey cocked his head, flashed a quick smile, and nodded. "I'm not your enemy, James. In fact, in this situation, I'm your best friend. You're paying me to keep you out of prison, something I can't do effectively if you won't tell me the truth. So, let me tell you this: I know you were racing. The detectives, the District Attorney, and your family, they all know you were racing. Hell, even the victims' family knows you were racing. You're the only one associated with this case who says this wasn't a race that ended in tragedy."

"And since I'm the only person alive who would know," said James, "why is everyone so keen on me implementing myself in a double murder. Look," said James, standing up, "let me know if I need to look for another lawyer. It's kind of hard for me to see you fighting for me if you think I'm a liar."

Shaking his head, Corey said, "What I think doesn't matter. I'm going to represent you because I fulfill my obligations. But I'm warning you now; I'm preparing your defense based off the notion of them finding evidence this was a race. The fact is, if they can't come up with something to support that theory, there won't be a case anyway."

Before either of them could say another word, the door to the room opened, and the person who entered caused an atmospheric shift of epic proportions. While the two of them argued, a frustrating tension had filled the space. With the new arrival, a different kind of tension evolved.

The soft, distinctly Hispanic voice said, "The officer told me it was okay to come in. I can leave if I'm..."

"No, no," said Corey quickly. "You can come on in. Me and James were just finishing up." As the lawyer said this, his eyes never stopped roving over the figure who closed the door and then stepped to the side out of the way.

James cleared his throat in annoyance, and said, "So, we'll talk again some other time, Mr. McCann. As you can see, I have a visitor."

Like he was waking from a trance, Corey's whole body jerked, and he said, "Oh, sorry." He shook the hand James offered and made his way to the door. "Yeah, uh, I'll call you if I hear anything. In the meantime, think about what I said. We don't need any surprises." During the whole speech his eyes never ventured from the visitor. At the door, he nodded and said, "Ms. Salazar, it's a pleasure to see you again." She repeated the sentiment and the lawyer slipped out the door after one last lingering look, leaving them alone.

In the silence that followed, James took a few seconds to take in the sight of the girl turned woman who used to be his best friend in the world. Showing a shyness that she hadn't displayed since early on in her life, her eyes stayed glued to the white Reebok Classics adorning her feet, while he continued to take her measure.

The first thing he noticed was the huge platinum and diamond pendant that hung from her chain, which spelled out his nickname for her: YAZZY. The second thing was the

55

rings made of precious metals and coated with colorful gems surrounding her fingers. The teardrop diamonds hanging from her earlobes spoke of a wealth and prosperity she'd never had in her youth. But, in his opinion, Yazmine Salazar was more fascinating than any piece of jewelry ever invented. And that fact pissed him off to no end.

It had been almost two years since he last saw her, but he used a ghost account to keep up with her on social media. He knew that she was a successful Instagram model, as well as a bartender and bottle service girl at the biggest club in Charlotte. Based on the videos and pictures she routinely post, he knew that she was doing very well for herself.

Finally, after about two minutes of silence, she looked up at him, her devastatingly familiar hazel eyes connecting with his. There was no doubt about it, the Mexican-American had grown to be one of the sexiest women in the world.

Before your gaze ventured below her neck, you would already find yourself infatuated if you stared for too long. Her lips were a soft, natural pink that you knew would taste like some long-forbidden fruit if you were ever lucky enough to taste them. If you could pull your eyes from that perfect cupid's bow of a mouth, you'd be blessed with the view of her small, oval-shaped face covered with an unblemished compilation of all things Latin.

From her eyebrows, to her cheeks, to her rounded chin, she had that look of vulnerability that made men want to wrap her up and never let her go. But, the angel stopped at her neck. Everything after that was built for pure sin.

Today, the voluptuous 20-year-old was wearing a white, long-sleeved, form-fitting stretch top that put her succulent, unencumbered breast on full display. He wasn't sure if he could really see the duskiness of her nipples through the material, or if it was just his imagination's wishful thinking.

Traveling down her slim but curvy waist, his eyes encountered a pair of matching white, hip-hugging bike shorts that were just this side of decent. The thin, skin-tight material left little doubt that panties had been left off the menu for today.

Her bare legs were caramel colored and looked as smooth and creamy as a favored treat. As always, her waist-length, stygian-black hair was left free to frame her sensational body. Yazzy was every man's walking wet dream. He knew because, growing up, he'd waken up plenty of mornings in tangled up, sweaty sheets having to wash his underwear out so his mom didn't find them.

Sitting back down in an attempt to hide his reaction to her, he asked, "What are you doing here, Yazmine?"

Her mouth opened and closed a couple times before she dropped her eyes and said, "I just came to make sure you were okay." This was the fourth time she'd showed up since he'd been admitted. Twice, his parents told him, while he'd been in the coma. The last time was yesterday, but he'd faked sleep until she gave up and left. He knew he was being childish, but he had enough problems on his plate without adding hers to the mix.

"Oh yeah, I'm fine," he said sarcastically. "My future wife is dead. My future sister-in-law is dead. My mom won't stop crying. My dad just wants to glare and yell at me. Alex quit the shop because he said I murdered his little girls. But, other than that, I'm doing just fine!"

She opened her mouth to respond, but he cut her off before she could utter a word. "Oh! I forgot. I have a compound concussion from the crash and then the police kicking my ass. I'm being investigated for seven assault charges on the first responders. The insurance won't pay for the car until the police clear me in their investigation. And now I got you in here asking me dumb ass questions. So, you tell me how I'm doing, Yazmine!" he yelled as he angrily swiped the tears from his face.

Clearing his own sight revealed to him the silent tears flowing down her face. She whispered, "I'm sorry." Turning to leave, she said, "I won't bother you again."

"Yazmine," he said, feeling like a dick. She wrapped her hand around the knob. "Yazmine," he said a little louder. She pulled the door open. "YAZZY!" he jumped up and shouted, finally causing her to stop. They both realized he hadn't called her by that nickname since they were 17-years-old.

When she didn't turn around, just stood in the open doorway, he said, "Yazmine, I'm sorry. You didn't deserve that. Thank you for checking on me, and if you want to stay, I could really use the company." Her head cocked a couple times like she was having an internal debate. Then she turned around and came back into the room after closing the door.

With tears still shining bright in her eyes, she threw her Louis Vuitton bag onto one of the chairs, walked right up to him, and wrapped her arms around his neck. She didn't care that his clothes were sweaty, or that he probably didn't smell too good. She just molded her body to his and attempted to give him all the comfort she could. After a brief hesitation, he returned the embrace as they both mourned the two lives lost, but for their own reasons.

So many times, in their youth, they had cried in each other's arms just like this. From small things like skinned knees, to big things like lost family members. James had missed this. Not being able to turn to her had left a void in his heart. Looking back on it now, his decision to push her away had hurt him just as much as it had her. Maybe now that they were grown, they could find a way to fix what had been broken for the last three years.

After the tears stopped and they separated a little, Yazmine brought her hand up to his face and wiped away the lingering moisture. As her cucumber melon scent drifted into his nostrils, their eyes locked, but he quickly turned from her to hide a reaction that he was helpless against. He eased back down on the side of the bed as Yazmine gathered her hair in front of her and sat down in the nearby chair.

He cleared his throat, his eyes everywhere but on her, and asked, "So, how have you been?"

"Um, I guess I'm doing good. I spend most of the day working. If I'm not at the club, I'm at home making new content online." After a nervous pause, she said, "I know I just asked you this, but how are you really doing?"

His eyes tracked over to her cross-legged form, and he met her eyes before he said, "To tell you the truth, I'm messed up. It hasn't even been two weeks but I feel like I've been missing them for years." Silent tears started falling, but when she went to get back up, he waved her down and rose himself.

As he gathered his composure, he paced from the foot of the bed to the door, over and over again. He wasn't sure if Yazmine was on her way to work or on her way home, but she just sat patiently, waiting in a supportive silence. Finally, he just started to talk.

"You know, growing up, you were basically my only friend. I didn't play sports, so I didn't really connect with a lot of the guys. I just felt so comfortable hanging around you that I didn't need anyone else. I did talk to some of the boys, and I went through the whole video games thing for a while, but there was nothing that compared to having your presence near me.

"I remember when my dad became concerned because I was with you so much. One day he asked me, 'James, do you and Yazmine talk about boys together.' I think I was 11 at the time and I didn't understand what he was getting at. Then he asked me if I ever felt like dressing up in your clothes and I figured out really quick where he was going. I laughed and assured him I wasn't gay, but he didn't seem convinced. He asked me if I thought you were pretty."

James stopped pacing and made his way back over to the bed. Sitting on the side, he stared into Yazmine's eyes before saying, "Until that moment, I'd never really thought about it. You were just my best friend, Yazzy. But, after that conversation with him, I started to notice girls in a different way.

"When Alanah came along, it wasn't just her looks, it was something deep down that sort of called to me. You know I'm not really the religious type, but our instant bond had to be from a Higher Power. I mean, it just didn't make sense. I never wanted to be away from her. I actually felt a pain deep in my soul when we weren't in harmony."

He leaned forward and let his dreads hide his face. "Me and you, we had a bond, Yazmine, but it had a sister\brother vibe to it. I could talk to you about things I'd never even bring up with another living person. But, with Alanah, there was this... I don't know... A... Completeness. Like discovering you'd been breathing with one lung your whole life, and then gaining access to the other one. It was like she provided something spiritual and gave my life meaning."

They sat in silence for a few minutes before he swung his hair back behind his head and looked at her once more. She was staring across the room at the wall, deep in thought, and he couldn't even guess what she was thinking. After Alanah entered into his life, he had made it abundantly clear to her that Yazmine was his ride or die. In that special way she had, Alanah just smiled and told him, "If she's good enough to be your best friend, then she's good enough to be mine, also."

At first, Yazmine hadn't trusted Alanah's acceptance. She told James she thought Alanah was just bidding her time before she demanded he kick her to the curb. After a couple girls-only nights together, Yazmine developed a different opinion of Alanah. They became good friends and James was happy and content with the direction his life was heading.

"Yazmine," he said, causing her head to jerk in his direction. "I know things have been different lately, but she was your friend, too. How are you doing?"

She looked down at her lap and fiddled with her hair before exhaling audibly. "Uh, my relationship with her, as you know, ended a while back. I hate that she and Amia are gone, but to be honest, I'm only sad because I know it hurts you." She rushed on when she saw him about to speak. "Don't get me wrong, they were both good, young women, but my feelings for them are only an extension of my feelings for you."

He rose to his feet at the same time that Yazmine stood up and gathered her stuff. So many comments filled his head. Things he'd wanted to say to her for years, but the words just wouldn't come out. She walked over to him and gave him a quick hug before stepping back. Toying with her long trusses, she said, "Anyway, I need to get home and get some sleep. We had inventory at the club and I've been up all night." With a bashful look, she asked, "Do you know when they're gonna release you?"

"The doctor is saying I'll be here at least until Friday. Something about the delayed effects of concussions."

With a hopeful look, she said, "I don't have to go in again until Friday. If you want me to, I can come back and we can catch up? You know, just to take your mind off things."

His first reaction was to refuse. Their relationship over the past three years had been tremulous at best. His soulmate had only been dead for 12 days and he felt like he was being disloyal even talking to Yazmine. But, looking into her earnest eyes, he couldn't bring himself to crush her hope.

"Uh, yeah, sure. I'd love to catch up with you." Her smile was so brilliant, it lit up the whole room. She bounced on her toes and hugged him once again, issuing a girlish squeal. Laughing, he bounced with her saying, "Okay, okay, calm down, Yazmine."

Pulling away, she made her way to the door, but she paused to send him one more message. "I'll go home and get some sleep and I'll be back tonight." Sobering a little, she said, "It was nice to see you again, JJ. I hate it was under these circumstances, but I don't want to leave you alone with your thoughts. Just do me one favor." He inclined his head for her to continue. She said, "Please take a shower before I…." Then she paused as her eyes went wide in shock.

They stood staring at each other as she stumbled to explain. "I mean… I was just… I'm sorry…" Closing her eyes, she yanked the door open and started to flee.

James said, "Hey!" Just like the first time she tried to run, she paused, but didn't turn around. "It's okay, Yazmine. I know what you meant. Just come back later so we can talk." Still facing the hallway, she nodded and left quickly like she feared he would change his mind.

Shaking his head, he gathered up some clothes and made his way to the bathroom. Upon seeing the shower enclosure, he groaned as erotic images assaulted his mind. He hated the feelings of guilt, but he'd lived with them for a long time now. He could almost hear Alanah saying, 'I forgave you years ago. It's time for you to forgive yourself.'

That's one of the things that made her so special. Holding a grudge just wasn't in her. Even after he almost torpedoed the special bond they shared, she had only been concerned with rebuilding and fortifying what she said wasn't lost at all.

Getting into the shower, tears pour out of his eyes because of the visions swirling around in his mind. When he should have been imagining the sparkling teal eyes belonging to the love of his life, he was too busy remembering the passion filled, hazel eyes of his former best friend, Yazmine Salazar.

• •

Stupid, thought Yazmine. Stupid! Stupid! Stupid! Without even thinking, she'd brought up the one topic that was sure to get her kicked out of his life again. In her defense, it had been innocent, but she couldn't allow a mistake like that to happen again.

Before she even made it out the hospital, she felt the phone vibrating in her bag. Rolling her eyes, she ignored it and continued the trek back to her car. She knew who the caller was, and his impatience was starting to get on her last nerve. The idiot had to know she was on the way out. He was the one who installed the listening device in the lining of her Louis Vuitton bag.

Stepping into the parking lot, the late morning sun was torturous in its brightness. The phone vibrated again as she reached in her bag and pulled out her Prada shades. Slipping them on her face, she ignored the call as she increased her pace, trying in vain to escape the brutal, smothering heat.

The little white Porsche 911 she was driving was a few years old, but it was a huge step up from the busted Pontiac Grand AM she used to drive. She hit the remote start and heard the engine purr to life, hoping the air conditioner cooled the interior somewhat before she got in. Just about arriving at the vehicle, her phone vibrated again.

Yazmine snatched the driver's side door open, flopped down inside the oven-hot car, and finally answered the call.

She didn't even get a word in before she heard, "Don't play games with me, Ms. Salazar! When I call you, I don't care what you're doing, you answer the phone!"

The cool air coming out of the vents did a lot to calm her. She was already sweating from nerves, the heat damn near made her skin soggy. Calmly, she said, "I'm not playing games, Sir, I was just trying to get back to the car and then I would have called you."

"Well, next time don't wait. Take the call when you get it," demanded the terse voice.

"Sorry, I just didn't want to talk business in the middle of a bunch of strangers." After a pause to put her car in gear, she asked, "Was there something important you wanted to talk about?"

"Yeah," said the man. "Come by the meeting spot before you go home. I need to remove the device from your purse."

Turning the car in the direction of the Wal-Mart parking lot, she said, "I'm on my way now. Give me about ten minutes." With the cold air now wicking away the sweat floating on her skin, the confident Yazzy was making a return. "Is something wrong? Why are you taking the device?"

"Your services are no longer needed. I'm gonna see if I can find something better than a staticky audio recording to hang my hopes on. Anyway, it's not like you were making much progress."

"But what about our deal?" she asked, desperately. "I only got to talk to him once. I'm supposed to go back…"

"Like I said," he rudely cut her off. "I'm gonna try a different route. So, the deal we had is no longer valid."

"That's bullshit!" she screamed. "You can't do this to me! Just give me one more chance. I know I can get what you need."

"Ms. Salazar, it's over. You had your shot and you blew it. You can't blame anyone but yourself." With an air of finality, the man said, "I'll see you when you get here," and hung up.

Despite the cooling temperature inside the car, the sweat came back in full force. She hammered the steering wheel as she envisioned the life she'd built for herself being stripped away. Greed had gotten her into this situation, and betrayal would have gotten her out. Now that that wasn't even an option, she had no idea what she was gonna do.

Pulling up next to the white Dodge Durango, with its blacked-out windows, she felt herself close to panic. It had been two years since she last had an anxiety attack, but she could feel one close at hand. Her phone signaled an incoming text and the vibration damn near made her wet her shorts. She looked at the message, cut the car off, grabbed the bag, and exited her vehicle.

On shaky legs, she made her way over to the passenger door and climbed into the SUV. The interior of the vehicle, mostly black leather and woodgrain, was dark and cool. It still had that new car smell, and the enclosed space was spotless and tidy. Lecherous eyes scanned her from the top of her head, to the Reeboks protecting her feet. Without a word, he held out his hand and she placed the bag within his grasp.

Carelessly, he tore at the inside and ripped the mic and transmitter from under the hidden seam. Tossing the bag back at her, he put the SUV in gear, signaling that she was being dismissed.

Nervously, she asked, "What about me?"

"What about you?" he said, unsympathetically.

"Are we even now? I mean, I did what you asked."

Laughing, he said, "You didn't do anything I asked you to do. Asking him how he feels and reminiscing about old times isn't gonna make us even."

With tears of fear flowing down her face, she said, "I tried to make him trust me first. We haven't really talked in three years. I couldn't just go in there and interrogate him."

"Ms. Salazar," he said in exasperation. "A deal is a deal. I was ready to hold up my end, but you didn't hold up yours. So, you're on your own now. I have no reason to help you."

In a last-ditch effort, she said, "There has to be something else I can do. I can't do this on my own." Placing her hand on his leg, she said, "I really need your help."

His eyes locked onto her hand, then tracked up to her eyes. With a smirk, he pushed her hand away from him. "Don't play games with me, little girl. You can take your cheap tricks to someone else."

Putting her hand a little higher this time, she said, "I'm not playing any games. I'm just trying to do something for you so you can do something for me." When she started making circles on his inner thigh and he didn't stop her, she said, "I see the way you look at me." Cupping the evidence of his arousal, she said, "So, do we have a new deal, or do I go back to my car?"

Meeting her eyes, he nodded and gestured her into the back of the SUV. She gave him one more squeeze before she smiled and slithered her way between the seats.

Cutting the vehicle off, he looked around the area for a minute before eyeing her in the rearview mirror. He watched as she peeled out of her tight outfit and spread herself out for him on the backseat. When she was ready, she beckoned him to join her, and he wasted no time following in her wake, eager to solidify the terms of their new deal.

Chapter 5

Before Yazmine went back to work on Friday night, she pretty much spent every waking moment in the hospital room with James. When she showed up Tuesday night in a pair of shape defining, black, leather pants, black and white Jordan's, and a gray hoodie, all the moisture dried up in his mouth. He almost sent her away because her sensual nature was pushing him to the brink of madness. But that wouldn't have been fair to her, she was just being herself. It was his own messed up thoughts that turned everything she did into an amorous invitation.

At first, they had both been tense and reserved, picking every word they used with care and caution. About the same time, they noticed how stupid they were acting, and the conversation turned more playful and natural. By the time she left, around 3:30 Wednesday morning, he had to admit she was doing an excellent job of keeping his mind off of his grief.

But the times she wasn't around, his thoughts bounced all over the place. Alanah and Amia were definitely at the forefront, but other things jockeyed for that number one spot. He thought about the investigation he was under, all the time wondering if they were gonna come in and slap the cuffs around his wrist. Thoughts of his family also drifted through on a regular basis. He hated the disappointed looks his parents cast his way whenever they visited. Mostly they came from his dad, but he'd caught his mother sending him the look a few times, also.

And he thought about Yazmine. They had been best friends since kindergarten. He still remembered the pretty little girl who stumbled with her adorable broken English. As kids do, she was picked on mercilessly, not just because of her speech, but because she wore ragged clothes and was always dirty and hungry. That was until James revealed that he also knew Spanish and became the girl's protector.

She had latched onto him like a lifeline. They played together, ate together, and integrated each other in every aspect of their lives. James hadn't had many friends because he was so shy, but kids left him alone because everyone knew about his rich family. Even the young kids understood that wealth and power went hand and hand. So, in a sense, he latched onto her just as hard. She offered some much-needed relief from his otherwise lonely life.

Those were not the parts of their relationship that he dwelled on though. His mind chose to circulate all the tragedies that turned their friendship into this falsehood of polite conversations. But, even that wasn't the loudest detractor from his remembrance of Alanah and Amia. No, that title belonged to the murdering son of a bitch that he couldn't wait to get his hands on.

James wasn't a rat. And in this situation, it would hurt him just as much as the other guy if he did decide to tell. But James didn't want to see him in jail, anyway. He wanted to see him on a dark, back road where he could give him a dose of his own medicine. He could just imagine how the man was going around spreading his propaganda against him. Safe in the knowledge that James couldn't take him down without following him into the abyss. In his mind, James made a promise to himself, as well as to Alanah and Amia: If it was the last thing he did, he would make sure the bastard got what he deserved for his treachery.

He'd been ruminating over how he was gonna exact some revenge, when the doctor pushed the door open and breezed over to the bed. He said, "I got some good news and some bad news. Which do you wanna hear first?"

Thinking that any news couldn't be as bad as the past two weeks, James said, "Give me the bad."

"Well, it's not all that bad," the doctor clarified. "I just know you're ready to get out of here. With that being said, I'm not going to release you until Sunday morning."

"But I feel fine," James complained. "I work out every day. I'm not nauseous or weak or tired. Why are you holding me?"

"James, you were in a coma for over a week. Now, the crash just rattled your brain around a little bit, but that baton to the head could have killed you. The brain is funny sometimes. You can feel good in the morning, and die in the afternoon. And that can be the response to an injury from months ago." Patting James on the shoulder, he said, "It's not gonna kill you, and it might just save your life. Anyway, I'll be back to check on you in the morning."

The doctor turned to walk out and James stopped him at the door. "Wait! What's the good news?"

"Oh, almost forgot. Detective Hall came by here earlier to ask me about your injuries. I explained to him that, if you were charged with any kind of assault on an officer, I would

71

testify to the excessive and unnecessary hit to your head. I told him that I would push for the officer getting charged with attempted murder because it had to have been a full force swing. So, I don't know anything about the crash investigation, but I think you're clear on the assault charges."

Getting up and shaking the man's hand, James said, "Thank you, Sir. I wouldn't have had a way to defend against it because I can't remember the incident at all."

Nodding with a smile, the doctor said, "Don't mention it. I was just telling the truth." He then turned on his heels and exited the room.

James went ahead and took his shower and then put on a pair of shorts to sleep in. Jumping in the bed, he flipped through the channels for a while but soon concluded that he wasn't really in the mood for any of the asinine movies or shows being played.

He checked his phone to see if his parents had left any messages for him. No dice. In the hopes of getting this day over with, James laid his phone down, turned off the TV, and got into a comfortable position. With millions of thoughts fighting for dominance in his mind, he thought he would be awake for hours. But within minutes, his eyes started to feel heavy. The next thing he knew, he was thrown back into a memory that could be classified as a dream or a nightmare. Tonight, his body couldn't decide which it was as the scenes played out in vivid detail.

Life didn't get any better than this, thought the 17-year-old James as he glanced around his parent's backyard. It was absolutely beautiful outside, with the sun blazing and the wind pretty much nonexistent. As he laid out on the lounge chair beside the Olympic sized pool, he let the summer heat dry the droplets off his skin from his latest dip in the water.

It was the first day of summer vacation and James didn't have a thing on his agenda. Well, other than doing nothing more strenuous than swimming and sleeping. Normally, with it being close to noon, he would just be finishing up his workout. But this summer, he was going to start off his break by taking some time off.

With shades in place, and his shorts-clad body feeling extremely lazy, James was preparing himself to take a quick nap. That was until the screamed, "Cannonball!" and the buckets of water splashing all over him.

He jerked up with a startled cry to see a beaming and laughing Yazmine swimming away in a mad dash to escape what she knew was coming. He ran and dove in, delivering powerful strokes in his effort to catch her before she reached the other side. Right as her hands went to propel her out of the pool, he snagged her foot and yanked her back into the water.

What followed was an hour of untamed chaos as they wrestled and splashed and dunked one another until they both had to lay down to catch their breath. Yazmine asked, "When are your parents coming home?"

James glanced over at her as she wrung the water out of her drenched hair. He said, "Not until Monday. My mom said they needed to get away for a few days." As it was only Friday, that left James on the huge estate by himself for the whole weekend.

"And what about Alanah? Isn't she at some kind of basketball camp?"

"Yeah," he responded, sadly. "14 days with nothing but Facetime and phone calls. And I can only call her between 9:00pm and 10:00pm because of how busy she is during the day, and then lights out at night."

"Aw! You poor baby!" she said in a teasing voice. Laughing, she said, "Well, we'll just have to stay busy so you don't miss her too much." Despite her words, she then laid down and put her shades on to soak up some sun.

His chair was to the right and slightly behind Yazmine's. For the next 20 or so minutes, while she dozed, his eyes roamed all over the valleys and hills of her body. This was still the little girl he remembered from when they were five years old, but then again, it wasn't. Although they had childishly made out in their youth, they had never been more than friends. But recently, it had become harder and harder for his eyes not to track her movements. Especially when Alanah wasn't around to hold his attention.

She was just so magnificent. Even his mom had had to pull her to the side and talk to her about her clothing, or lack thereof. At 17-years-old, her body was plump and healthy and drove the male population at their school insane. In response, she would wear the tightest and skimpiest outfits she could find to cause the most discomfort.

Once, she had emerged from the pool house in a slingshot swimsuit during one of their weekend get-togethers and all conversation had ceased. Brianna had jumped up and led her back inside, fussing her out the whole way. Since then, whenever she knew his parents would be around, she would cover up the essentials. Today, knowing they were out of town, wasn't one of the times when modesty was on her mind.

The suit she chose to wear in celebration of their first day of freedom was cheap, thin, about two sizes too small, and white. Once the flimsy material got wet, it was damn near like she was naked. While they'd been playing in the water, his mind had focused on having fun with his buddy, Yazzy. Now, seeing her bountiful assets on full display, he groaned in misery.

Her head turned in his direction, and she asked, "You alright, JJ? What's wrong?"

He looked out over the acres of rolling lawns comprising the Jordan land as he clenched his jaw and said, "Nothing. Just thinking." She smiled knowingly and then turned over on her stomach.

DON'T LOOK! Don't even think about looking! Those were the demands running through his mind. Of course, at 17-years-old, not looking at a sight so illustrious was next to impossible.

Alanah loved to wear revealing clothes that showcased her long, toned limbs. As a basketball player, not much fat remained on her thin, but sexy, body. But, the one place she remained plump and curvaceous was her heart shaped butt.

Yazmine, on the other hand, took thickness to a whole new level. She ran track and she worked out religiously trying to get faster and more explosive. The result was a firm and prominent backside that seemed to jiggle and undulate with every move she made.

When James couldn't resist the temptation any longer, he allowed his eyes to take in the sight of her mounded, caramel-colored cheeks separated by a dental floss sized string.

She reached over and grabbed her phone off the side table and spent the next ten minutes updating her numerous followers on her actions so far today. Absentmindedly, at least he thought so, she wiggled her feet and fluttered her legs from side to side. Her movements created the effect of her twerking while she was laying facedown. He became mesmerized by the slight clapping sound, and the wave-like motion playing out only a few feet away.

He wasn't aware she was playing with him until she giggled and asked, "You liking the show?"

His eyes shot to her smiling face as he blundered to explain. "Uh, I was just… It was a… I thought I saw…"

A sensual laugh issued from her throat before she saved him. "I'm getting a little dried out. Can you please go get me something to drink?"

In his haste to hide his embarrassment, he said, "Yeah, sure," and almost knocked his chair over during his retreat into the house.

Once inside the cool, open-air kitchen, he took a deep breath and tried to get control of himself. He was acting ridiculous. This was Yazzy, the closest thing to a sister he had, and here he was ogling her body. He had seen her hundreds of times over the years in stages of undress, he couldn't understand why these lustful thoughts were now bombarding his mind. With a new resolve to stop acting like a horndog, he grabbed two Cokes out of the Subzero fridge, and made his way back out to Yazzy.

They spent the rest of the afternoon swimming and wrestling and just having a good time. Eventually, the sun drained them so much they found themselves watching videos and shooting pool in the game room connected to his bedroom. Neither one of them were any good at the game, so they spent most of the time dancing and goofing off.

Everything was back to normal now. In the air-conditioned space, James had changed out of his wet clothes, and Yazzy, still barefoot, had dried off and put on one of his long T-shirts. She had braided her long hair to keep it out of the way, and the brother\sister, best friend atmosphere was back. And then the stupid ass song came on and everything changed again.

Trey Songz was Yazmine's favorite singer. Normally, when one of his songs came on, she would rock her hips, close her eyes, and sing the lyrics along with him. But this one song, *Love Faces,* seemed to transport her to this euphoric state that was not good for his present mental health.

She gasped and looked at him wide eyed as she abandoned the pool stick and moved over in front of the 80-

inch screen. With a blissful look on her face, she slithered her body left and right, up and down, as her hands roamed over her curves. She sang along with Trey in a soft, dream-like voice as James made his way over to the recliner, sat down, and watched her performance.

After the song went off, she turned, searching for him. Finally spotting him on the chair, she said, "That's my song. You know I can't hear it and not dance." While she talked, she walked over to stand in front of him. All he could do was swallow the lump in his throat and nod at her. She laughed and asked, "What's wrong with you? What, you're too cool to dance now?" Just as the joking banter was about to pick back up, the devil said, "Oh no, not so fast."

The conspiracy continued as Summer Walker's, *Girls Need Love Too*, video started piping out it's opening notes. Yazzy squealed and reached for his hands. "Come on, JJ! Dance with me!"

"Um, not right now, Yazzy…" he started, but it was too late. Using the strength of her lower half, she pulled him to his feet and their bodies meshed as one. There was no way that he could hide his arousal from her, but she didn't seem to mind. She wrapped her arms tightly around him, laid her head on his chest, and swayed as Summer Walker's raunchy lyrics led them to a world of sexual fantasy.

"Honestly, I'm tryna stay focused, You must think I got to be joking when I say,

I don't think I can wait, I just need it now, Better swing my way,

I just need some dick, I just need some love,

Tired of fucking wit these lame niggas, baby I just need a thug,

Would you be my plug, You could be the one,

You can start with a handshake, baby Imma need more than a hug."

By the time the chorus came on, James was more aware than ever that Yazzy was naked under the T-shirt.

Her perfume, mixed with her natural scent, was leading his brain into dangerous territory. During her hunching and grinding, the shirt had ridden up and he was staring down at her bare cheeks while they continued to move in unison. Without conscious thought, his hands found themselves squeezing and rubbing all over her exposed flesh.

She moaned and her rolling motion became more pronounced and focused. Leaning back slightly, she stared up at him with a dazed look on her face. He had no idea who kissed who, but the next thing he knew, her legs were around his waist and they were locked mouth to mouth.

Within seconds, her gyrations took on a frenzied cadence and she moaned deep in her core as her body began to shudder. He was close to exploding himself when he realized how far he had let this situation escalate. Tenderly, but forcefully, he separated them and set her back on her feet. They both looked down at the same time and saw the wet stain she had left on his shorts. It was also painfully obvious that he hadn't found his own pleasure during the exchange.

Close to tears and looking flustered, she said, "I'm so sorry, James. I just got caught up and…"

"Yazzy, it's okay," he cut her off. "We both got a little carried away. But nothing happened. Let's just act like the last few minutes didn't take place."

She wiped the fallen tears off her face, and said, "I don't know if I can do that JJ, but I understand your situation. We can talk about this later, but for now, I think you need a shower." Once again, they both looked at the wet stain before he nodded and took off for his room.

James entered the luxurious, marble shower enclosure with its frosted glass and six separate water jets, and peeled out of his clothes. He decided to start with cold water, but all that did was make him cold and horny. He switched the water over to hot and tried to think about anything other than what had just happened with Yazzy.

Alanah and James had promised to be each other's first. Even though they had experienced orgasms with each other, it had never gone beyond kissing and roaming hands. He had never held a girl in his arms while she hunched on him and felt the orgasm rip threw her body. With the new sensations torturing his mind, he had no idea how he could face Yazmine and not become aroused every time.

With his mind playing back the encounter over and over again, he wasn't even aware of the shower door opening. Only when she started to speak did he notice her. "JJ, I'm sorry but I can't control myself right now."

His head jerked in her direction, and he backpedaled until his body hit the far wall. She was gloriously naked and, while in his mind he was screaming for her to stay away, his eyes devoured the hidden treasures being revealed to him. She advanced on him, but he was shaking his head and looking around like a cornered, wild animal.

Creeping slowly, with her hands raised in a calming gesture, she said, "I just want to give you what you gave me. I want to make you feel good."

When she was close enough to touch him, he tried to gain some semblance of control over the situation. Standing up tall and ignoring her repeated glances at his jutting lower region, he said, "Yazmine, what the hell is wrong with you? You know I'm with Alanah, and she's your friend. We had a moment of weakness in the game room, but now we need to think clearly. Neither one of us is ready for this, and I'm sure neither of us wants to hurt Alanah."

She paused for a second with her head cocked in thought. He felt like he had gotten through to her until she shrugged and said, "You might feel those things, but I don't feel them in the slightest." Then she stroked her hand over him while brushing her nipples against his chest. He went blank for a second, then they were kissing once again.

Somewhere in the delirium of her climbing his body, they became one. The pleasure was so unexpected it set fireworks off in his skull. He couldn't think. He couldn't reason. All he could do was ride the waves of pleasure that Yazmine was giving him.

He stopped fighting the attraction after that first time and they spent every free minute of the next two weeks exploring their sexuality. Even after his parents returned, they would make the trek over to the guest house, which belonged to him, and continued their discovery of each other's bodies.

James would call Alanah every night and act as if nothing was going on and that he missed her greatly. But Alanah would ask questions that let him know she wasn't fooled by his act. Finally, on the night before she was scheduled to come home, he broke down and told her the truth. He originally told her over the phone, but she hung up and Facetimed him immediately.

He answered, but couldn't look at her face on the screen. She said, "I knew there was an attraction between you two, I just never thought you would let it go so far." His head came up at her matter-of-fact tone because, even though she sounded hurt, she didn't sound angry at all. Continuing, she said, "When I met the two of you, I couldn't quite understand the dynamics of your relationship. Both of you were invested in being friends, but both of you hungered for each other."

Not knowing what else to say, he said, "I'm so sorry, Alanah. You know I love you and I never meant to hurt you. I told her yesterday that I couldn't be around her anymore, so I can promise you this will never happen again."

Smiling sadly, she asked, "Do you love her?"

With downcast eyes, he said, "Yes, but not in the way I love you. I just made a huge mistake, but it's you I want to be with."

After a long pause, he looked up at the screen to see her wiping the tears from her face. She finally said, "We'll talk about this when I come see you tomorrow." Showing a maturity far beyond her years, she said, "We can work through this. We're young. I know I love you and you love me, this is just a bump in our journey. See you tomorrow, James." She then hung up.

The next day, after dodging the repeated attempts of Yazmine to connect with him, Alanah called and told him she was at the guest house's front door. He raced over to the property and eyed Alanah warily as she sat on the front steps.

He sat down next to her and they stayed silent for ten minutes before she asked, "Why didn't you tell me you were ready?"

He couldn't pretend like he didn't know what she was referring to. "I didn't know if you were and I didn't want to put any pressure on you." When she didn't say anything, he said, "I don't really know if I was ready or not. Yazmine just kind of swept me up in her wave."

For the first time since the revelation, she showed anger. "Don't you dare try to put this off on her! I've watched you watching her. She's very desirable and you let your lust control you."

Dropping his head, he said, "You're right. I'm sorry." With tears streaming down his face, he turned to her and said, "I love you Alanah, and whatever I have to do to earn your forgiveness, I'll do. Please! Just tell me what to do!" She scooted over next to him and wrapped her arms around his neck. For the next few minutes, she held him as he continued to plead with her to stay with him.

Finally, she hushed him and stood up, grabbing ahold to his hand. He looked up at her in confusion until she smiled and said, "I told you yesterday I wasn't going anywhere. As long as you promise you will never cheat on me again, we can put this behind us." He gave his word on everything he could think of as he nuzzled her bare leg like a lovelorn puppy. Laughing, she pulled him to his feet and said, "Let's go."

Frowning as she led him up the steps, he asked, "What's up? What are we doing?"

With a look of determination laced with fear, she turned and kissed him softly. Looking into his eyes, she said, "I'm ready," and pushed him into the house. What followed was the true definition of love making. It was soft and gentle and every movement was geared towards bringing the other pleasure.

After they were both cuddled up and satisfied, they had their first serious talk about forever. Around 9:00pm with Alanah sleeping on his chest, he cursed silently because he knew he had to get her home soon. He was just about to shake her awake when he noticed a figure standing in the doorway. His breath hitched and Alanah woke up and glanced in the direction he was looking.

Yazmine was leaning on the doorjamb with tears of devastation flowing down her face. James was mortified, but Alanah, being the angel she is, hopped out of the bed, threw his t-shirt on to hide her naked body, and rushed over to comfort the crying girl.

They went off and James cleaned up and got dressed while they talked in the living room. When he emerged, Alanah had Yazmine laughing and looking like her old self. Surprisingly, Alanah excused herself to get cleaned up and left them alone.

As soon as Alanah was gone, he spun on Yazmine. "What are you doing here? I told you I can't be around you anymore!"

Ignoring his question and tone, she said, "You really do love her. I see that now. I hate that I jeopardized that and I will stay away from both of you from now on." She got up and walked to the front door, but he stopped her with his next statement.

"I've known you since we were 5-years-old. I don't think more than three days has passed in a row without me seeing you or talking to you. I'm inexperienced so I didn't realize the difference until I was with Alanah. Now that I know the feeling, you care to tell me when you lost your virginity?" He didn't try to hide the hurt or disappointment at the fact she'd kept him in the dark.

Turning slowly, she studied his face before she responded. "Not that it's any concern of yours anymore, but I was 12-years-old and I didn't really have a say in the matter." Her disclosure shocked him so much he didn't realize she'd fled until the door latched behind her.

In a daze he drove Alanah home in his Elkhart blue Z06 Corvette convertible and he left her with a promise to call later that night. But that was the night he decided to race some idiot at a red light to let off some steam and he got busted. His dad didn't come get him until 2:00am, and by then he was exhausted and feeling like a complete failure. Only someone like him could continually mess up such a good life.

At 2:30am his cellphone rang and Alanah's sweet voice filled his ear. She said, "I was so worried about you, but I'm glad you're safe. Get some rest and I love you." He responded in kind before they hung up and he went to sleep. During the night, he woke up several times with one question burning in his mind: How could his best friend in the whole world be raped at 12-years-old and he not know a thing about it?

• •

Sometime during the night, James woke up with his arms wrapped around the soft, fragrant body of a female. He pulled the pliant body closer to his and whispered, "I had this horrible dream that you had left me. I love you, Alanah. Don't ever leave my side again."

A soft voice whispered back, "I won't ever leave you. I love you, JJ."

Only later, when he woke up in the hospital bed alone with the sun shining through the window pane, did he realize what he had done. The cucumber melon fragrance was still on his clothes and sheets. His alert self knew that Alanah was gone and she would never return. His subconscious, on the other hand, had concluded that any female body pressed to his side in the middle of the night had to belong to Alanah.

Yazmine was smart and practical, so he had no doubt that she would understand he was still half asleep when he uttered those words. Practical or not, he still realized the words would have hurt her. He reached for his phone to give her a quick call, but his parents chose that moment to enter his room.

He sighed as he looked at his father's anger filled eyes and sat up to endure whatever lectures he had for him today. The good news was, if the doctor was telling the truth, tomorrow his lecture filled days would be over.

Chapter 6

Saturday nights, in towns and cities all across the world, usually saw a large uptick in crime. A lot of people celebrating the weekend, end up with a little too much alcohol in their systems, which adds to the incorrigible behavior. For that reason, Detective Maxwell Hall was cruising the streets in his unmarked, prepared to be on hand if help was needed nearby. And this also gave him additional time to spot a black racing car with damage to its front passenger side.

Already, he'd responded to five drunk drivers, two bar fights, two shootings, and three traffic accidents. Since he was a Homicide detective, when he responded to scenes like these, he just provided an extra set of hands to whomever was in charge. Really, he was just bored, and sitting at home all alone with nothing to do but paperwork, didn't appeal to him.

So, there he was, driving around listening to the scanner, coming up on 18 hours of active duty, when he noticed about 15 cars sitting in a Burger King parking lot. This sight normally wouldn't have caught his attention, this particular nightspot being a popular hangout for local high school students. But tonight, there seemed to be a different element in attendance, one that might provide just the kind of clue he was looking for.

Around this area, the weekends brought out a bunch of Honda Accords, maybe a Corvette or two, and a spattering of Mustangs. Most of them would be dented and old with the only aftermarket accessories being a few stickers or LED lights. But the vehicles dominating the area tonight, cost more than most houses in the city.

He made a U-turn and drove back pass just to get a better idea of what he was seeing. A Lamborghini worth about $300K. What looked like a 1970's Ferrari which ran about $500K. Porsche, Maserati, and Jaguar all had representatives that cost hundreds of thousands of dollars. What really drew him in was not the price of the cars, it was that every one of them looked to be supped up for racing.

Max parked his car at a nearby Wendy's and walked over because he didn't want to spook the crowd. He was glad he was in jeans and t-shirt because his usual suit would have stood out like a sore thumb. Not wanting to draw attention to himself, he didn't talk to anyone, just walked around pretending to be like everyone else enjoying the sights.

Now that he was actually in the middle of the group, he could see that these were no show cars. Their owners, who were a lot older than the high schoolers milling about, had cleaned the vehicles up, but Max could clearly see that these cars were used on the tracks and streets. Some of them didn't even look street legal, but it seemed like the owners were just giving the younger crowd something to look at. Something to keep them away from the bad elements that came out at night.

Looking around, Max saw the older crowd gracefully answering questions thrown their way. All the cars had North Carolina plates, but he was certain he'd never seen the cars or the men before. Standing close to the Lambo, he heard the owner telling one of the kids they were all from Charlotte and had brought their cars out to have a little fun.

Max walked around for a while longer before he decided that nothing nefarious was going on and the out of towners were genuine in their quest to give the kids a fun Saturday night. He was turning to leave when something all the way in the back corner of the lot caught his eye.

All the younger kids had parked their cars in the hospital lot about 50 yards away. So, he thought it was odd that a gleaming, black racing car, with what had to be illegal tint, sat tucked away all by itself. He thought it could belong to one of the Burger King employees, but something just didn't sit right with him. He headed that way to investigate.

As he got closer, he saw that it was a totally blacked out, Ford Mustang, Shelby GT-500. Not on the scale with the other cars in the parking lot tonight, but definitely several steps up from the normal cars the kids trolled around in. Feeling uneasy for reasons he couldn't explain, he glanced around to see if anyone was paying him any attention, then unsnapped the flap holding his gun in his holster.

Without some form of internal light, there was no way to see if anyone was inside the vehicle. Max stayed about 20 feet back for protection, and started circling the Mustang. At first, he was circling in the direction of the back so he could get a good look at the license plate, but some interesting marks on the front passenger side caused him to change directions.

When he got close enough to the car, he glanced around the area once more, and then bent over and pressed his face to the windshield on the passenger side. He couldn't make out too many details, almost no light filtered through the illegal tint. What he could see was that the vehicle didn't appear to be occupied. Standing up straight to make sure he was still alone, he quickly squatted next to the front tire to get a look at the damage.

Max was not a crime scene specialist or any kind of forensics expert, but he had seen a lot of traffic accidents during his career. Plus, at the Police Academy, almost every car in the driving pool had these same marks in the exact same place. The dint that signified the impact, and the scrapes that identified the push. A classic signature of a car used to perform a PIT maneuver.

Once again, not being an expert, he couldn't tell if the marks were new or old, but if he could get a sample of the paint, Kimberly Gibson could match it to the flakes they had and achieve justice for Amia and Alanah. In order for it to stand up in court, he had to do this the right way. So, he jerked upright to head over to his car and get a couple evidence bags and a swab kit. Thinking he should at least take a few pictures with his phone before leaving, he reached for the device. A toe scrape on the asphalt was the only warning of danger he got.

The first blow to his head splayed him out on the hood of the car before he slid off and crumpled to the ground, face first. He could feel the blood dripping down his neck and face as he moaned from the pain. Floating in and out of consciousness, he heard someone whisper, "Should have minded your business, cop," before the next blow brought darkness to his world.

• •

The early morning June sun brought only moderate heat, but intense illumination to the dismal scene being played out. Sundays in this region normally displayed ghost-town like qualities as residents slept off their debauchery of the night before, and prepared to ask for forgiveness in one of God's houses. The crowd of gawkers made Max feel like everyone in the area had heard about the cop being assaulted at the Burger King.

As he sat on the back bumper of the ambulance, waiting for the paramedic to finish applying the compression to his head wounds, he steamed at his own personal mistakes and failures. Max knew he could have done a hundred things differently last night and it would have led to justice for Alanah and Amia Knight. Because of his own stupidity, he was sure the driver of the black Ford would now get rid of all the evidence linking him to the crime.

The paramedic tapped him on the shoulder and said, "I've done my best to make sure you won't bleed out, but I still think you should see a doctor." Gesturing to the nearby hospital, he said, "I would hate to see you die from a brain bleed this close to a hundred doctors." Max looked at the young man, nodded, and stood up to make his way over to the detectives investigating his assault.

There was no way in the world he was gonna let some doctor take him off duty for a couple of lumps on the head. Plus, since he had no idea who attacked him, the bastard could be watching from the crowd. He wasn't gonna give him the satisfaction of thinking he'd taken him out of the hunt. All they needed was one clue, one witness, one shred of evidence, and this guy was grass.

Others might not make the same leap he would, but Max saw this as confirmation that a race had led to the murder of those two young women. It was too much of a coincidence that a black car with the perfect damage would turn up in this area only weeks after the initial crime. And no one who'd had a simple fender bender would attack a cop and compound their trouble just to get away.

The words of his attacker were the final nail in the coffin. The culprit knew he was a cop and was investigating the murders. Only someone with a vested interest in the case would have reason to know that. The whole situation just added fuel to the fire he was gonna pour over everyone involved.

One of the uniforms had been nice enough to get one of the t-shirts he kept in the trunk of his car, and wet wipes removed the traces of blood dried on his skin. He still felt sticky, but he made his way over to see if any of the detectives had found anything. When he got close, a short, Asian detective broke away from the group and made a beeline over to him.

Timothy Lehman was a few years older than his own 40 years of age. He was smart and detail oriented, but had been suspended a couple times for violating departmental drug policies. High or not, Max knew if there was anything in the area to find, Tim would damn sure find it.

The detective pushed his glasses up to the top of his nose and then shook his head. "We got nothing." He paused as he pulled out a small notepad Max was sure he didn't need, he was just doing something to fill the silence. "Witnesses said they remember the black car, but the guys from Charlotte swore the car hadn't come with them. Nobody saw the attack and, according to the video, you laid there for 18 minutes before anyone noticed you. A lot of cool cars around, who could blame them for not paying attention, right?" he asked with a dopey laugh. Seeing Max wasn't amused, he sobered up and continued with the report.

"Speaking of the cameras, they're low-grade bullshit. Maybe during the day, we could have picked up some detail from the car or the guy, but the quality is so low, the video is useless. Plus, the guy didn't come from the Burger King, he came from the street. We're running down videos from the hospital and surrounding businesses, but so far, nothing that shows the man, or the license plate clearly. It's not even clear what he hit you with."

Max glanced around the area and pictured it as it would have been the night before. The closest Supercar would have been a hundred feet away. With no adequate lighting on this end of the lot, it was easy to see why no one had seen what happened.

Detective Lehman smoothed his hair back, pushed his glasses up again, and said, "We issued a BOLO on a Ford Mustang, black, with damage on the front passenger side, but it's probably long gone. If it was mine, I'd already have the damage fixed, the paint sand blasted off, and listed on Facebook Market at a bargain price. We're still processing everything we find, but I don't think it will amount to anything. Sorry pal, but I think this one will get away." He walked off to rejoin the crime scene team.

Damn, thought Max. He'd been so close to taking down James Jordan, and by extension, Sammy. If only he'd looked at the license plate before exploring the damage. Then again, if the man had been watching the whole time, he might have beat him to death rather than just unconscious. Now, not only would James and the unsub get away with murder, this asshole would get away with assaulting him. Shaking his head after one last look around, he stalked back to his car.

He was already dripping with sweat by the time he made it back to the unmarked. He slumped down in the furnace-like interior, started the engine, and turned on the air conditioning, not even caring that the circulating air provided little relief. Fatigue was clouding his mind. Or, maybe it was the concussion. Whatever it was, he almost turned the ignition back off, lowered the window, and went to sleep. Max sighed and was just about to put the car in gear when his cellphone signaled an incoming call.

Looking at the display, he mumbled, "Probably just wants to give me crap," before he answered the call. "What's up, Kim?"

His colleague, probably alerted by his defeated tone, decided to cut him a little slack. "I heard that hard head of yours finally came in handy." Softly she asked, "How are you feeling?" She was usually all business, her attitude tending towards brash and rude. Every now and then, though, she showed that she really did have a heart.

Max said, "I've been better, but I think I'll live. The bumps on my head aren't what I'm worried about, it's the fact that I let this clown get away. I was this close to getting justice for those two girls," he stated, holding his fingers an inch apart.

"Well, if your attacker really is the missing race car driver, he's had a very busy night. I'm sending you a video right now, watch it and tell me what you think." Five seconds later, his phone signaled an incoming email.

"What should I be looking for?" he asked.

"Just watch the damn thing, Max! You'll see whatever you see."

He opened the attachment and hit the play icon on his screen. He frowned in confusion because he had no idea what he was looking at. There was no sound, and everything was illuminated with a red glow. The camera appeared to be vibrating, other than that, nothing moved. Then, for just a brief second, everything was bathed in a green hue and then things became clear.

His heartrate accelerated right along with the cars on the screen. Now he could tell that the camera was attached to a car on the left, and it was pointed towards another car on the right. He'd seen this setup before. It was used in street races to settle any disputes if the results were contested. All his exhaustion faded away as he smiled with glee. This would be all the evidence he needed to lean on James.

A fraction of a second into the race, a silver blur separated itself from the right-side darkness on his screen, and sped off to the left. Because of the positioning of the camera, there was no way to see the license plate numbers. There was no doubt the lab could clean the video up, so he didn't stress too much over the lackluster details.

About eight seconds later, the green glow emerged again, but only for a second, then it was all darkness again. In a sequence so fast, if you blinked you'd miss it, red brake lights appeared on the right side of the video, then a violent collision took place.

This guy is a pro, thought Max. Even though he'd swerved with enough force to wreck the other car, not once did the video swing, which would have signified his own car losing control. No, this guy used his car as a deadly weapon and then coolly drove away from the scene. Based on where the wrecked Nissan had been, the other driver had to have used the grass lined shoulder to get by, otherwise the camera would have picked up the wreckage.

Remembering Kim, who was still on the call, he asked, "How much was the lab able to clean up?" When she unleashed one of her famous sighs, he almost slammed his still aching head on the steering wheel. "Just give it to me straight, Kim."

"Let me start at the beginning so you get the whole story." He could hear her flipping through some papers before she said, "Okay. Based off the time line from your attack, 15 minutes after the perpetrator left that scene, the video was sent to the department by email. The account and phone used were burners and have not been active since that initial use.

"Since the video reached me, which was minutes after the department got it, I've been working to gather all I could from it. The truth is, it's not much."

"Is this enough to go after James Jordan?" he asked her.

"Hold on, Max! I'm getting to that." More paper rustling, then she continued. "The lab put a rush on it because of its connection to the two murders. So, they cleaned it up, but it's almost impossible to use any of it as real evidence."

Max was confused by that. "This is evidence of a race! You can even see the point where the car driven by James is hit by the other car."

"What we infer and what the video shows is two different things," she went on to explain. "There's no time stamp, so the video could be ten years old. The background is dark as pitch, so we have no references to determine speed. We do have the glow of the street lights, but who's to say the video is unedited. Then, the major missing element, we never see anybody in the silver car. We also never see the car crash, which means we have no proof that this video was taken June 10th."

"So, you're telling me we have nothing!" Max exclaimed.

"Nothing concrete," she said in a calming tone. "This situation is very serious. With two dead young women, and now the assault on you, people are a little more willing to step out on a limb. I've already talked to the Cabarrus county DA, as well as the Police Commissioner."

When she paused, Max said, "Stop fucking around, Kim! What did they say?"

"Well, everything we have is circumstantial, but it is compelling. Too many coincidences for them not to be connected. So, while you were laying around being babied for your little booboo, we were talking to a judge trying to get an arrest warrant. We couldn't find one willing to go that far, but we did find one to sign off on an order to bring James Jordan in for questioning. Once we get him in interrogation, we can arrest him at our discretion for suspicion of murder."

"That's good," Max said. "But, an order for questioning won't override his doctor's orders for medical care. All I could do is take him to the County Jail and place him in the medical wing. I won't even be able to question him before he has a hearing and is bonded out."

"Oh! I forgot to mention the last part. James Jordan's doctor signed his release papers about 20 minutes ago. We have three officers over there waiting for him to exit the hospital."

"Why the hell didn't you start with that!" he yelled, putting the car in gear. "You better pray I'm not too late to be the one slapping cuffs on this lying little shit!"

Chapter 7

"Knock! Knock!" Yazmine said before she poked her head into the room. Entering, she said, "I hope you're ready to go, I got the whole day off and I got plans to spend it with my best bud."

After closing the door, she turned to him with a huge smile on her face, and swung her curtain of hair behind her back. She stood, hands clasped in front of her, with a look of expectancy in her eyes. She was wearing a short, denim Chanel skirt that drew his gaze to her well-toned thighs. The black tube-top bared her midriff and molded to her perfectly formed breast. The only reason he knew they were natural and not implants was because they were the same shape, just a tad bigger than when they'd been mashed against his chest about three years ago.

His eyes traveled back down her body to the pink and black Balenciaga tennis shoes before returning to her face. She looked down at her outfit and frowned. "What?" she asked. "It's hot as hell outside!" All he could do was sigh and shake his head as he turned to gather the backpack that was the only luggage he had left after sending the rest home with his parents the day before.

Yazmine, trying to regain her excitement, said, "First, we going to McDonalds to get some bacon, egg, and cheese biscuits. You've lost some weight and we need to fatten you back up. Then, we going to your house so you can relax and chill until it's time to go to the park. I got some workout clothes in the car and we can jog or play some hoops, maybe do some yoga. Then I got some picnic…. What?" she asked as he just stood there staring at her.

James had expected his parents to pick him up, but got a text early this morning that Yazmine was coming instead. This was their first communication since he'd mistakenly called her Alanah while she slept in his arms Friday night. He'd called her a hundred times, but she just sent him to voicemail. Now, she was here acting as if everything was okay.

"Yazmine, I'm sorry."

Her head cocked and he could tell she wanted to act like she didn't know what he was talking about. Then her smile faded and she started looking down, toying with the strands of her hair. She said, "I know what Alanah was and still is to you. I've known you for 15 years, JJ. I know when you feel something, you feel it down to your toes. You've loved her with all your heart and soul for the past six plus years. Even if your mind knows that she's gone, your body still hasn't reached that conclusion." She paused as her eyes met his. "After Friday night, I really tried to stay away from you. I know you still have love for me, but we both know that my feelings run a little deeper."

Shaking his head, James said, "Yazmine, I don't think…"

"Hold on JJ, let me finish," she interrupted. "When we were children, I pictured us being together forever. That image has never changed, but now I'm just happy to have you in my life again. You're my best friend, my only real friend in the world, and I've let you down over and over again. I promise I'm not looking for anything more, I just want to be your friend, JJ. Yes, I love you. Yes, I would love to be with you. But, trust me, I won't do anything to jeopardize our friendship. Now, can we please get the hell out of here! I'm hungry!"

James smiled and opened his arms for his best friend. She stepped into him like she had thousands of times in her life, and he wrapped her up tightly. He willed his body not to respond to her smell and feel as he buried his face in the hair he loved. He whispered, "I'm so sorry, Yazmine. You know I'll always love you." They stayed locked in the embrace until he kissed her head and pulled away.

They held hands, staring into each other's eyes, and smiled as they acknowledged their relationship was on the mend. James pulled her under his arm and jokingly said, "Don't be posting our day on your timeline. If you rolling with me, it's just gonna be us."

She slapped his chest but smiled brilliantly. "I don't post everything. Plus, the followers I have wouldn't be thrilled to see me hanging with some fine ass man."

"Yeah, I know," he said before he could catch himself.

She stopped them at the door and looked up at him in surprise. "The last I checked, you weren't on my followers list. Let me find out you been keeping up with me through a ghost account!"

He blushed and said, "No comment."

They exited the room, laughing and joking as they passed the officer still stationed outside his room. They ignored him, but James did notice the man pull his phone out and fall in behind them. As far as he knew, nothing had changed, so he didn't pay him any more mind.

Yazmine said, "I always park my car at one of the back exits to stay away from traffic. I'm still in love with my Porsche, and I don't want her getting dinged up. It's a bit more of a walk, but at least we're in the air conditioning."

"Hey, it's better than my dad. He pays a hospital employee to run out and reserve a spot for him whenever he's on his way." Shaking his head, he added, "Sometimes the man's ego and entitlement is unbelievable."

She murmured, "The apple doesn't fall far from the tree." She tried to run when he reached for her, but he noticed she didn't put a whole lot of effort into getting away.

He wrapped her around the waist and she squealed as he swung her around. An older white couple smiled at them and clutched each other tightly as they watched what they thought was a young couple in love.

When he set her down, she smoothed her skirt down and said, "Boy! You just showed the whole hospital my ass!" She looked around at all the people in embarrassment.

"What? You mad because they aint subscribed to your OnlyFans for the opportunity?" She gasped and he took off running when she swung at his head.

"You low life bastard! How do you know what's on my OnlyFans?" She caught up with him at the exit and was about to attack when she noticed how ridged his posture had become. She swung her gaze to the parking lot just as five

103

officers exited their vehicles and made their way towards them. When she looked up at James, she noticed the officer from outside of his hospital room had cut off any retreat back through the doors.

The detective, in his grubby looking street clothes, already had a pair of cuffs in his hand. One of the four uniforms branched off and said, "Miss, can you please take a few steps to your right?" Just in case she thought about not complying, he grabbed her arm and pulled her away.

James, with bewildered eyes, asked, "Detective Hall? What's going on? What's wrong?" He noticed the bandages wrapping the man's head that he tried to hide, unsuccessfully, with a baseball cap.

All business, Det. Hall said, "Turn around and put your hands behind your back." He followed the order and his backpack was ripped from his body as rough hands searched for any weapons on his person.

"Hey!" he exclaimed. "I'm cooperating! You don't have to be so rough. Just tell me what's going on!"

"Two counts of murder are what's going on," said the detective. As he locked the cuffs on his wrist, he said, "You have the right to remain silent. Anything you say can and will be used against you in a court of law. You have the right…" As he went on, James turned his head and focused on Yazmine.

"Call my parents, Yazzy! Tell them what's going on." Yazmine reached into the Burberry sack she had strapped around her waist and pulled out her phone. He watched her as she talked animatedly, but couldn't hear her because he was already in the back of the cop car.

The detective walked around and got into the driver's seat and turned with a smirk. "Should have talked when you had the chance. Now, you'll spend the rest of your life in prison." He turned back around, started the car, and pulled off. The smile never left the detectives face.

James watched a frantic Yazmine crying and pulling her hair while she talked into her phone. Then they turned and he couldn't see her anymore. One thing was for sure, James was anything but stupid. He didn't care what evidence they thought they had; he wouldn't be saying a word until his lawyer arrived on the scene.

• •

Detective Hall didn't take him to the Cabarrus County Detention Center, instead he took him to the Concord Police department. Once they arrived, James was ushered into an interrogation room, uncuffed, and left on his own. The detective hadn't asked him any questions or made any demands, just left him in this room about an hour ago.

The space wasn't hot or cold, it seemed the temperature was perfect for his shorts and t-shirt clad body. Everything in the room was concrete or metal, and the metal table and chairs were bolted down to the floor. There was a two-way mirror, a TV in a plexiglass enclosure, and a camera mounted directly over the table. Although the chair was a little uncomfortable, nothing about the room screamed intimidation. He was just about to get up and pace when the door was pushed open and three people entered.

Detective Hall entered first, wearing the same dirty clothes he'd had on earlier. The next person was a woman with crinkly, dark hair, wearing khakis and a man's dress shirt, carrying a thick file. The last person to enter was a huge officer who James assumed was there just in case he decided to act up. The uniform stayed next to the door after he closed it.

The two plain clothes people came in and claimed the seats across from him with the two-way mirror behind them. Det. Hall pointed up and said, "That camera will be recording everything said in this room. You've already been read your rights; did you understand them?"

James didn't respond at first, he just used the silence to study the pair. Det. Hall looked tired and beat up. His small body looked as if a strong breeze could blow him over. The woman, on the other hand, seemed sturdy and in control. Her eyes were alert with intelligence and readiness. It didn't take him long to figure that she was the real threat out of the two of them.

In response to the detective's question, James said, "Yes, I understand, but I don't want to talk until I've had a chance to consult with my lawyer."

Nodding, Det. Hall said, "That's your right, but it won't stop us from talking to you. By the way," he said, gesturing to his left, "this is Kimberly Gibson. She's the Crash Investigator who's going to put you in prison for the rest of your life." After a few beats of silence, he added, "Now, I know you want to wait for your attorney, but if you want to save yourself from that fate, I'm giving you the opportunity, right now, to tell me your side of things."

James shook his head and said, "I'm not talking until…"

"We have the video, Mr. Jordan," Ms. Gibson cut him off softly. "Early this morning, the driver of the black Mustang sent us the video of the race. We had our lab enhance the video and we got some pretty compelling evidence. It was enough that we have you sitting here now. You know anything about Felony Murder?"

James was reeling. He was replaying the images he'd watched from hundreds of videos through his mind. He had no idea what kind of capabilities their lab had, and he didn't know what type of camera the man had used. Some of the HD cameras he'd seen could have picked up all three of the occupants in his car. There was really no way to know what they had unless he saw it.

Ms. Gibson said, "Mr. Jordan!" His head snapped in her direction, and she asked, "Do you know anything about Felony Murder?" He shrugged noncommittal, so she explained the relevancy of the question. "In a typical murder case, there are elements that have to be proven before we can move forward. You have motives and thoughts and actions that have to line up in a certain way for a death to be ruled a murder. Most cases get reduced down because of how hard it is to prove a number of these elements.

"With the Felony Murder rule, it's different. The burden of proof is simple: Was a felony being committed when a death occurred? That's pretty much it. As long as you were a knowing and willing participant in the felony, everyone involved is responsible for the death.

"Even if you were just a lookout. Or if a coconspirator is killed. Any death that comes about during the commission of a felony, it makes the case immediately open for the Felony Murder rule."

She stopped talking but Det. Hall picked up the diatribe. "But, not only did your buddy send us a video leaving no doubt that you're guilty, when I located his black Ford Mustang this morning, he attacked me to get away."

James was shaken by the information being thrown in his face. Until this conversation, he'd forgotten all about the camera the man said he attached to his car. This guy obviously had no quarrels with throwing James under the bus. If memory served him right, no part of the other car would be visible, only his own. Outwardly, he was stone faced and solid as a rock. On the inside, he was a quivering mass of worry and fear.

Detective Hall continued. "This opens the door wide for you to make a deal. We can see from the video that the race was over when this guy struck you. With that information, it gives a little wiggle room on whether you were still in the commission of a felony when the deaths happened. Now, if you cooperate fully, tell us who this guy is, and agree to testify against him, we've been authorized to offer you a plea for illegal street racing and immunity for the two murders. You can get justice against this guy for Alanah and Amia, and you can reduce your risk of ever touching a jail cell. What you have to understand is, this deal expires the second we leave this room."

For a couple of minutes, they all sat in silence. The officers watching him trying to pick up on any hidden signals, and James thinking about how best to play this situation. What were the rules of the streets when it came to snitching on someone who was actively trying to snitch on you? Hell, do people even care about who's snitching anymore? With all these rappers cooperating with authorities and still selling out shows, James thought that was answer enough.

Once again though, James was far from stupid. Cops lied. All! The! Time! Most of them lied so much, they didn't even know what the truth was. He could spill his guts right now and then end up with no deal, spending the rest of his life in prison. Some kind of doubt must have shown on his face because Det. Hall felt the need to do more convincing.

"Look Son, we all make mistakes. Old, young, male, female, all of us make decisions that later on we wish we could do over again. The thing is, we as adults have to claim our mistakes and learn from them. Now, your choice to race this guy with those two women in your car can't be undone, but I'm giving you the opportunity to claim your mistake and make this right."

"I won't pretend that I know you James," said Ms. Gibson, joining the conversation, "but from what I've seen, you seem like a good and decent young man. One thing that comes across loud and clear from everyone who does know you is your love for Alanah and Amia. What I want you to do is close your eyes and picture their faces before they got into your car that night."

James didn't close his eyes, but only because he didn't need to in order to picture the two women. Their smiles and shining eyes as they playfully insulted each other was the memory on replay in his mind. He swallowed deeply as he tried to keep his emotions from welling up. When that didn't work, he swiped angrily at the tears rolling down his face.

"Now," she continued, "I want you to picture their faces at the crime scene when you snatched those sheets off of them." After a short deliberate pause, she said forcefully, "He did that! This animal, who you are protecting, took those young ladies from you. Alanah, your future bride, future mother of your children, college basketball star. This asshole decided that her life was worth scarifying because he lost a race.

"Amia, just entering adulthood, set to go to UNC-Chapel Hill in the fall. Another casualty of this guy being a sore loser. Make him hurt like they hurt. Like you hurt. Don't allow him to go free after he's taken so much good from this earth!"

She fell silent as James took deep breath after deep breath trying to staunch the flow of tears. Clip after clip of his life with Alanah and Amia flashed in his mind. While he loved Alanah with every fiber of his being, Amia was just as important to him. She had never been the annoying girl who was always in the way. Amia had been the little sister who he'd been proud to call his family.

The detective and investigator were good. They knew just what to say and which emotions to play on. The truth was right on the tip of his tongue, but self-preservation was stronger than his need for vengeance. He couldn't take the chance that the police were playing him just to get a confession.

Clearing his throat, he said, "I wish to speak to my lawyer before I agree to anything."

Det. Hall exploded. "You stupid little shit!" he yelled, slamming his fist on the table. He jumped up and snatched his hat off so the bandages were now clearly visible. "You see what he did to me to keep his identity a secret. If you ever see the streets again, what do you think he'll do to you? Other than his car, which is probably at the bottom of a lake by now, you're the only person who can link him to this crime. I have a nerve to release you and let him have a go at you!" Pulling out his cuffs again, he said, "But, I'm good with taking one of you off the streets for now. Get up!"

The detective secured his wrist behind his back, and he marched him back through the precinct out into the late afternoon sun. James had his head down, trying to shield his eyes from the punishing rays, when he heard, "You better not have talked to my client without me being present! I'll have your badge if you did!" His lawyer, Corey McCann, was standing next to the unmarked cruiser in a light gray, summer weight suit. He looked at James and asked, "Did you invoke your right to counsel?"

The detective never stopped his march to the backseat of the car. James said, "Yes! From the very beginning. They tried to get me to talk but I wouldn't say anything." By now, the detective was pushing on his head in an attempt to get him in the car. "They tried to offer me immunity for the identity of some guy who doesn't exist." That was all he had time to say before the door was slammed shut.

The situation didn't end there. Corey pointed at Det. Hall and said, "I'm gonna have your ass over this! You dare to violate one of my client's civil rights? Your career is over!"

Det. Hall smirked and said, "Interfere with my duty again and we'll see whose ass is had. I know how to do my job, and none of your fancy lawyer tricks are gonna save your boy. I offered him a way out, but you know what, I was hoping he wouldn't take it. Now, I get to march his ass to county with two counts of Felony Murder. No judge will grant him bond with these charges. His ass now belongs to the state. Let's see what all that money can do for him and his Pops now!"

While the detective laughed and walked around to the driver's side, Corey turned his focus to James. "I'll be over at the jail to see you after you're processed. Don't say anything to anybody. I'll see you later." The car started up and pulled off with Corey standing at the curb watching them go. The detective just continued to laugh as he drove the quick mile over to the Cabarrus County Detention Center.

Once inside, James went through the same process he'd went through when he was 17-years-old. Mug shot, fingerprinting, strip search, and his clothes being changed out for an orange jumpsuit. His shoes were taken and he was given shower shoes before he was walked to a back room where he encountered the magistrate.

The older white man in glasses never even looked at him as he asked for all his personal information. At the end of the Q&A, he handed James a few sheets of paper and said, "I'm holding you with no bond until you go before a judge for a hearing." Then he turned away like James was already forgotten.

Next, the correction staff led him down a long corridor to an elevator which they rode a couple floors up and then got off.

He had immediately bonded out the last time, so this part was new to him. At his assigned block, he was handed a small toiletry bag, a roll of linens and clothes, and led into the block. At this moment, the seriousness of his situation hit him.

He heard people talking about the jail all the time around The Strip. He knew the blocks consisted of 16 cells, eight on each of the two levels, with two men assigned to each cell. He knew about the metal bunks and the stainless-steel sinks and toilets. No one had ever mentioned the dread that came over you when the sights and smells assaulted your senses on entry.

The C.O. said, "You're lucky. We have an empty cell in this wing, which is reserved for people with more serious crimes. So, unless someone kills or rapes somebody tonight, you'll get a cell to yourself." Even though no one was out in the dayroom area, the officer still had to yell to be heard over the noise.

People were shouting and banging and singing. Radios were blasting. Inmates were arguing and hurling insults back and forth. It actually sounded like prison did in the movies. He even heard a few guys yelling "fresh fish" in reference to him. The noise was enough to drive a man crazy, but the smells were even worse.

Burnt food, urine, and body odor were the smells competing for dominancy. A hint of some weak cleaning solution hung in the air, but it was overpowered by the foul scents billowing out of an overflowing trash can in the middle of the floor. Flies and ants seemed to be working together to make sure enough food was spread over the area so the whole insect kingdom could eat. Overall, the stench was enough to make him gag.

The officer yelled for the door to the last cell to be opened, and said, "I'll see if I can get you some food and some cleaning supplies. The last two guys in this room damn near killed each other and the result was never cleaned up. Be careful what you touch until I come back." The door closed between them and James turned to survey his new home.

It wasn't all that bad. Most of the blood splatters were centered around a desk hanging from the wall opposite the beds. The mattress and pillow were both plastic and didn't have too many stains on them. The mirror bolted over the toilet was so scratched up, he couldn't see his reflection. The best thing about the cell was that it drastically cut down on the smell and the noise. He probably wouldn't be able to sleep, but he definitely could spend his new-found free time thinking. He located a relatively clean spot on the mattress and sat down to wait on the officer's return.

Hours later, while he was thinking about spending the rest of his life in a cell just like this, the door opened. He hadn't eaten anything all day, so he looked forward to whatever meal was on the way. Instead of food, the officer said, "Kitchen is closed for the day, but your lawyer is here to see you. I told him you hadn't gotten any food and he went back to the vending machines out front. Don't give me any trouble and I'll let you eat whatever he brings. I'll have the cleaning supplies waiting when you're done."

The young, heavyset officer led him back to the elevator which they rode down to the main floor once again. He directed him down the hall until they came to a small room with a window on the door. James could see Corey sitting anxiously inside. The officer eyed him speculatively when they stopped at the door.

He said, "I've never been wrong about these things, don't make this the first time. I'm supposed to shackle you, but I don't get any deranged-killer vibes off of you, despite your charges. I'm stepping out on a limb with you in regards to the food and the restraints. Don't make me regret it." After his speech, he opened the door and closed it once James stepped in.

Corey McCann was pissed. Even as he directed James to sit down and eat the chips, jerky, and candy he'd spread on the table, he was lighting into him. "You know James, you're a real piece of work! I told you to be honest with me. I could have put a stop to this before it went this far. You understand that they have evidence that can put you in prison forever? And, if I can't get you bail, today might have been your last free day on earth."

James polished off the jerky, and was now working his way through the bag of party mix. He closed his eyes and almost moaned from the salty goodness. He was listening to his lawyer, but he was so damn hungry! For the second time that day, a man slammed his fist down in exasperation because of him.

"You better start taking this seriously, boy!" he exploded. "Your dad is at the police department raising hell and he might end up being your roommate by the end of the night. Your mom and Ms. Salazar just left from here trying to see you, both looking like the world was ending when they were turned away. Everyone understands how serious this is, except for you. You better get with the program quick, or get prepared for the snacks you're eating now becoming a delicacy."

James finished the chips and felt somewhat better. Opening the bag of Sour Skittles, he looked up and said, "I am taking this serious, but what is it you expect me to do?"

"Well, for starters, you can tell me the truth about what happened that night."

Shrugging, James said, "I already told you what I remember. We were on our way back from the party and I woke up on the road with an EMT leaning over me."

"James, this is your life at stake, not mine. The evidence they have, it's not ironclad proof, but it's pretty damning. They have a video, which doesn't prove much, but it was enough for a judge to issue a warrant. I talked to a couple sources and they assured me that their whole case is so far built on circumstantial evidence, but plenty of people have been convicted on a fraction of what they have now. I need you to trust me and tell me the truth."

James leaned back in his chair and studied the man sitting across from him. Corey and his dad had become close once Victoria Jordan, Sammy's mother, had died and Corey became his estate lawyer. Since James was 10-years-old at the time, his dad's lawyer represented him, also. Grandma Victoria had split her money between her son and grandson and Corey had picked up a hefty commission for his good work. James couldn't question the man's loyalty, he had never let them down so far, but nothing short of Jesus resurrecting was gonna make James confess and put his life in someone else's hands.

"Listen, Mr. McCann, I know you're trying to help me. I understand that I might be making the situation difficult for you. What I need you to understand is, this is what you have to work with. I'm not changing my story, and I'm not taking any deals. If they have some video of a street race, it isn't me driving. And any other "proof" they drum up, it has to be manufactured because the only thing happened on that road was a tragic accident. Anybody saying differently is lying or guessing because I'm the only person who knows the truth."

After a long silence with them staring at each other, Corey nodded with resolve and lumbered to his feet. "Bail hearing at 9:00am tomorrow. If I can't get you bail, you could spend the next few years in here waiting for trial. Or, I could talk to the DA and try to get you that deal the detective was talking about?" he asked, in a last-ditch effort.

James just shook his head and finished off the rest of the Skittles. Corey said, "See you tomorrow," and left when the officer answered his knock.

The officer patted him down to make sure his lawyer hadn't slipped him any contraband, and then escorted him back to his cell. He spent about 30 minutes cleaning, made up his bed, and laid there until the lights suddenly dimmed.

Just like every night since the accident, thoughts of Alanah filled his mind. They had hardly ever argued, but that was mainly because Alanah always got her way. At first, he was petrified that she would leave him if he dared to disagree with her. Over time, he realized how much she sacrificed just to keep their relationship moving in the right direction. She had truly been his guardian angel, and he'd paid her back by ending her life.

For the first time, though, no tears came to his eyes. Instead, rage took over his heart. Not only had The Black Sheep taken Alanah and Amia from him, now he was trying to finish what he'd started on that backroad. By getting him life in prison, that would effectively end the third life that he'd tried to extinguish weeks ago.

The Golden Boy wasn't done yet. If he could somehow get bail tomorrow, he was definitely gonna pay the man a visit. James was sure the bastard wasn't hiding. In fact, he was probably making himself as visible as possible. His visibility showing the world he was innocent and providing all the cover he needed.

Chapter 8

James was ushered into the courtroom the next morning at 9:15. He was wearing his orange prison jumpsuit, but he was unencumbered by any restraints as the detention center officer led him over to the defendant's table. The room was quite impressive with its soaring ceilings and gleaming wood furnishings, but he was more focused on what was waiting for him behind his seat.

Sammy, Brianna, and Yazmine were drinking him in like they were checking for damage. He smiled and waved to assure them he was good before he turned his focus to the front of the courtroom.

Corey had prepared him about an hour ago on the actors in this drama. The judge, Timothy Kennedy, was exactly what he'd pictured in his mind. An older, bald, black man who appeared to be slightly overweight and about 60-years-old. His eyes, behind the small rimmed glasses, made him look mean and hard. Corey assured him the man would be fair, but with 15 years under his belt, he wouldn't take any crap. Since he was flipping through some papers, and didn't appear to be ready yet, James turned his head to the left and studied the District Attorney.

Jennifer Morrison was tall, thin, and everything about her screamed no-nonsense. Her blond hair was pulled back into a tight ponytail. Her dark blue pantsuit was pressed to perfection and her black flats were for function only. She was standing at the prosecutor's table staring at the judge like she could will him into hurrying up. Corey had told him she was only in her second year as a DA, but she was very good, if not a little too dramatic. She would definitely be pushing for no bail.

Without preamble, Judge Kennedy looked up at James and said, "This is just an arraignment to find out how you're going to plead to these charges and figure out any bail considerations. You are being charged with two counts of Felony Murder for the deaths of Alanah and Amia Knight during an illegal street race. This race allegedly took place in the early hours of Friday, June 10th. How do you plead to these charges?"

Corey stood up and said, "I'm representing James Jordan in this matter and my client pleads not guilty to any and all charges stemming from the accident on June 10th."

"Alright," said the judge, jotting down something on a piece of paper. After a few seconds of silence, he glanced up at the DA and asked, "You have anything in request about bail?"

"Yes, Your Honor," she said walking out from behind the table. "The defendant is being charged with two Capital crimes. Even though the State will not be pursuing the Death Penalty, Mr. Jordan is still facing the rest of his life behind bars. I recommend that the defendant be remanded in the custody of the Cabarrus County Detention Center pending the outcome of a trial." If the situation wasn't so serious, James would have fell out laughing. She was strolling and posing as if she was in front of a jury on Law & Order.

The judge didn't seem like he enjoyed the performance much himself. He fumbled through a stack of papers looking perplexed before glancing at the DA. "Ms. Morrison, I'm not seeing an indictment here. You did take this to the Grand Jury before processing these charges, right?"

Looking somewhat flustered, she said, "Your Honor, I felt it was pertinent to get this dangerous man off our streets as soon as possible. After one of our detectives was attacked while gathering evidence for this case…"

"Are you accusing Mr. Jordan of committing or orchestrating this assault?" Judge Kennedy asked her.

"Well… No, not necessarily, but our detective had found the car that the defendant was racing…"

"And you have evidence that this other car was racing Mr. Jordan on June 10th?"

"Um… That's the evidence Det. Hall was in the process of getting before he was savagely attacked from behind."

"But this evidence was never gathered, so you're assuming the evidence would have led to this conclusion. Am I correct?" he asked the DA.

Slumping in defeat, Ms. Morrison said, "That is correct, Sir."

Judge Kennedy stared at her for a beat in admonishment before focusing on the papers in front of him. After a minute of silence, he looked at her again and said, "I'm not seeing anything here that would have made me even issue an arrest warrant in this case. But, we're here now." Turning to Corey, he asked, "You have anything to add?"

Corey stayed where he was and said, "Absolutely, Your Honor. There is not one shred of evidence that my client did anything wrong. The police department and the DA, justifiably, wants someone to pay for the deaths of Alanah and Amia Knight. Because Mr. Jordan was driving the car when it wrecked, he's the easiest target for them to go after. They assume that the wreck was a direct result of an illegal street race, but nothing they've uncovered substantiates that claim. I know I'll have to wait for an evidential hearing to file for a dismissal, but to hold my client in jail for even one more day on these fictious charges would be a grossly negligent act by this court."

The judge leaned back in his chair and looked at each of them in turn. Finally, he turned to the DA and asked, "You have anything more, Ms. Morrison?"

"One last thing, Your Honor. Based off the latest tax records summitted by the defendant, he is worth slightly over $100 Million. I feel that, because of his resources, if he is released on bond, we will never see him again."

"Your Honor," interjected Corey. "My client, just as his father, grandmother, and great grandfather, was born and raised right here in Concord, North Carolina. His family has been prevalent in this community for 100 years. To suggest that he is a flight risk just because he is rich is asinine and foolish."

Judge Kennedy held his hand up for silence when the DA started to make a rebuttal. "Both of you, take your seats and be quiet for a minute." He looked at James and said, "Stand up, son." When he jerked to his feet, hitting his knee on the table in the process, Judge Kennedy asked, "You want to add anything to this discussion?"

James took a deep breath and said, "Yes, Your Honor, I would." The court was packed to the brim with members of the community. Most were there just to be nosy. Others were there to either support James or the Knight family. Whatever purpose each individual was there for, they now sat in silence, raptly awaiting what would come out of his mouth.

"Running has never crossed my mind, Sir. Concord is my home. And, with all due respect, I'm not a coward. I don't skirt my responsibilities and I won't hide from the justice process. But I'm innocent. I'm mourning the loss of two people who were very dear to me. No matter how you rule, whether you grant me bail or keep me locked up, nothing will bring Alanah and Amia back." Pointing at his chest, he said, "I was driving, so I hold myself responsible for their deaths. But I didn't commit any crimes. It was just a horrible accident that I have to live with for the rest of my life."

Tears of pain accompanied his words, but they weren't for show. They were a real release of the emotions boiling up from deep inside him. He was doing all he could to keep from curling up on the floor and bawling like a baby.

James sat back down and the judge once again took a minute to contemplate. He leaned forward, wrote something on the paper again, and then sat up to address the court. "One thing everyone knows I am against is the misuse of the criminal justice process. When steps are skipped and corners are cut, it puts us rule abiders in a tough situation. We are forced to fix things that should never have been broken."

He focused him attention on Jennifer Morrison. "I have a nerve to file a misconduct report on you! These charges are a travesty to our justice system. You didn't go through any of the suggested steps to protect the integrity of this court or the public. But I won't file any reports, I just want you to use this as a learning experience. Don't ever let the police, or even a judge, dictate what you know is right. I've worked with you enough to know that you are very much aware of what's going on in this case."

Turning to the defense table, he said, "With all that being said, Mr. Jordan, you are still charged with two counts of Felony Murder, and I've never granted bail on any type of murder charge. However I feel about these charges, they are in the system now and I have to rule accordingly.

"An Evidential Hearing will be set for Tuesday of next week because of the holiday on Monday. Depending on the outcome of that hearing, we will revisit the topic of bail. For now, bail is set at $500,000 for each of the counts!" *BANG!* He hammered his gavel signifying a close to the hearing.

Corey jumped to his feet and said, "Your Honor, my client is ready to post a cash bond right now!"

The judge nodded and said, "Very well. Pending the payment, the defendant is free to go."

His mom and Yazmine squealed and he leaned to give them both quick hugs. When he got to his dad, he was pulled into a tight embrace and Sammy whispered, "When you get home, we need to talk!" Then he was released from the hold and the detention officer led him back through the side door to the jail.

Corey followed him and stopped him halfway down the corridor. "This shouldn't take more than an hour. Your dad is putting up the cash, so you're being signed out to his custody." Pausing, he leaned in closer and said, "Get ready because he's pretty damn mad. He saw the video and he wants me to bring you to the house, immediately."

"I have the cash. Why couldn't I pay my own bond?"

Wincing, Corey said, "This is how Sammy wanted it. I think he wanted it this way so, if the conversation doesn't go how he likes, he can revoke the bond and get you tossed back in jail. My advice, try not to piss him off any more than you already have."

The officer then told him it was time to go, so he shook Corey's hand and continued the walk back to his jail cell.

• •

After the judge announced that James would indeed be let out on bail, Alex grabbed the hand of his quietly crying wife, and exited the courtroom. He was livid. He knew the little bastard was gonna work his magic on the judge, pretend to be oh so innocent, and His Honor was gonna fall for the act. Justice against the rich happened only seldomly, why he thought it would prevail this time was a mystery even to him.

To tell the truth, that's why he'd sat at the back of the courtroom anyway. He didn't want to see the corrupt Jordan family celebrating another bought victory. Nothing ever seemed to stick to them. He was convinced that, anytime trouble came their way, money would change hands and the problem would soon disappear. No one cared that his two daughters were dead, all they wanted to do was keep the image of the legendary Jordans clean.

Alex turned on his way to the elevator and saw his son AJ only a couple steps behind. When they entered the enclosure, Alex hugged his wife to his side and glanced over at AJ. Shaking his head, he said, "That fucker is gonna get away with it. We all know it. Either he's gonna run, or they're gonna pay off that judge to dismiss the case. No matter what, The Golden Boy won't do any real time. The one night he's done is gonna be all we get in exchange for Alanah and Amia."

They were all pretty much dressed alike. Khakis, dress shoes, and white shirts, with the men wearing Polo's, and Amanda wearing a polyester blouse. Alex and AJ also sported angry expressions, thoroughly upset by the outcome of the hearing. Amanda, on the other hand, wore a peaceful, tranquil expression as nothing ever really ruffled her feathers. She was quietly dabbing at the corners of her eyes, but that was the extent of her outward emotions.

AJ asked, "Well, what do you want to do? You wanna catch him when he leaves the courthouse? Maybe get a little preemptive justice?"

"Why would you do something like that when it'll just land the two of you in jail and add more sympathy from the public towards James?" asked Amanda.

One of the things Alex always loved about his wife was how absolutely gorgeous and classy she was. Now, he could barely stand to look at her for more than a few seconds. She and Alanah looked so much alike, it was uncanny. Same Italian coloring, same brilliant smile, same teal-colored eyes and dark blond hair. The only difference physically was that, since Amanda was 45-years-old, she carried slightly more weight. When he looked at her face it just made it that much sharper, the pain he felt from the loss of his oldest girl.

"Listen, Mom," said AJ. "I'm not talking about killing him. Just letting him know that we aren't buying his act. One thing I know about him is, he can drive. No way does he flip a car if he was just driving back from the party. Bottom line, we have to do something to avenge the girls. We can't let him murder them and then continue on like he's done nothing wrong."

"But none of us really knows what happened on that road," said Amanda. "What if he's telling the truth?" Looking at Alex, she said, "What if you just quit the best job you've ever had for no reason other than your anger and pride? The Jordans have been good to us over the years. They gave both of you jobs when neither of you were qualified for the positions. They paid for your educations and treated us like family from the beginning. Don't you think they deserve the benefit of the doubt until something proves he's guilty? You both know James is hurting also. He loved our girls!"

Both men remained silent as they thought about her words. Alex hated to admit it, but she had a point. Eleven years ago, he was a janitor and his wife worked at Wal-Mart. Both made close to minimum wage, and they were struggling to take care of their young family. When he was laid off because of budget cuts at the company, his family ended up in dire straits.

Out looking for a job one day, he saw a mechanics wanted sign by the road in front of a garage under construction. On a whim, he went in and talked to the owner.

Sammy listened to his spiel about doing anything that needed to be done, but he admitted he didn't know a thing about working on cars. Sammy asked, "Did you graduate from high school?"

Alex said, "Yeah, and I played football at Duke until I hurt my knee."

Sammy asked, after some consideration, "Can you do a year of technical school?"

Alex shook his head. "I got three hungry kids at the house ages seven, nine, and eleven. Right now, we're living off my wife's wages from Wal-Mart. I can't pay for school or take that much time away from the job search."

Sammy had studied him for a few minutes before he leaned forward, seeming to reach a conclusion. "How about if I pay for school, and while you're going, I'll pay you a thousand dollars a week to come by on the weekends to clean up a little? Maybe get you a little more hands-on training with the cars?"

Alex had broken down crying, very much aware of the blessing that had just fell in his lap. After finishing up the classes, Sammy doubled his wages and made him a mechanic. Over time, he increased his pay to $12,000 a month and made him a manager. He also took AJ through the same process. They didn't get rich off of the wages, but they were able to get a bigger house and live very comfortably.

Alex would always be grateful for what Sammy had done for him and his family, but none of those feelings could bring his babies back. And nothing from the past lessened his anger over the fact that James was gonna walk away from this situation unscathed. It was bad enough he came out of the wreck without a scratch, now he was gonna come out of the legal battle the same way.

Exiting the courthouse, all three of them were feeling somewhat melancholy. Walking down the front steps, a flash of cobalt blue in the corner of his eye caused Alex to turn to his right. Coming as fast as her low-heeled boots would allow, a reporter was waving, trying to get his attention.

He said, "Hold up," to his family and they all stopped and waited until the woman in the dress, with her camera crew, caught up to them.

She walked directly to Alex and extended her hand, which he immediately shook. "My name is Savannah Harris and you were pointed out to me as the father of Alanah and Amia Knight. I was just wondering if I could speak to you for a moment?"

Her voice was forceful and confident, in direct contrast to her small, slim body. He could clearly see the intelligence dancing in her bright, ion-blue eyes as she tucked her blond hair behind her elven ears. She was pretty, with her shining hair and delicate features, but he could tell she didn't want to be defined by her looks. He was distracted from his study of her by his wife gently pulling on his arm.

Amanda said, "Excuse us for a minute," before pulling Alex and AJ a few steps away. Looking at Alex, she said, "I don't think you should be talking to a reporter while you're upset. All it would take is one wrong comment and the public could turn on us."

"I don't give a rat's ass about the public, Amanda!" he whispered, emphatically. "If I can send a message to the DA and judge that we're not gonna allow the Jordans and their money to decide the outcome of this case, then I owe that to our girls. And I'm not stupid, you know? I might say something that will force the public to back us."

Shaking her head, Amanda said, "I don't think you're stupid, sweetie. I think you're too emotional right now." To prove her point, she reached up and wiped a tear off his cheek. "Now that we're at odds with the Jordans, you know how Sammy can get. He's liable to sue you if you say anything against James."

Taking a deep breath, Alex glanced over at the reporter waiting patiently for him to make his decision. Focusing back on Amanda, he said, "People like us don't get a chance to tell our story often. The world is so fixated on the 1% they forget about the fact that they themselves fall into the other 99%. This is an opportunity for us to tell the world that we matter too. You might not like it, but I'm doing the interview."

"But Alex…"

"But nothing, Amanda! I'm doing it! If you're that much against it, then leave. I'll catch a ride with AJ." They engaged in a brief stare-off before Amanda turned and stormed off towards the parking lot.

AJ stepped up next to him and said, "Dad, you know I got your back and I'm down for whatever you want to do. But Mom might have a point on this one. Why don't we setup an interview for later in the day and we can come up with…"

"You know what, AJ?" Alex cut his son off. "You were never built for stuff like this. Your problem is you're soft. Always trying to put on this tough guy act, but when it's time to stop talking and put the work in, you clam up." Looking at his son in disgust, Alex said, "Go on and get out of here. Follow behind your mom like you always do, and I'll find my own way home."

"Dad, I'm just saying…"

"Go AJ!" screamed Alex. "I'm done talking to you!" He stared his son down until he too walked off towards the parking lot with a shaking head. Alex turned back to the reporter and raised a hand before she could speak. He said, "I'll talk to you here and now, but I'm warning you, don't try and make a fool out of me. I have a message I want to convey to the world, and I don't want you distorting my words."

Smiling and nodding, Ms. Harris said, "I'll let you tell your story in your own words. All I'll do is ask questions and you say as much or as little as you like. I promise I'll be fair and unbiased."

Nodding in thought, Alex rubbed his bald head and glanced around the now empty area. He did consider what his wife had said, but he saw this as a once in a lifetime opportunity. The world hadn't cared about his life since he blew his knee out in college. All he wanted to do was make sure the world cared about his wonderful daughters, Amia and Alanah.

Focusing back on Ms. Harris, he said, "I'm gonna trust you to do right by me and my daughters." After pausing a beat, he said, "Let's do this."

Chapter 9

When the palatial estate finally came into view, James breathed a huge sigh of relief. He was very much aware that, had the bail hearing drifted in a different direction, he might have never seen the familial grounds ever again. He was worried about the reception he would get from his parents, but it would definitely be better than the reception he'd have gotten at the jail.

Glancing over at Corey, he said, "I don't understand why I have to go to the main house. My house is on the same property. Take me home, let me rest and clean up, and I'll go to my parent's house later."

Corey just shook his head and explained again why that was impossible. "Your father holds custody of your bond. I am legally obligated to turn you over to him. If not, he can have me thrown in jail for aiding a fugitive, and he can revoke your bond and have you tossed back inside. I know it's just a bullshit power play, but you know your dad is an expert at these types of games."

Mr. McCann pulled in well over a million dollars a year handling all the Jordan family affairs. There was no shortage of legal rigmarole for him to wade through when dealing with the family's more than a quarter billion-dollar fortune. Corey didn't mind though, it made it possible for him to live the lifestyle he felt he deserved. Like today, he had on a $2,000 suit and was jauntily driving a blood-red Maserati Grand Turismo Sport. James complained, but he knew the

133

man wouldn't risk his bread and butter by not following a direct order from Sammy.

Pulling to a stop under the columned stone awning, Corey said, "James, your father loves you and he has high expectations for you to be great. I know he's been on your behind since you chose not to go to college, but he only wants what's best for you. Listen to what he says and don't argue too much. Just be honest and forthright and everything will be okay."

James shook the older man's hand, smiled and nodded, then exited the car, waving when the car pulled off. Alone now, he turned and studied the monolithic structure before him.

This was not the original home that his great grandfather, Thomas Little, built in the mid-1900's. Back then, it was a modest sized farm house that sat directly in the middle of an 1800-acre tobacco field. Since Thomas and his wife liked a simple life, and only had one daughter, they were content to save all their money and not put their wealth on display. After his great grandparents died, his grandmother, Victoria Little, had a different view on life.

She was a beautiful, and well-educated woman, but she was black in a time and place where she was expected to be quiet and subservient. Neither of those attributes were in her nature. So, her first middle finger to the cultural norms thrusted upon her was the knocking down of the old, decrepit structure, and the building of the 30,000 square foot abode that her future family would call home.

To further show her disdain for her hateful community, she cleared all the tobacco plants from her land, married a banker from Philadelphia, and turned over her vast fortune for her new husband to invest.

Samuel Jordan Sr. had been a wiz when it came to the markets and soon the couple had more money than they knew what to do with. So, Sam did what every smart, rich person on the planet does; he started buying up all the property he could get his hands on.

After a while, Samuel Jordan Jr. came along and Victoria was content to stay at home and raise her baby boy. Sam Sr., on the other hand, started to methodically buy all the property from their neighbors until he owned a big portion of Concord NC. They had estates and farms and retreats all over the world, but Sam Sr. wanted to make his wife's hometown their private oasis.

Rolling lawns, forested escapes, and magical gardens ruled their land until the mid-nineties when the developers showed major interest in their open fields. Instead of selling the land to the power-hungry town faction, Sam Sr. used a big portion of their cash to hire builders to come in, section off the property for new home builds, leaving 50 acres for the family to maintain their peace.

Millions upon millions were sunk into the project because Sam didn't sell one home until the project was complete. By this time, the market value of the property had grown 10-fold. With their opulent estate right in the middle of all the luxury mansions, the who's who of North Carolina were jockeying to buy the most exclusive homes.

Being the vindictive man he was, Sam remembered how the town folk had treated him and his wife so, regardless of how much money the locals came with, he wouldn't sell them any of the premium homes. Instead, he sold the properties to his friends and colleagues from up north.

No one knows if the locals were responsible for the tragedy that occurred, but when Sammy Jr. was 20-years-old, a year before James was born, Sam Sr. was shot and killed coming out of a Wal-Mart in broad daylight. The culprit was never identified and no evidence was ever recovered to point to a specific suspect. Victoria and Sammy always suspected the locals of the murder, but without proof, they were left with just their suspicions.

When James was 10-years-old, and Victoria was 60, she died from a stroke suffered while she slept. James remembered her as loving and kind, but also fiery and firm. Her will left Sammy Jr. $100 Million cash, the family estate, and several of the properties spread out all over the world. James was left with $100 Million cash, the guest house on the family estate, which has its own ten acres, and a few stateside properties if he ever wanted to get away. Victoria wanted to make sure that her and Sam's legacy would live on for a long time.

While he was standing under the awning day dreaming, obviously Sammy had grown impatient. The massive, 14-foot, solid oak door was snatched open and his dad said, "What you waiting for, me to die of old age? Don't keep me waiting on your ass!" James just sighed as he watched the retreating Sammy. He wanted to take off running to his own house situated around behind his father's huge property, but he needed to man up and face whatever his dad had instore for him.

When he stepped into the marbled interior, closing the door behind him, he ignored the twin, winding staircases leading to the second floor, and walked on through until he entered his father's library.

Sammy's massive desk was directly across from the door. Technically, the room was a library. It boasted row after row, shelf after shelf, of leather-bound volumes of great value, all the way down to ragged dime westerns. When James was a kid, he'd spend hours jumping from book to book. One thing he'd never seen, and probably never would, was Sammy reading any of the material surrounding him. So, for him, this was less a library and more a meeting room that contained books.

James took a seat in one of the plush visitor chairs and sat staring at his father's angry face. This conversation wasn't gonna be a good one. Whenever Sammy got into a mood like this it was best to avoid him at all cost. Over the past few years, several of their interactions had turned violent, as Sammy took any defiance from his son as a personal attack on his authority.

After a couple minutes of the staring contest, Sammy finally said, "You lied to me." His words were calm, but his whole body vibrated with pent up energy. "I saw the video and, while it might not hold up in court, that was your car racing down that road."

James, not knowing what his father wanted, sat quietly in the hopes that Sammy would vent his anger and then let him go home. There was nothing James could think to say to hurry the process, so the best course of action was silence.

"I went out to the crash site, also," Sammy continued. "I saw the marks in the road and it's clear that somebody hit your car and made you flip." Leaning forward, Sammy said, "Tell me the truth, James. What happened?"

"I already told you what I know. I wasn't racing. We were on our way to drop Amia off at home, and then Alanah was spending the night with me. One second, we were listening to music, the next I was laying in the road. If somebody hit me, it wasn't because of a race. It must have been an accident."

Sammy chuckled. "You think this is a game, don't you? You think I'm playing? You think these people won't throw your ass in prison?" Slamming his fist on the desk, Sammy screamed, "Tell me the truth, or so help me God!"

James absorbed the angry outburst and shrugged with indifference. "I can only tell you what I know." Looking at his dad with suspicion, James asked, "Why are you so adamant I confess to this? You wearing a wire or something? Should I have my lawyer present?"

A deadly calm settled over Sammy's face as he rolled his chair back and stood up. James watched him as he slowly walked around the desk and stopped by his side. With violence vibrating through each word, Sammy said, "Get up!"

James glanced to his left and looked up at the menacing form of his father. Pasting a mocking smile on his face, James stood up and stared his dad right in the eyes. Sammy was slightly taller, and about 20-pounds heavier, but both men were formidable in their own right.

Sammy's jaw clenched as he moved chest to chest with his son. "Say that shit again. Call me a rat to my face." There was no mistaking that this situation was out of control, but James wasn't scared of his dad. If Sammy wanted things to turn physical, James was ready for a fight.

"Dad, why are you acting like you're a thug or something? You grew up just like I did. You're not from the hood and you're not a child. Why don't you start acting like a grown man who has a grown son?" With that, James turned to the side and headed towards the library's exit.

Sammy reached out and grabbed his shoulder, spinning him back around. "Don't turn your back on me, boy! I'm not done with you!"

James jerked out of his father's grasp and yelled, "Don't put your hands on me again! You might not like the result." Turning to leave this time, he caught the aggressive move with his peripheral vision. He leaned to his left and the right hook his father had thrown sailed over his shoulder. James spun back around with a left hook of his own, catching his father flush in the face. Sammy looked at him in stunned surprise, then the fight was on.

Squeaks from their sneakers and muffled grunts was the symphony of their engagement. The two men shuffled and struggled for dominance, trading blows and destroying the entrance to the library. Both of them were in shape, and both were committed to winning the fight. After a particularly vicious blow delivered by Sammy to his son, they both careened out of the room and continued their battle in the front hall.

"Hey! Hey! What the hell is wrong with ya'll? Stop!" yelled Brianna. She was running fast as she could down the staircase as both men continued to grapple. James got off a perfect overhand right that exploded blood out of Sammy's nose and laid him out across the marble floor. Brianna ran up and shoved James so hard, he lost his footing and crashed to the floor beside his dad.

"What the hell!" she screamed. "Ya'll down here fighting like two animals. Both of ya'll, get the hell out of my house until you can act like you got some sense."

James looked up at his mother's pain-filled face and felt shame engulf his heart. He rolled over and got to his feet, then extended his hand down to his father. After a moment of hesitation, Sammy wiped the blood from his hands onto his t-shirt, then reached for his son's hand.

They both mumbled apologies to Brianna, but she wasn't trying to hear it. "Yeah, yeah. I know you're sorry. Now, OUT!" she demanded, pointing at the front door. Heads down and shoulders slumped, James and Sammy marched to the front door and exited the home.

Without thought, they both turned left, following the stone path that would take them to the back of the house. They bypassed the 12-car garage, the sauna, the hot tub, and the pool, and made their way onto the pickleball court. Neither of them said a word as James went to the far side and served the ball.

The match was just as intense as the fight had been. Each trying to outwit the other. At times, it was all about power, but more often than not, it was about finesse. They didn't even keep score, winning by points was never the goal. Father and son just needed to burn off some steam before re-engaging in their man to man talk.

One prolonged volley led to another, and another, until both men stored their paddles and made their way over to the pool. They stripped down to their boxers and both dove in for a leisurely swim. After about 15 minutes, they found themselves silently sitting on the steps leading into the pool.

Sammy leaned his shoulder into his son and said, "I love you boy."

James nodded and leaned on his father. "I know," was all he said.

Looking out across his land, Sammy said, "I understand you're grown, but that doesn't make me any less your father. I will always do everything in my power to protect you. Normally, as you know, I don't get in your business. I've always shown you trust and respect. This time, the consequences are more serious. You have to understand that I can't let you go to prison for the rest of your life."

Again, James nodded, and said, "I know."

Sammy looked over at his son. "No more lies, JJ. No more games. I need you to tell me the truth. I promise I will never tell anyone, not even your mother. You don't even have to say the words. Just nod your head. Tell me James, was it a race?"

James took a deep breath and lowered his head so his hair hid his face. Tears swam into view and blurred his vision. He tossed his dreads out of the way and looked his dad directly in the eyes. The tears spilled down his face as he nodded to answer the question.

Hours ago, Sammy would have exploded. He would have ranted and raved and called James every name in the book for being so stupid. Reading the defeat in his child, Sammy didn't do any of that. He instead wrapped James up in his arms and they cried together.

Minutes passed until Sammy stood up and patted his son on the shoulder. He said, "Go home, son. Yasmine is at the house waiting for you." With that, Sammy walked over to the sliding glass door and disappeared inside.

James stood up, got dressed in the same clothes he'd been arrested in, and started the journey back to his own slice of Jordan land. On the way, he wondered what the future would hold. Could he sell the lie convincingly enough to avoid prison? If he couldn't, what would he do if he was sentenced to life in prison? And what would the bastard who killed Alanah and Amia do next? He seemed to be trying his damnedest to get James locked up. What would be his next move?

Maybe it was time for James to stop letting everyone dictate his actions. Maybe it was time for him to go on the offense. He had to be extremely careful while he was out on bond, but if everything went right at the hearing next week, James was gonna shake some people up.

Opening the side door of the guest house, which was a miniature of the big house, James realized he had a problem he'd have to deal with before he even went to the hearing. As the cucumber melon scent drifted to his brain, causing an instant reaction, he wondered how he could suppress his desire for Yazmine Salazar. Or, if he even wanted to.

Part Two

Chapter 10

Rockwell, North Carolina was jumping. To be more precise, The Strip was jumping. It didn't matter that it was a Wednesday night, it was summer, so every night drew large crowds and fast cars ready to speed down the quarter mile track.

This wasn't one of the sponsored events, drivers had to stipulate their own races and their own rewards. Some racers only participated on these nights because they couldn't afford the steep entry fees of the formal tournaments. Other drivers liked these freestyle races because it gave them a chance to settle some perceived beefs.

These were the most dangerous nights when anything could happen. From entertaining cat-fights, to multiple murders. When a driver felt slighted, violence often followed. The Strip owners took 5% of all purses to ensure all antes were paid. Most of the time, it wasn't a driver who sparked the violence, it was one of the collection men who had to get rough to collect a debt.

The event so far had been surprisingly free from drama, but the night was still young. 11:00pm meant there were still hours of competition to come. All of the parents who had young kids were gone and the alcohol consumption kicked up a notch. The pungent aroma of marijuana became thick around the track.

It hadn't been easy for him to slip away, but James "The Golden Boy" Jordan had managed it. This wasn't a night when you would hear the crowd chanting his name. No one would be asking for his autograph. He wouldn't have awestruck groupies trying to peek under his hood. None of that would be going on because no one knew he was there.

James didn't have a lot of cars that could blend in, and the $200,000 Aston Martin Vantage Coupe wouldn't either, in the light of day. But, with its onyx-black paint job, and its blackened chrome, outside of the stadium light's reach, the car was invisible.

He'd left the vehicle about a half mile away, parked at an abandoned airport and walked the rest of the way in. He had spotted his target within minutes of arrival. James had been lurking around the perimeter of The Strip for about an hour, just waiting for the right opportunity to present itself. He had to get in and out clean. The only person who could ever know he'd been here was the bastard he'd come to see.

The Black Sheep had obviously called it a night after his last race because he started drinking immediately. It was clear that he'd won big as he was showing a huge knot of cash to anyone who cared to see it. The man was feeling good, didn't seem to have a care in the world. No one would guess that less than a month ago this evil asshole had murdered two innocent women.

And like God had reached down from heaven and delivered up his enemy, The Black Sheep finally separated himself from the crowd and made his way over to the long line of porta-johns. This late at night, there was only a trickle of people making the long trek. The owners, never wanting the smell to offend their customers, placed the blue enclosures as far from the stands as possible. This made the job easy for James because the whole area was shrouded in darkness.

James wanted the man to feel safe and secure, just as Alanah and Amia had. So, he stayed hidden as the other man strutted up, whistling a jaunty tune. Hearing one of the doors open and close, he jumped up from behind the bushes and searched the area for any stray witnesses. Seeing nobody coming or leaving, and hearing his target still whistling, James smiled and walked around to greet The Black Sheep when he emerged.

Dressed in all black, with a pair of weighted leather gloves, and a toboggan covering his dreads, James felt his body fill with anticipation. His adrenaline was pumping. His blood was boiling. He wasn't anyone's gangster or thug, but the vision of Alanah and Amia, dead in the middle of the road, filled him with all the motivation he needed.

The off-beat tune stopped and the latch was pulled back. The door was pushed open and James gave the man the same consideration he'd given Alanah and Amia: None.

The first blow was brutal and effective as the man's head jerked to the right and he sank to his knees. Another well placed punch folded him backwards so he was half in half out of the porta-john. Eyes wide, The Black Sheep stared up at The Golden Boy and knew that he was in deep shit.

Half-drunk from alcohol and dazed from the blows to his face, the man could do nothing but beg. "Please man! I'm sorry! I didn't want anyone to die!"

James saw red. "You dare ask me for mercy? Did you have any for Alanah or Amia? I'll tell you what, don't apologize to me, apologize to Jesus on judgement day!" Stradling the man, James didn't have any more words for the coward. All he wanted to hear was the screams of pain while he died an agonizing death.

Blow after blow was delivered to bring about the most pain. The screams turned to pleas and the pleas turned to moans. Ribs cracked. Bones broke. Bruises spread. Blood pooled. At no time did James get tired or even think about cutting the man some slack. He wasn't a born killer, in fact, he knew he'd be sick about this tomorrow. But, that was a concern for later. Right now, all he was focused on was the death sentence he had come to administer.

"Hey! What the hell are you doing?" The shouted question was hurled from maybe a hundred feet away. James glanced up from the unconscious man and saw a middle-aged white guy hurrying in his direction. Looking beyond the newcomer, James could see three other men not far behind.

Lunging to his feet, James took off full speed around the side of the porta-johns. With his black clothes on, unless they had a spotlight with them, the men had no chance of catching him. Hearing the men still yelling for him to stop, he pushed even harder to get back to his car. If they called the cops fast enough, they would quickly figure out where he was headed, it was the only thing in this direction.

Chancing a look over his shoulder, the group of men were still at the toilets, trying in vain to see using their cellphone flashlights. He was positive at least the lead guy had been drunk, he just had to hope the man's thinking was as slow as his running had been.

Finally entering the airport, James ran to the side of the hanger where his car was hidden in the shadows behind a dumpster. Quickly, he stripped out of his bloodstained gloves and clothes and stuffed everything, including his shoes and toboggan, into a black bag he'd stashed under the car. He pulled out a tub of wet-wipes next and cleaned his face and neck to make sure nothing would transfer from him to the car.

Opening the door, he popped the trunk and put on the outfit he'd brought to change into. After he was fully dressed, he grabbed the black bag and stashed it in the false floor compartment that was impossible to detect unless you deconstructed the whole car.

He had just turned the car on and put it in gear when a cop car slowly turned the corner at the far end of the hanger. If the cop continued on, there was no way he could miss him where he sat. James wasn't about to go to prison for murdering the son of a bitch who killed his girls, so he did the only thing he could possibly do, he ran.

The car was not registered in his name, it was owned by a shell corporation set up by Corey McCann that couldn't be traced to any person. The vehicle had over 800hp and a complete blackout mode that made it damn near invisible at night. So, when he slammed on the accelerator and roared towards the exit, the blue lights flashed, but he was already pulling away.

His only hope of escape was the long, dark backroads that would actually take him farther from home. To try and out run cops on the interstate was foolish, but if he could find a place to lose the police and hide the car until a later date, he'd be home free. As the thought was entering his head, he figured on the perfect place. It pained him to do it, but coming out of the airfield parking lot, he made a left to go deeper into Rockwell.

James could almost hear the cop calling for backup. Trying to outrun numerous radios was just as foolhardy as trying to escape using the interstate. So, James needed to get some fast separation from his pursuer to turn this into a search and not a chase.

With nothing at all to illuminate his vehicle, the police tried their hardest to keep him in sight. He used every bit of speed he could until James couldn't even see the blue lights except for on straightaways. When he had enough distance to slow down a bit, he pulled out his phone and made a quick call. Even though it was close to midnight on a Wednesday, the call was answered on the second ring.

"Hey Buddy! Long time no hear. You must be in some kind of trouble to be calling me this late." Timothy Earnhardt wasn't exactly a friend, but the 30-year-old white man was a magical mechanic when it came to race cars. James had paid the man $250,000 two years ago and pretty much told him he was on retainer for any car troubles he experienced. Tim was by no means broke, as he was a cousin to the legendary racing Earnhardt's, but he had a little bit of a gambling problem. Through stories the man told while fixing this or that, James felt like he could trust the man in a situation like this.

"Hey, Tim. I'm in a bit of a bind and I need to swing by your place. I might need to borrow one of your cars in the morning."

"Sure man, whatever you need." Revealing the criminal mind state he had, he added, "Just pull around back and we'll hide whatever you're driving in the garage. No windows, so the cops would need a warrant for a peek inside."

"Alright man, I'll be there in about five minutes," said James.

"I'll have everything ready. See you soon," Tim said before hanging up.

The five minutes turned into 15 as James had to dodge two more cops by pulling into someone's driveway, and then out running another one who had to turn around to give chase. True to his word, the tall, slim figure of Tim Earnhardt was waiting for him at the top of the driveway. He trotted around the side of the house with James following, and pointed to an open barn-style door where he wanted James to proceed.

After parking and leaving the enclosure, the two men headed towards the two-story home with the sound of distant sirens echoing through the night. Neither said a word until after Tim had ventured into the kitchen and returned to the living room with a beer for himself, and a Coke for James.

Tim told James to make himself at home and then went about turning off all the lights so any passersby would think the occupants were long sleep. Sure that no one had a reason to believe the house was harboring a fugitive, Tim sat down and asked, "Do I even want to know what the hell is going on?"

His blond hair was fashionably cut, but his clothes were a little ragged. They only socialized when James had a problem with one of his many cars, but anytime they came into contact, rain, sleet, hail, snow, or sunshine, Tim had on a pair of beat-up blue jeans and a t-shirt. He was always smiling and happy and smelled of Marlboro Lites. But, the man was a genius. He could figure out and fix some of the most complicated racing configurations in minutes. James felt blessed to have the man on his side.

To answer Tim's question, James said, "Had to settle a beef. I was interrupted in the middle of it, but I'm sure I got my point across."

Deep in thought, Tim nodded. Finally, he said, "I heard about what happened with you and the girls. First off, let me say I'm sorry for your loss." James thanked the man before Tim continued. "Rumor is, someone hit you with a PIT maneuver after you won a street race. They also say you were in a GT-R50 and you were racing a Shelby GT500. There's only one person I know who would have been stupid enough, or cocky enough, to think he could win that race." After a pause, he asked, "Was it him?"

James trusted Tim or he wouldn't be in the man's home right now, but there were probably thousands of people in prison for trusting people they shouldn't have. Even though the feud between him and The Black Sheep was well known, there was no way he was admitting to anything. So, James just shrugged and took a gulp of his soda.

They could vaguely hear police cars still out searching for him in the area, so they continued to sit in silence until James had a thought. "Where did all those rumors come from? How does someone spread them without implementing themselves in the crime?"

This time, it was Tim who shrugged. "Someone said something to someone who said something to someone else. You know how these things go. Some cop talked to their cousin who talked to his wife, and the conversation was overheard by her sister. To tell you the truth, I believe it all came from The Black Sheep, but no one can confirm that. There had been a detective, um, Hall or something like that, asking a lot of questions. For obvious reasons, he's not buying The Black Sheep theory."

Huffing out a laugh, James remarked, "Yeah, who would?"

After that exchange, Tim excused himself to get some sleep and left James the keys to an apple-green Camaro. About 3:00am, having not heard any police for over an hour, James grabbed some lighter fluid, a long handled lighter, and retrieved the bag of evidence out of the hidden compartment in his trunk.

He made his way through the pitch-black night over to a metal barrel where Tim normally burned his trash. He torn the bag open and doused the contents with the super-flammable liquid and threw the whole bag inside. Picking up a piece of newspaper off the ground, he lit it and dropped it in the barrel. The flames jumped high enough that he had to take a step back or risk his hair catching fire. But he didn't go far, he stood right there, poking into the clothes with a stick, until everything in the bag turned to ash.

James returned the lighter and fluid back to the kitchen and then walked outside to the Camaro. It was a car the police would see and know it wasn't the car they were looking for, but he still took a circular route to get back to his home in Concord. He never saw a cop during the whole ride.

He parked the Camaro in his own garage and then made his way into the house. Only after he'd showered and eaten a quick snack did he turn on the news to see if anything was mentioned. Surprisingly, there was nothing.

It was still early, but none of the local channels were reporting anything on the incident. James didn't know if he was relieved or angry, but the lack of news meant the bastard was still breathing. A murder in Rockwell would have been headline news. It made James wonder how bad the man was and what he planned to do about the ass whipping he'd just taken.

As the thought crossed his mind, his cellphone vibrated. Looking at the number, he wasn't surprised to see who was calling him. He answered after about the tenth ring, but he said nothing, giving his nemesis the chance to speak first.

Heavy breathing was all he heard for the first 30 seconds. James laughed and said, "If this is supposed to scare me, you're not doing a very good job."

Shifting the phone around, The Black Sheep said, "You should have stayed and made sure I was dead, or left the situation alone. I guess you didn't learn the lesson the first time around. Now, I'll have to take something else you love." A few more menacing breaths and the man hung up.

James slowly put the phone on his nightstand and laid back down. The man's voice had been filled with pain, but also a fierce determination. He'd meant every word he'd just said. There was no way James would sleep anytime soon as he thought about the wisdom behind The Black Sheep's words. Yes, James should have made sure the man was dead, or he should have left the whole thing alone. Only time would tell just how bad he would regret the decision he'd made tonight.

Chapter 11

Alex was up early, driving to a meet that he felt didn't make sense to go to, but his curiosity had gotten the best of him. It was Sunday, two days before the murdering bastard was due back in court, and Alex was doing everything he could think of to make sure the kid stayed locked up this time around. This meeting, in his opinion, was a last-ditch effort to make sure justice was served one way or the other.

The sun was blasting through his windshield and driver's side window as he traveled down the highway to his destination. He grabbed some cheap gas station shades out of the center console of his F-150 and slipped them over his eyes. Even though it was only 6:15am, this early in July, the sun was already making its presence felt. The meteorologist said there was a zero chance of rain and the temperature would float just above 100 degrees with no relief in sight. Alex hoped this little get together would be in an air-conditioned space. If not, the heat might make this a quick visit.

For some reason, the idiot wanted to meet at a firework stand in South Carolina. Alex didn't understand why they couldn't have gone to a park if they needed privacy. Thinking on that, he couldn't understand why they would need privacy, anyway. What could the fool want to talk about that required them to leave the state? Well, Alex wasn't gonna drive himself crazy trying to guess. In the next 15 minutes he should know why all the secrecy was needed.

Exiting the highway, he made the left turn away from Carowinds, the amusement park he hadn't been to since he was a boy. The traffic was thick as everyone from North Carolina flooded the area to buy their last-minute celebratory items. Because of some outdated law, people still couldn't buy fireworks in North Carolina, at least none of the good stuff. So, with the Independence Day shows coming up tomorrow, this whole area would be jammed pack until no more product remained.

Alex turned into the parking lot where the guy had instructed him to go and immediately understood why this particular stand was chosen. It was small, ragged, and mostly sold out of anything useful. The wizened Hispanic man sitting inside the enclosure was the same shade of brown as the weather-beaten planks on the structure. With all the other painted and shiny buildings dotting the nearby landscape, only two vehicles sat beside the dilapidated domicile. One was a 30-year-old Honda, the other was a white Dodge Durango with blacked out windows.

Alex had known the guy for several years, but had never seen this vehicle before. Obviously, coming to the same conclusion, as soon as he parked his truck, he received a text telling him to come over to the passenger side of the Durango. Thinking he had nothing to lose by hearing the guy out, Alex shrugged and exited his vehicle.

Trying to be careful of a setup, he walked around the structure to make sure no one was nearby waiting to jump him. It's not like he had any training in spotting something out of place, but nothing in the area made him suspicious. So, he walked over to the SUV and climbed inside.

The vehicle was cool and clean, just like its driver. Alex glanced around the interior as the man watched him with an amused grin on his face. Finally, Alex sat back and said, "You called me. Why am I here and why couldn't we have talked about this at my house?"

"You're here because you're angry and you know this bullshit case isn't gonna hold up in court. You're here because you know that James is gonna get away with murdering your two girls. And, that little interview you did at the courthouse, yeah, it might have caused a few tears to fall in sympathy, but the people who feel your pain don't matter. The ones who have the power to do something about this injustice are firmly in his corner."

Alex understood where he was coming from, but he felt his interview had done more than cause a few tears from unimportant people. Politicians from all over the country had lambasted the criminal justice system that catered to the wealthy. Since he'd done the interview, all his social media accounts have been bombarded with messages from people offering their help. He knew that if James walked out of that courtroom, the public outcry would be tremendous.

The man continued. "The reason why we had to come down here is because no one can see us together. For this plan to work, no one can ever guess that we have any kind of connection. After we leave this place, there will be no more interaction between us. You will do your part, and I will do mine."

"But, whatever you have planned would only be necessary if he walks out of the courtroom on Tuesday."

Shaking his head to show his disappointment, he said, "Alex, James is gonna walk. Either the DA is dirty or the judge, or maybe both. One of them will make sure some kind of error or rule or law will lead to the case being dismissed. The Jordans are worth over a quarter Billion dollars, but their power is the problem. They hold stakes in some of the biggest and most important businesses in Cabarrus County. They do so much for the community, and invest so much in local politics, no one can afford for the Jordans to leave and take their money elsewhere. If you're looking for justice, you're searching in the wrong places thinking the courts or the community will turn on James."

Alex was still suspicious. "So, why do you need me? And, why do you care one way or the other if James walks? Why are you willing to help me get justice?"

The man paused and looked over at Alex. "I have my own reasons for wanting James to go down. Trust me, I'm not helping you out of the kindness of my heart. With or without you, I'm gonna carry out my plan. I just figured I'd let you join me so you can get the satisfaction of knowing you played an active role in his downfall."

That was part of the reason, but Alex was sure there was more to it. He hated being manipulated, but if he was aware of the attempt, and willing to push forward, was it still manipulation? Deciding he was willing to take a chance for his lost daughters, he said, "Alright. If your plan sounds feasible, I'm in. If it sounds like some bullshit, you're gonna have to find some other patsy to be your puppet." The man nodded and began to lay out his devious plot.

The plan was good. Not great, but certainly doable. When he had answered his phone five o'clock this morning, and the caller had identified himself, no way would he have foreseen the conversation leading down this path. After listening to the man talk steadily for 15 minutes, Alex actually hoped James did get off. He felt that now, prison was too good for the no-good son of a bitch. Alex didn't even try to hide his giddiness as he rubbed his hands together and grinned.

The man finished with, "You'll have to get your son involved, or at least someone that knows James and you can trust."

"Don't worry about that. AJ will be more than willing to help out."

"Alright then, any questions you have, we need to go over them now. When you leave this SUV, we'll have little to no contact."

They talked and hammered out details for about another hour. Not one car entered the parking lot during that time. When both parties were satisfied, they shook hands and Alex jumped out and made his way back to his truck. As the Durango was pulling off, he changed his direction and went to the building to make a purchase. $40 got him all he would need to celebrate after this job was done. With a smile on his face, and a pep in his step, he climbed into the F-150 and made his way back home.

It was still early, about 9:30am, when he opened his front door and entered his living room. The space was open and airy, but after the death of his two girls, the whole house seemed dark and gloomy. He'd already mentioned selling the place, but Amanda had vetoed the notion. Her stated reason was her need to be around things that reminded her of Alanah and Amia. He didn't think it was a healthy reaction to death, but what the hell did he know? He just hated seeing the defeated look on her face, and thought a change of scenery was exactly what she needed to heal.

Speaking of his wife, turning around after closing the door, he noticed her staring intently in his direction from the couch. "Where have you been, Alex? Why didn't you wake me up?"

Tossing the keys in a bowl sitting on the entrance table, he said, "I just went for a drive. Needed to clear my head a little bit."

Standing up, he saw that she had on a blue, slip-on dress, and a pair of low-heeled, white sandals on her feet. She said, "Well, go get dressed. We still have time to make it to the 10:00am service."

"Service?" he asked before remembering it was Sunday. "Oh, um, I don't really feel like going to church today, Amanda. Maybe we can go next week."

The look that crossed her face was classic Amanda Knight. He'd been on the receiving end of her disappointed, yet severe, looks since he'd met her at a Duke campus party his Junior year. Tears threatened to spill down his face because it was an expression that she'd passed down to both of their daughters, but he'd never get to see it on them again. Before she could launch into her diatribe of rebuke, he sagged down into his recliner and prepared for the argument to come.

"Don't you think we need to go to church and pray that the truth comes out at the hearing on Tuesday?" she asked.

On a sigh, he said, "Amanda, if you wanna go to church, go to church. Me, I'm going to sit here and watch TV for a bit. Maybe take a nap." He reached over, picked up the remote off the coffee table, and turned the TV on.

"I think we need to represent a unified front to the public. With the hearing being only two days away, we need to remind them that Alanah and Amia would be there if they were still alive." Her voice broke when she got to their daughters' names.

Rubbing his head in agitation, Alex said, "Who are we supposed to be reminding? You think the judge is gonna be at the church? Maybe the DA? The public doesn't matter, don't you understand that?"

"Alex, don't yell at me," she said in response to his raised voice.

"Well, stop pestering me! I said I don't wanna go to church." Jumping to his feet, he said, "Why the hell would I wanna pray to some God who just took my daughters from me? Obviously, He doesn't give a damn about how I feel. So, unless Jesus is gonna bring the bodies from the cemetery, lay them out at the front of the church, and bring them back like He did Lazarus, then I don't have a use for any of this religious bullshit!"

And then the look again. He gritted his teeth and sat back down when the tears started falling from her teal eyes. Shaking her head and wiping her eyes, she turned her back on him and gathered up her bag. She didn't even look at him as she scooped up the keys to her Toyota Sequoia and breezed out the door.

Forget prayer, he thought as he cut the TV off and leaned back in the chair. What he had planned was real and didn't require any help from some imaginary force. All he needed was for James to be released and then he could settle up on a more personal note. Thinking on it, there was one more thing he needed to do. Even though he'd showed confidence on the subject at the meeting, he was positive a little bit of persuasion would have to be used to complete this task.

He pulled his phone out and dialed his son. On the second ring, AJ answered with, "What's up, Dad?"

"A lot. I need you to come over to the house so we can talk."

Alex could almost hear his son rolling his eyes. "I can be there sometime tomorrow. I've been feeling a little sick the last few days."

"Boy!" proclaimed Alex. "You live a block and a half away! Get your lazy ass up and get over here in the next ten minutes!" Attempting to calm himself, he took a deep breath before continuing. "Listen, I need to talk to you about something very important. This can't wait until tomorrow, I need to see you, ASAP."

On a sigh, AJ said, "Alright, Dad, but don't give me any shit. I told you I'm not feeling good."

"Just get over here as soon as you can." Alex hung up wondering where he went wrong raising his oldest child.

AJ had always been a mean child. Not always the biggest kid in the room, but definitely the most aggressive. He seems to resent all kinds of authority, and since he turned 8-years-old, he'd shown total disdain for his parents. After a couple years of hoping the kid would grow up, Alex had had enough.

When AJ was 10-years-old, Alex told him, "You think you're a man, okay son, I'll treat you like a man." From that moment on, Alex would beat the shit out of AJ anytime he went against one of his directives. Because Alanah and Amia never caused any trouble, AJ thought Alex loved the girls more than him. So, secretly, the boy started taking his anger out on them.

Kids being kids, Alex didn't think anything of it when the two girls would show up with bruises and scrapes. They would never complain and they both seemed to idolize their older brother. Only when Alex came home from work early one day and heard Alanah screaming, did he learn the truth. AJ had been physically abusing both girls for as long as they could remember. After beating his 16-year-old son to the brink of death, he allowed him a few weeks to heal up, then kicked him out of the house.

Alex had washed his hands of the brute he'd once called his son, but Amanda and her soft heart had implored him to give AJ another chance. Alex assured her that this would force the boy to grow up and maybe, after he learned to be respectful, he could return to the family home. Well, that never happened.

By this time, Alex had been working for Sammy for about four years. Knowing his family needed a bigger home, he set his eyes on buying a house right up the street that was almost twice as big. The price was right and Alex moved his family with the plan to sell the other house if the need arose.

Since Sammy was paying him a very generous salary, the need never came up, so the small house remained in his possession. About eight months later, the cleaning crew he hired to maintain his first home called and said they believed he had a squatter. Alex raced over, ready to physically expel whoever dared to breach his property. What he found was a sleeping AJ, and a semi-furnished house that looked like it'd been occupied for a while.

Alex didn't bother to wake him, but he did step out to call his wife. They had a huge fight about it but, bottom line, four months prior, AJ had come home after getting his ass whipped for trying to steal someone's money. Amanda had immediately gone to their storage unit, loaded up her SUV, and set AJ up in the other house. Alex didn't like the fact that everything was done behind his back, but after having a long talk with his son, it seemed the 17-year-old was finally growing up.

AJ never went back to school until Sammy hired him on at the auto shop and made him get a GED before going to trade school. He and the girls had seemed to renew their relationship. Pretty much, him moving into the other house had been the perfect solution. Alex charged him rent, the boy paid all his bills on time, and the time on the street had instilled in him a genuine respect for others.

His front door opening jerked him out of his reprieve and thrust him back into the very real present. One look at his son and all he could do was chuckle and shake his head. Maybe the streets hadn't straightened him up as much as he'd thought. Anyway, they had a lot to go over and Alex launched right into his spiel.

AJ sat and listened, never interrupting or asking questions. After Alex finished going over the plan, minus who the guy was doing the organizing, AJ stared at him like he believed his father had finally lost his mind. Shaking his head, he actually said, "What the hell is wrong with you? Have you lost your mind? I'm not doing that dumbass shit! We'll both end up in jail for life!"

On an audible exhale, Alex said, "AJ, the plan is foolproof. If we stick to the script the way it's written, James will get exactly what he deserves."

"Yeah, and if any part of it goes wrong before the end, I'm the only one in the hot seat," stated AJ.

"This boy murdered your sisters. I know growing up ya'll didn't have the best of relationships, but that was on you, not them. Those girls loved you and cherished you as an older brother. And their reward for loving you was pain and humiliation."

"Dad, I was a kid…"

"And you made the majority of their lives hell," Alex stated firmly. "You never did anything to earn their love, but they gave it to you freely. Now they're gone. And the fucker who did it is gonna walk out of that courtroom two days from now having spent one day in jail. You think that's a fair exchange?"

Shaking his head, AJ said, "Dad, I don't think…"

"Dammit, AJ!" Alex exploded, jumping to his feet. "Stop being a fucking coward for once in your life! You've never done a thing for this family. I don't need you to think, I need you to do!" he shouted. Visibly trying to collect himself, he sat back down and focused on his son. "I've never asked you for anything. My baby girls never asked you for anything. In response, you've given us nothing. Two lives lost and your mother and father devastated, and you can't muster up enough courage to help this family get its dignity back?"

"It's not that, Dad." Leaning forward, AJ said, "The plan is foolish. We're relying on too many maybes and ifs. Since I'll be the one on the front line, I think I should have a say on how this can work."

Even though the man had adamantly repeated his need for secrecy, Alex felt his son needed to know who was behind the plan for him to realize it could work. "AJ, I'm not supposed to tell you this, but I want you to understand that we'll be protected in this. The plan was setup by…."

AJ couldn't believe it. "No way! Why would he involve himself in something like this?"

"I asked the same thing and he said he has his own agenda that doesn't concern us. What matters is, with him on our side, we're good as golden."

168

Looking serious, AJ said, "I have a very bad feeling about this."

"Son, it doesn't matter how you feel, we're doing this." Holding up his hand to silence AJ's objection, Alex added, "You said that you're on the front line, but this guy has way more to lose than either one of us. He'll be the first person who can be linked to this. So, he's gonna do his part, then you're gonna do yours, and then I'll do mine."

"But what's the end game here?"

"Justice, AJ. Justice and accountability. James isn't gonna get away with killing Alanah and Amia, even if we have to handle this on our own,"

Shaking his head again, AJ said, "I don't like this. We're either gonna end up in jail or dead. Either way, what good is it gonna do Alanah and Amia? They're already dead."

Standing up, Alex told AJ, "Get up son." When they were face to face, Alex smiled and said, "I love you, AJ. I know I didn't say it a lot while you were growing up, but I really do love you. I tried everything I could think of to turn you into a good man. Looking at you now, I can honestly say that I failed miserably. There has never been a time when I looked at you and felt proud to call you my son. And for a man like me, that makes me a failure right along with you.

"Now, I've tried to get you on board by speaking to your manhood. I even tried to invoke a little bit of familial pride and obligation. None of that seems to be having an effect on you at all. So, I'm gonna try this one last thing and then we'll see where the chips fall."

Gathering his thoughts, Alex continued to stare at his son. Finally, he said, "Son, you won't do this for your sisters. You won't do it for me or your mother. Well, do it for yourself." Letting all the emotion he felt enter his eyes, he proclaimed, "Like most cowards, you're only concerned with yourself. So, you tell me right here, right now, that you're in, or I will kill you myself."

They both stood in silence as the words filled the room. Alex stared intently at his son until AJ dropped his eyes and nodded his head. Alex smiled and patted his shoulder. "Good, good. I'll call you and let you know when everything is set." He released him and AJ walked dejectedly to the door. Before he could open it, Alex said, "Oh! One more thing."

AJ stopped and turned, inclining his head for Alex to continue. "I meant what I said. If you start having doubts, use that selfishness to tamp them down. It would break your mother's heart, but I will really kill you if you don't follow through on this." They stared for a few more seconds and then AJ turned and exited the house.

Alex wasn't proud of everything he'd said to his child, but every word had been the truth. Deciding that he'd put in enough work for the time being, he laid back down on the recliner to take a quick nap. As soon as Amanda returned home from church, their earlier argument would be renewed. He really needed to get some rest before that happened. If not, he might end up saying something he would later regret.

Lately, whenever he closed his eyes, all he could see were the sad faces of his two beautiful baby girls. This time, they seemed to give him a stamp of approval for what was floating in his mind. They looked happy and content, and in turn, Alex fell asleep with a light heart and a huge smile on his face.

Chapter 12

The courtroom was packed. Neither the Jordans nor the Knights socialized a lot, so most of the attendees were just spectators wanting a front row seat to the drama. Standing in the back, reporter after reporter lined the wall, holding up their cellphones to record every sound and scene they could capture. They were all quiet and reserved, maybe not by their nature, but because Judge Kennedy had already warned them that any interruptions would get them all banned from the room.

James was seated at the defense table with Corey, both of whom were clothed in expensive, dark blue suits. Corey's head was freshly shaved and gleaming while James had his dreads tied to stay out of his face. They both wore solemn expressions, both knowing that the next couple of hours would determine the fate of the whole Jordan clan.

Behind them sat Sammy, Brianna, and Yazmine. They were also decked out in dark, conservative attire. All three tried their best to put forth a brave front, but fear for James made them a little shaky. Corey had warned them to stay quiet and respectful as any perceived misbehavior could reflect badly on James.

Jennifer Morrison sat at the prosecutor's table wearing what looked like the same severe, skirt suit she'd worn at the last hearing, but dyed black. Her hair was once again pulled back into a tight ponytail and she sported a no-nonsense expression on her face.

Alex and Amanda sat behind her wearing their usual boring khakis. That was one of the reasons Alanah used to dress how she did. She hated the drab clothes the rest of her family wore. Until James had brought the pink bodysuit for Amia, she'd dressed in the same muted colors to fit with the rest of her family. Neither of them had spoken to the Jordan's when they entered the courtroom, but Amanda had sent him a quick smile and small wave before she sat down. AJ was nowhere in sight.

Corey had already handed Judge Kennedy a motion to dismiss all charges against James due to the lack of any evidence of a crime even being committed. The judge had ordered everyone to be quiet as he reviewed the motion and its validity. When his head finally came up, he looked at the DA and said, "Ms. Morrison, I hope you have something to contradict this motion or this is gonna be a very quick hearing."

Jumping to her feet, the DA said, "Your Honor…"

Waving his hand at her, Judge Kennedy said, "Retake your seat, Ms. Morrison. This isn't a trial and you have no jury to try and work your acting skills on. Just remain seated and tell me what you have."

Face blazing with embarrassment, she sat back down and started her comment once again. "Your Honor, two women are dead and now their right to justice is in my hands. And your hands. And potentially, the hands of a jury. There is no doubt in my mind that the defendant, James Jordan, was racing another car when the two collided and the resulting accident caused Alanah and Amia Knight to lose their lives. I have a written report from a highly decorated Crash Scene

Investigator, who is also ready and willing to testify to her findings. I have the ME's report on the trauma the wreck had on the bodies that brought about their deaths. The defendant is a well known racer who goes by the handle, 'The Golden Boy.' And finally, I'm in possession of a video that shows the race and the resulting accident. It also clearly depicts the car owned by the defendant racing down the road where the wreck occurred."

The judge, clearly interested, looked over at his bailiff and said, "Set everything up so I can have a look at this video." While the officer went about his task, he turned back to Ms. Morrison and said, "Let me see these reports you have and any other relevant content for this case." She immediately jumped up and carried a stack of papers to the bench.

James glanced over at Corey who didn't seem the least bothered by any of the activity going on. Tapping his arm, James looked at him in puzzlement. Corey just made a calm down gesture and focused his attention back to the front of the room.

After about ten minutes of absolute silence, the judge looked over at the bailiff and told him to play the video. The lights dimmed and the 80-inch monitor blinked on, then the silent video started to play.

Heart pounding with fear, James watched the video for the first time. It was edited in a way so that it slowed down at certain points to draw attention to one detail or another. After the video ended, James wanted to jump up and shout with joy. Leave it to The Black Sheep to use the cheapest, low-quality equipment on the market. The video was so bad,

James had been there and could barely make sense of it. He didn't know what was in those reports, but if they were relying on the video, he was home free.

The judge glanced over at the DA and then told the bailiff to turn the lights back on. His focus returned to the paperwork in front of him and the distressed look on his face grew with every page he turned. When he reached the bottom of the stack, he snatched the glasses off his face, shook his head, and leaned back in his chair.

He sat with his eyes closed for a couple minutes before his gaze landed on the DA. He said, "You still didn't get an indictment. And most of these reports have contradictory statements right next to each other." Flipping through the papers, he pulled one out and said, "The Crash Scene Investigator, Kimberly Gibson, I've known her for years and I've never seen a report from her like this. On one line she says the car could have been bumped, on the next she says it could have loss control. Right here it says the car was traveling 100mph when it flipped, but states the car could have been going as slow as 80mph. This report is useless."

Standing up, Ms. Morrison said, "Your Honor…"

"Sit down, Ms. Morrison!" Judge Kennedy demanded.

Flouncing down, she said, "The Grand Jury has been on vacation and they don't reconvene until tomorrow. I didn't think it was necessary to call a Special Jury when the indictment would only be one day late. As far as the CSI report, Ms. Gibson specified what she thought based on her 20 years of experience, but she had to include all possibilities. I understand that looking at it piece by piece, this case is a stretch, but when you look at everything together, the only conclusion that makes sense is James Jordan racing, getting bumped, and the resulting crash killing Amia and Alanah Knight."

The judge continued to stare at Ms. Morrison. "Anything else?" he asked. When she got ready to jump up and sell her case, Judge Kennedy quickly stated, "Anything that's not in one of the reports I've just went over?"

That seemed to knock the wind right out of her sails. With eyes downcast, she murmured, "No, Your Honor."

His focus shifted to Mr. McCann. "Anything you want to add to the motion?"

Corey sat back and said, "Your Honor, I hate to speak ill of our justice system, but this is the shoddy work that's becoming so prevalent when it comes to the prosecution side of things. They get so comfortable with scaring defendants with numbers, and sometimes letters, that they have no clue how to handle a case where there is no plea to be had. When someone is truly innocent and they have the desire and the means to prove what they proclaim.

"This case was never about whether my client was innocent or guilty. Ms. Morrison expressed her personal bias against rich, young, black men by consistently ignoring every sign he was innocent. Instead, she focused all her resources on trying to twist the facts to further her agenda."

"Objection, Your Honor! I have no such bias against anyone!" yelled the DA.

"Then explain to me why we're in this courtroom when you don't have a shred of evidence that a crime was even committed!" Corey screamed back.

"Order! Order!" *Bang! Bang! Bang!* "One more outburst from either one of you and you'll find yourself with a state sponsored meal tonight." Turning to the DA, he said, "This is an evidence hearing, who are you objecting to? You were allowed to give me a stack of papers that the defense had no clue what was in them. Mr. McCann sat quietly through your video and your impassioned speech. Why do you feel like you don't have to give him the same respect he gave you?"

Turning to Corey, Judge Kennedy said, "I gave you a lot of leeway with your statements, but keep your words focused on the case and not on the DA or politics. You may proceed and I'll make my judgement when you're finished."

"Your Honor, I'll make one more point and then I'll pass to the Court." Corey paused and looked over at James. "This kid has been through hell. James lost, not just the love of his life, but also her sister, who he felt was his family also. In his delirium, brought about by grief and a concussion, he was beat up by a cop and put in a coma for over a week. During that time, Alanah and Amia Knight's family went ahead with the funeral and he never got to say goodbye.

"After waking up and spending a little over a week recovering in the hospital, he was released, only to have the police waiting to arrest him outside. A move that was deliberate in its coldness, because it caused a confused and vulnerable man to spend the night in jail. The time to stop punishing James is now. The DA could have showed

177

compassion and let James grieve with his family. Instead, she showed a vindictive ruthlessness by continuing to threaten and pursue a man who has already been punishing himself for having an accident. At this time, I'd like to reiterate my motion for all charges against my client to be dropped, with prejudice. That's the only way my client and his family can begin to heal."

The courtroom was dead silent. James was quaking on the inside because his life would be decided in the next couple of minutes. He couldn't get his breathing right. His heart was pounding. He felt like he was about to pass out. He wasn't aware how much he was shaking until Corey reached over and laid a hand on his arm. Just that small contact with reality brought him back from the brink. When he could focus on the judge again, his breath hitched from the amount of compassion he saw in the man's eyes.

With little fanfare, Judge Kennedy picked up his gavel, said, "Motion granted. Mr. Jordan, you're free to go," and banged the gavel once more before getting up and exiting the courtroom.

The celebration was loud and swift. He was grabbed and squeezed by his family as tears flowed all around. Thank you's were thrown at Mr. McCann and he nodded graciously before walking over to the DA. But when James was released, he saw a sight that made the joyous feeling evaporate from his heart.

Amanda Knight, who in his mind was the perfect representation of what Alanah would have looked like in her 40s, was bent at the waist, crying her heart out. Alex was standing in front of her trying to coax her out of the seat, but her grief had made her dead weight. She had always been so calm and controlled, it devastated him to see her in this state. His feet actually started to move in their direction when a hand stopped his progress.

Turning around, Sammy was staring intensely into his eyes. He said, "Now is not the time. The same way we need time to heal, they need it too. Leave them alone until we're all in a better head space." Sammy then focused his attention on something Brianna was saying and James took one last glance at the Knights.

This time, he was greeted with a sight that almost made him take a step back. Alex had finally gotten Amanda to her feet, but at the moment, even though she was wrapped in his arms, he was paying her little attention. Instead, his hate filled gaze was locked directly on James.

Trying to show how sorry he was, James stared at the man with apology and empathy on his face. Alex just stared back with a glacier-like coldness that froze James on the spot. Then, like he'd imagined the whole episode, Alex blinked and tears spilled from his eyes. He directed his wife down the aisle and disappeared out the back door.

James felt a small hand grasp his and he turned to see Yazmine looking up at him with all her feelings on her sleeve. They stayed shoulder to shoulder as they followed his parents out to their waiting vehicles. When they all started talking about going to lunch to celebrate, he looked at them and said, "I think I just want to go home and chill." Focusing on Yazmine, he said, "Alone."

Deciding to give them privacy, his parents hugged him once more, got into his father's Range Rover, and drove away.

Yazmine said, "I know you're conflicted right now. On one hand, you're happy, on the other, you're sad and filled with grief. I'll give you time to yourself because I know you need it. But, I'm warning you now: Today is all you get. Tomorrow, I'm gonna be on your ass like white on rice." Smiling, she stepped up and gave him a lingering kiss on the cheek. She said, "Don't push me away, James. I'm willing to be whatever you need me to be." With that, she jumped in her little white Porsche and drove away.

That morning, not knowing if he would ever drive again, he'd pulled out a storm purple, $4.6 Million Ferrari LaFerrari Aperta he kept in a special atmosphere-controlled enclosure in his garage. He had wanted the pleasure of driving a car that only 200 other people in the world owned. This wasn't a car people raced, even though technically it was a race car. This was a vehicle that reaffirmed there were things bigger than man. For a guy like him, driving a car like this took his brain to a euphoric state. Right now, he was glad he'd made the choice because he needed something to erase the guilty feelings floating around in his head.

He took the long way home, but even the legendary LaFerrari couldn't completely wipe out his melancholy. He was free, but only because of a legal system that catered to people like him. Rich, from a good, influential family. He was under no illusions that, if he was poor, he'd be sitting in jail right now waiting for a trial that wouldn't start for years.

Making it to his room, he fell on the bed and wished for sleep to come and carry him away. He was exhausted. The range of emotions from the day had stripped him of any excess energy. Plus, guilt was eating him alive. No matter what the law said, he had killed Alanah and Amia. Now, they would forever be classified as accidental deaths. No justice. No responsibility. He could almost feel the disappointment strangling his soul.

All day and all night, he slept and mourned. Ignoring his phone and focusing on wallowing in a debilitating grief that he felt he deserved. Several times, he woke from nightmares containing the staring eyes of Alex, but those weren't the worst. The most crushing dream was of a smiling Alanah wrapping him in her arms and saying, "Me and Amia died, but you survived without a scratch. Can you explain to me why?"

After that doozey, he stayed awake for hours. Heart aching and soul tortured, because no matter what answer he came up with, it seemed inadequate. Finally, he came to the conclusion that there was no explanation. There was no answer to why he had survived. The shocker came when the truth entered his heart: If he couldn't explain why he survived, was it possible to have a reason to live? Realizing what the answer had to be, he laid in the dark with tears streaming down his face until he eventually succumbed to sleep.

Chapter 13

The doorbell was loud and persistent, but not totally unexpected. His phone had been vibrating constantly for the past hour. If any of the calls had been from his parents, the second he didn't answer they would have rushed over and entered the house. So, just using the process of elimination, he guessed it was Yazzy calling. When the doorbell began ringing off the wall, the words yelled at his door confirmed his assumption.

"Come on, JJ! Get up! I know you can hear me. I'm not going away until you come to the door. James! Stop acting like a child and answer the door!"

Even though the master suite was on the top floor at the back of the house, James had never used it. All the bedrooms were roughly the same size, so he used the one down the hall from the living room for convenience. Up until now, he'd thought it a good decision. Being able to hear every shout by Yazmine forced him to rethink his assessment.

Knowing she would stand there all day harassing him, if necessary, he rolled out of bed and made his way to the front door. Still wearing the clothes from court, minus the suit jacket and tie, he snatched the door open and stared at a smiling Yazzy. Not waiting for an invitation, she leaned up, kissed him on the cheek, and brushed pass him to enter the house.

"If you think for one minute I'm gonna let you sit around sulking all day, you can think again." Flopping down on the couch, she said, "We're celebrating today. Go put on something comfortable, grab a couple of your bank cards, and we're spending the day together tearing up the mall."

Closing the door after watching her strut to the couch, he asked, "And you're wearing that?"

Yazmine glanced down at her bright-red Nike bodysuit that wrapped her curves like a lover's embrace. The top of her perky breast sat so far out of the designed cups, the edge of her areolas was visible. The stretchy material also molded to her chest in a way that detailed every bump and ridge of her nipples.

Their eyes locked as she said, "There is nothing wrong with what I have on." Pulling the top up to cover a millimeter more of cleavage, she said, "It's summer, JJ. It's only 9 o'clock and it already feels like a hundred degrees." Flashing her brilliant smile, she added, "And, you'll no doubt be with the baddest chick everywhere we go. Now, hurry up and get ready so we can celebrate your freedom!"

Her enthusiasm finally breached his walls, forcing him to smile at her antics. Shaking his head, he headed back to his bedroom to get ready. Showered and dressed, he returned after about 20 minutes to find Yazzy posing, taking selfies with her phone. Seeing him, her eyes traveled up and down his body before she quickly brought the phone up and snapped a picture of him. She said, "You look nice."

The Louis Vuitton shorts and t-shirt he had on were lightweight and comfortable. The ensemble was white and gold and he accessorized the outfit with gold-rimmed Louis V shades, a white and gold Hublot Big Bang watch, worth about $90,000, and an all-white pair of Jordan 11s. He had no doubt that he cut a dashing picture with his dreads brushing his shoulders, but no one would be looking at him. Every eye, both male and female, would be stuck on his partner for today.

The Nike bodysuit covered the essentials, and now that he wasn't half sleep, he could clearly see how much it emphasized her flat stomach, legs, and bubble butt. Even the small, red and white Nike Foamposites covering her feet made her look cute and sexy. Her hair had been tamed into a long braid that tickled the shelf created by her plump ass. Which left her stunning face, with its delicate features, blasting the world with full force.

Doing a slow spin so he could see all her barely covered attributes, she asked, "Do I look good enough to chill with a multi-millionaire?"

Trying to work up some lubrication for his suddenly dry mouth, he settled for a few quick nods as Yazmine giggled evilly, knowing the effect she had on him. Showing a little mercy, she gathered up her Nike bag, grabbed his hand, and pulled him towards the door. "Let's go show those Charlotte natives that everyone from Concord isn't as country as they think."

They exited out the front door, but James slammed on the brakes when it became apparent where she was leading him. "Um, your little Porsche is cute, but I'm not riding around in that cramped car all day."

Putting on a saucy grin, she said, "That should give you a little motivation to make a purchase at our first stop."

When he cocked his head at her, she laughed and said, "Come on, JJ! We're not holding anything back today. Let's just have fun and enjoy each other's company." Reluctantly, he walked around and jumped in the passenger side.

For the next 30 minutes, Yazmine drove while telling him story after story about the people who subscribed to her OnlyFans. He laughed at most of the inappropriate request and kinks people possessed, but the images floating in his own mind made him think he was just as depraved. By the time they pulled up to the luxury car dealership, he was damn near sweating with the restraint it took to keep his hands off of her luscious body. If she kept him in this state all day, when they returned to his house, there wouldn't be any doubt on how the night would end.

Parking the Porsche, she turned to say something, but he must have been showing his thoughts on his face. She sucked in a breath and continued to stare deep into his eyes. The atmosphere was charged with sexual attraction and damned if James didn't enjoy the feeling. Leaning towards her, he wrapped his hand gently around her thigh, causing a hiss to issue out through her clinched teeth. A slight rubbing motion resulted in her turning slightly towards him and her legs splaying open to provide room if he wanted to explore more.

Still locked in their eye-to-eye connection, James withdrew his hand and leaned back against the passenger side door. With her heavy breathing and her body spread out in invitation, it took everything in him to say, "We can't do this, Yazzy. I mean, you know I love you. I've loved you my whole life. You're the only person in the whole world who knows all there is to know about me. I don't know what the future will hold, but for right now, I really need you to just be my best friend. Okay?"

Eyes shining, she turned her body around in the seat and nodded her head. Biting her lower lip, she turned to him again and extended her hand up to his face, rubbing his clean-shaven jaw. "I love you too, JJ, and right now I will respect your wishes. But I want you." After a pause where her eyes shot to his lap, she said, "And I know you want me too. For today, we'll let this go and have a good time, but this conversation isn't over." She withdrew her hand, opened her door, exiting the vehicle to give him some alone time to collect himself.

Finally, able to get out of the car without embarrassing himself, he joined Yazzy and just stared at all the exotic vehicles surrounding them. There was no doubt that Yazmine knew him well. Most of the cars he bought, he did so through a proxy, online. Normally, he would never shop at a place like this because he would undoubtably spend too much money. Just looking around now, he could feel his bank account dwindle by a few million dollars.

Yazmine brushed his shoulder with her's, grabbed his hand, and said, "Let's go have some fun." And fun they had.

For the next few hours, he climbed in and out of Lamborghinis, Ferraris, Bentleys, McLarens, and even a Koenigsegg CCX that he was sure his father had been looking for. He and Yazzy oohed and aahed as they explored cars that most kids dreamed of owning. At one point, a salesman came out and politely informed them that only serious shoppers were allowed to enter the vehicles. James pulled out his wallet, showed the man his Black AmEx and several Platinum cards before saying, "Shut up," then went back to enjoying his day. The salesman watched them for a few moments then went back into the showroom.

They came upon a McLaren 570S with a creamy-purple exterior, and a leather, black and purple, interior and Yazmine squealed like a school girl. "Oh my God! This car is so beautiful. I can't wait until I can afford something like this." She climbed into the driver's seat and James walked around to join her.

With a shrug, James asked, "You want it?"

Initially, she laughed. But seeing the serious expression on his face, she said, "Boy, don't play with me."

Shaking his head, he said, "The sticker price is only $146,000. If I offer them $130,000 in cash, I know they'll jump on it."

"I can't let you spend that much money on me," she declared, after a moment of thought. "I know it might not be much to you, but that's life changing money to some people."

"Yazmine, that $100 Million assessment they said in court is so far off base, it's not even funny. That's what my grandmother left me, but that was ten years ago. All of my bills and living expenses come out of a separate trust that she set up for the Jordan family. So basically, for the past ten years, that $100 Million has been earning more money than I can ever spend in this lifetime. $130,000 for my best friend to be happy is the least I can do."

Leaning over with tears in her eyes, she kissed him lightly on the lips. "I really do love you JJ, and I appreciate the offer. But no. I don't feel right accepting gifts from you. I've always been that way and I'll probably never change, but thank you so much for making me feel loved." Getting out, she sent one last lingering look at the McLaren, and then they walked away.

Not being at all reserved like Yazmine, James found a metallic silver Ferrari F12 TDF and knew he'd found his next car. The leather and carbon fiber, white and purple, interior was streamlined and perfectly matched his taste. Yazzy gasped when she saw the $875,000 price tag. James threw out a counter-offer of $850,000 on the spot, which the dealership accepted, and about one o'clock that afternoon, he was following behind Yazmine's Porsche on the way to Concord Mills Mall.

The whole drive, the Ferrari groaned at him for not unleashing it on the open roads. It was extremely hard to act like an adult and not go tearing up the streets, but one day soon, he'd have to take a trip to the practice track and see what this baby could do. One thing it was already proving to be was a master at drawing attention. When they pulled up to the mall, people materialized out of nowhere for a chance to check out the exotic car.

For the next 20 minutes, James allowed the locals to explore the car. The people had no idea who he was, so several assumed he was famous and asked for his autograph. He took selfies and genuinely had a blast with all the young kids clambering on and around the vehicle. Finally, he was able to escape the melee and Yazmine grabbed his hand as they made their way to the mall entrance.

Halfway there, they looked at each other and laughed when they heard a guy ask his friend, "If you had to choose between the car or the girl, which one would you pick?"

The friend's reply was raunchy, but still funny. He said, "Neither. Either one I pick, I'd ride to an early grave."

They made their way into the mall and Yazzy asked if they could catch a quick bite before they entered the next phase of shopping. They both ordered Chinese food, sat down in a section without a lot of people, and talked as they ate. After drifting off a few times, and Yazmine having to question if he was okay, he decided it was time for him to say something that was long overdue.

"Yazzy?" When she stopped eating and looked up at him, he said, "I'm sorry for abandoning you, and I want you to know, if I had known what was going on, I would have never left your side."

Her face went pale. "No! No, James! We are not talking about this now."

"I think I need to talk…"

"James, stop! I'm serious. We're supposed to be celebrating. We can talk some other time."

After a lengthy pause, he nodded and said, "Okay." Reaching across the table and grabbing her hand, he added, "But I have to tell you this right now: No matter what happens in the future, I promise you that I will never turn my back on you again." She dropped her gaze and nodded as his thumb played over her knuckles. It was a vulnerable moment for both of them that was interrupted by the hateful words thrown their way.

"So, is this why you killed my sisters! You decided you couldn't live without your whore by your side!" James immediately jumped up and pushed AJ away from their table. AJ snarled and was about to throw a punch when Alex came from behind, grabbed him, and pulled him away.

James said, "You better watch your mouth, clown! Don't you ever disrespect Yazmine like that again." His muscles were jumping with the need for violence. He was praying that the men decided to try him like they'd done his father. He'd show them what a merciless Jordan could do.

With hate-filled eyes, Alex said, "It's okay son, he'll get what's coming to him. But this isn't the time or the place."

AJ, still being pulled away by his father, pointed at James and said, "You think you got away with it, but I'm gonna make you and your whore pay. You'll wish they'd kept you locked up when I get finished with you!"

James took a couple advancing steps, ready to do battle, when Yazmine said, "James! Please! Just let it go! It's okay."

He stopped, but gave the men a message as a farewell. "Either of you decide to come at me or mine again, I promise I'll kill you both." Focusing on AJ, he said, "Give me a reason, you son of a bitch. I dare you." After a brief stare off, AJ ripped himself from his father's grasp and stalked away. Alex looked back and forth between James and his retreating son before he too strolled away.

Yazmine pulled him back to his seat and she tried her best to bring him back to his pre-interruption self. Finally, she went quiet and just stared at him with sadness in her eyes. Seeing the self-loathing on her face made him realize how selfish he was being. She was doing everything in her power to make him happy, and he was choosing to embrace his anger instead of her love.

Smiling, he said, "It's been a while since I had to threaten someone for calling you names. At least he didn't accuse you of having cooties like Jahzion Wilson did in the 3rd grade. I don't think I could have restrained myself if he had." Their smiles morphed into full on belly-laughs, which had several people looking at them as if they were crazy. Eventually, they stood up, tossed their trash in the bin, and he tucked her under his arm as they jumped from store to store.

James chuckled as workers and customers alike tripped all over themselves in an effort to help Yazmine. From horny teens, to middle-aged men, eyes tracked every move she made and tried to anticipate any of her needs. What amused him the most was the combination of envious and admiring looks the women cast her way. Walking pass one group, a woman said, "She acting like she all that. I saw that same bodysuit on Amazon for like $30."

Another one sucked her teeth and said, "Well, you better buy one quick, because after the world sees her in it, Nike will be charging $300. She rocking that thing!"

They shopped. They talked. They ate again. Then they made their way to the movie theater. James vetoed any kind of rom-com or emotional film. They settled on a suspense\thriller that had gotten rave reviews from critics and customers alike.

In the darkened screening room, it didn't matter that the sounds of screams and gun battles filled the air. That damned cucumber melon scent was drifting in his nose, and her warm supple body was pressed up against his. They both behaved themselves, but after the movie was over, James had to remain in his seat for a few extra minutes to gather himself.

Their cars were full of purchases. Their stomachs were full of candy, popcorn, and soda. Their hearts were full of each other, and their minds were consumed with erotic thoughts. The drive to his place in separate cars did little to bank their flame, and sitting in his living room where their day had started, fantasies were floating in the air.

Yazmine soon had enough of the awkwardness and said, "I want to show you something." Grabbing a bag that she'd entered the house with, she said, "Stay out here until I call you." Then she walked down the hall to his bedroom.

He heard his shower kick on and his heart started to pound in his chest. He desperately wanted to see what Yazmine wanted to show him, but then again, he didn't. He'd been fighting his desires all day, and he wasn't sure he had the strength to keep it up. But hell, he was getting ahead of himself. Maybe she just wanted to show him a new game on her phone. Or a new, innocent tattoo she'd gotten on her ankle. Surely what she wanted to show him had nothing to do with the lingerie store she'd snuck off to while she thought he was occupied. As if he'd been able to peel his eyes away from her at any time during their day.

The shower turned off and he heard Yazmine fumbling around in his room. His palms were sweating, he was pacing back and forth nervously, and his mind was shouting, "RUN! Get away while you still can!" He was seconds away from yelling for Yazzy to abandon whatever she was planning, when he heard her say, "Alright JJ, you can come on back."

His body petrified. The forces at work were pulling him in two different directions. His heart and soul were telling him to leave the house because this wasn't right. His mind, and another part of his anatomy, were telling him that this is what he'd wanted all along. He had to admit that both feelings were accurate, but still, his feet propelled him in the direction of the bedroom in the end.

He pictured Yazzy, laid out on the bed with some asset baring material draped over her body. When he stepped in, however, candles were lit, the lighting was low, but Yazmine was nowhere in sight. He called her name and she responded from behind the bathroom door. "I laid out what I want you to put on. Change your clothes and then lay down on the bed."

The red, silk boxers were sitting on the end of the bed. The material was damn near see through and would do nothing to hide the state he was fast approaching. Holding up the underwear, he said, "Yazzy, I don't think..."

"That's your problem, JJ!" she yelled back. "Stop thinking so much and just do what I tell you!" Shaking his head at his own stupidity, he stripped out of his clothes, donned the thin boxers, then laid back on the bed. Since she had already removed the covers, he had nothing to block the view of his arousal. He glanced at the pillows, but thought he'd look like a high school virgin if she entered to the sight of him clutching one to his body. Plus, this is obviously what she wanted. He settled back and waited for what was sure to be a hell of a show.

"You ready?" she called out. He responded affirmatively seconds before soft music filled the room. Of course, what else would she use as her entrance song other than Trey Songz, *Love Faces*. His mind instantly transported back to the day she climaxed in his arms, then the bathroom door opened and he lost all train of thought.

The first thing that came into view was a glowing, caramel-colored, stiletto clad leg. The red, high-heeled shoes provided the perfect backdrop for her French pedicured toes. His eyes traveled up and down the delectable sight, until she swung her left hip into view, and the voluptuous flesh stole his attention.

He could barely make out the red strip of material at her waist, but her hand coming down to toy with it caught his full focus. Letting it go, she wrapped her leg and arm around the doorframe, bringing her luscious, free-flowing hair, and shapely shoulder into view.

Her hand reached down and slithered from her sculpted thigh, all the way up to the side of her face before she tossed her hair back and stepped out to reveal her full, scantly covered body. Literally breathtaking. He couldn't breathe as her hazel eyes, smoldering with love and desire, locked with his own, which were helpless to show the same emotions. He actually shivered when her eyes traveled down his body and she licked her glossy, pink lips in delight.

She struck a pose with her left hip cocked, and her hands by her side so he could inspect her magnificent body. The crotchless, red panties showed that she was clean shaven and, if the wetness shining in the candle light told the tale, she was ready for action. The half-cup matching bra did nothing except offer her breast a place to rest as her rock hard, jutting nipples were on full display. When his eyes went back up to her face, she must have assumed he was finished with that view and needed another. Slowly, she gathered her hair in front of her and then turned around.

Her oiled-up cheeks were glorious. The skin was smooth and unblemished from her ankles to her neck, but her ass was the perfect centerpiece of the full package. Suddenly, she glanced back over her shoulder, bit her bottom lip, and folded her body forward so her hands were touching the floor. He moaned and turned his head to the side because, just the view and the atmosphere, was pushing him towards an epic explosion.

He hadn't known she'd moved until he felt something brush his foot. His head whipped back around just as the song changed to Alicia Keys and Miguel's, *Show Me Love*. She stood at the foot of the bed and studied his body as she gave him a foot massage. Whispering just loud enough to be heard over the music, she said, "I've wanted to show you how much I love you for a long time. Let me show you what life can be like with me by your side."

She worked her way up his body using her hands, her eyes, and her mouth to drive him insane. This was the reason he'd had to push her out of his life three years ago. While he was deeply in love with Alanah, Yazmine could catapult him beyond reason in a matter of seconds. She was so sensual, so sexy, so…. Powerful. All he could do in defense was pray that she showed him mercy because, if she didn't, he was helpless to resist her call.

When she reached his bulging manhood, she stared down at it while he held his breath in anticipation. Glancing up at him with an almost evil smile, she pulled her hair around to make a silky black curtain to hide what she was about to do. She never removed him from the silk prison, but after two minutes of her hands and mouth teasing and tasting, the boxers were a gooey mess from both of their juices.

After she finished there, her tongue blazed a trail up his body until they shared a kiss that would have made a porn star blush. They attempted to devour each other. She tasted so good to him that he started to wrestle her for control of their pleasure. Both breathing hard, she used all her strength to pin him back to the bed to prove her dominance.

They stared at each other, him from his back, her straddling his waist. When the next song began to play, he understood that she had a specific soundtrack to go with the plan for her show. DVSN and Snow Aalegra proclaimed, "I don't want nothing in-between us." Yazmine worked her way back down his body, and said, "My sentiments exactly," before she snatched the ruined boxers down his legs.

When he was naked and standing firm, she clambered to her knees at his feet, removed her bra and panties, but kept on the stilettos. Her cat-like crawl brought her sensational form back up to his hips where she used her pelvic region to trap him between their bodies. Her undulations made him pant as her burning core dragged up and down his steel. With her head back, and her back arched, she soon worked herself into a frenzy. The shaking had just started when he craned his neck forward and captured her nipple, causing her to scream his name.

She collapsed on his chest, breathing out of control, as he rubbed and roamed her ass and back. He was still standing tall, the heat and moisture making him as hard as he'd ever been. Finally, her quaking subsided and she arranged herself to sit on his hips once again.

This time, it was Lloyd's, *One For Me*, that issued out of the speakers. James expected her to carry out the final act of their lovemaking. With just a shift, she could have him buried deep in her womanhood. Instead, she raised herself off of him so that no part of them was touching. Then, softly, she started telling him what she needed.

"I used to listen to this song when we were children and I'd picture you singing it to me. Even before I knew what some of the words meant, I envisioned you holding my hand, staring into my eyes, and telling me that I was the one for you. A girlish dream that the woman is still holding onto."

She pushed her hair behind her back so he could clearly see the emotions playing out over her face. "Our whole lives we've been a team. You've been my savior, my protector, and my best friend. But, there's one more role I've been dying for you to claim... Lover," she said, on a sigh.

"But James, that's a step that you and only you can take. I've loved you since I was 5-years-old. I loved you when we used to ride bikes together. When you used to tear the heads off my dolls. When we used to go on fishing trips with your father. Even when you told me to never speak to you again. Not one second has passed since you rescued me in kindergarten that my heart hasn't beat for you."

Looking down at his throbbing shaft, she said, "So, now it's time for you to make a decision. I know you lust after me, I even recognize that you love me. But, you have to take the step to become my lover." She reached and grabbed his hand, directing him until his fingers wrapped around himself. "I've never hid my wants or needs from you, what I need now is for you to make yours clear to me. Make us one. Show me that I'm the one for you."

He looked down the length of her torso and saw that he was mere millimeters from that final connection. He used his other hand to guild her hips where he needed them to be, and then he looked up at her beautiful face. The hope in her eyes warring with her doubts. She knew what his body wanted; it was staring both of them in the face. But, the heart, that was a different matter. She had no way of knowing if there was room left in his heart for her.

He could still feel her warmth and her sticky fluids all over his midsection. He lifted his hips and made contact with her opening. Her eyes closed, her mouth fell open, and her muscles seemed to be trying their best to pull him in. Then the visions hit.

Flick. Flick. Flick. Picture after picture flashed in his mind. His and Alanah's first time. Her face as she willingly gave him her body, mind, and soul. Her tears. Her smiles. Her victories. Her defeats. He closed his own eyes as visions of a lost future floated in his head. Teal eyed little boys and girls running around the Jordan estate. Nights of passion that ended with him and his wife still joined as they fell asleep. Sitting on the porch watching their grandkids play in the grass. Raindrops falling on his face.

Wait… What? Raindrops?

Opening his eyes, he looked up into the totally devastated face of Yazmine. Her tears raining down on his face as she let her pain and hurt wash through her body. She rolled off of him, but he jumped up quickly in pursuit. "Yazzy, wait! Dammit, wait!"

Spinning back around, she used her arms to hide her nakedness. "Wait for what, James? I'm tired of waiting for you! I'm tired of being good enough to fuck, but not good enough to love!" Turning on her heels, she launched herself towards the bathroom.

"Yazzy, stop! Come on! Stop!" he yelled, grabbing onto her arm.

She yanked her arm and spun, slapping him across his face. "Let me go, James!" She continued to rain blows on his chest and face until she collapsed against his body, sobbing in agony.

He gathered her to him and laid back down on the bed with them facing each other on their sides. They were holding each other tighter and closer than when they were in the throes of passion. But, this was a different kind of embrace. This had nothing to do with sex and everything to do with love.

As she sobbed, tears leaked out of James, also. He murmured and petted her in an effort to get her calm. After a while, her breathing evened out and he thought she had fallen asleep. When he went to untangle their limbs, she squeezed him tight and asked, "Why? Why do I have to keep living in hell, James?"

He used his fingers to comb her hair as he turned onto his back, carrying her with him so she was draped over his body. He said, "You're not in hell, sweetie. And, if you are, then I'm right there by your side."

"James, all I've known my whole life is pain and rejection. Why has God picked me to suffer so much? Why does He hate me? What did I do to deserve this?" He could feel her tears once again sliding down his neck.

Pulling her hair slightly, he said, "Yazmine, sit up and look at me." When she buried her head deeper, he said, "Please, Yazmine, I need you to look at me when I say this." Reluctantly, she eased herself around so she was still laying on his chest, but could look into his eyes. "I love you, Yazmine Salazar. I've loved you since the first time I laid eyes on you. It was never my intention to hurt you or let you be hurt. But, you know I had no idea what was happening to you. Until you said what you said that day before you left, I had no clue that you were going through that. I was a shitty friend, and I turned my back on you in your time of need. I promise you right here and now, I will never hurt you or turn away from you again. I swear it."

"But you always hurt me, James. Every time you reject me like you did tonight. I feel that rejection all the way down to my soul."

He reached up and brushed the tears from her face. "Yazmine, I'm just not ready yet. If I allow this to happen now, it would only be for my own selfishness. You know I've always had strong feelings for you, but my emotions are twisted right now. Just give me some time so I can work through my shit."

Nodding, she leaned forward and kissed him delicately on his lips. A gentle rocking led to him reaching around and grabbing her hips to stop her motion. Laughing saucily, she asked, "You sure we can't just make out a little longer?"

Hissing, he said, "I'm not against a little make out session here and there, but we definitely have to put some clothes on." She laughed again, gave him one more playful pelvic roll, and lunged off of the bed. He said, "Um, can you do one thing for me though?" After her nod, he said, "Can you walk as slow as possible to the bathroom?" She did. The gloom in her eyes floating away when she saw the love and appreciation in his.

For the rest of the week, they were inseparable. They shopped and drove and just enjoyed each other's company. Yazmine did have to go back to work every night, but she was back with James by three o'clock each morning. James was still working through his guilt for moving on from Alanah, so all of their make out sessions remained clothing mandatory. Every night they slept in the same bed together, every morning they felt their bond growing stronger.

Everything was going wonderfully, that's why Yazmine should have known something was about to go wrong. She and James had just finished one of their rounds on Saturday when James gave her one last smoking hot kiss before jumping in the shower. Yazzy fell back on the bed, smiling at the good fortune that had taken over her life. Then her phone rang.

She hit the ignore button five times before she concluded the man wasn't gonna give up. Hoping to be done before James returned, she finally answered the call.

"What the hell do you want? I'm done with you!" she hissed.

"Says who?" was his reply. "Since I know exactly where you are, tell me you're done again, and I'll send someone to come get you right now. Might have a little collateral damage in the process," subtly threatening James with the comment.

"Why are you doing this? The case was dismissed. It's over, so why are you calling me?"

"We still have our agreement in place. I hope you didn't think that one time was enough to satisfy me or our terms?"

Sitting up, she said, "You got what you wanted. I hope you didn't think I'd be your little sex slave forever," she tossed back at him.

"I'm done arguing with you, Yazmine. I'm sending you a text on where to meet me. Unless you want to spend the next ten years in prison, you'll be there within the hour. If you don't show, I'll figure you're nullifying our deal and I'll act accordingly. I know some cops who would love to get their hands on the evidence I have."

After a pause, she asked, "If I come this time, will this satisfy our terms?"

"Yes, Yazmine. I promise, if you make it on time and do what you need to do, I'll never contact you again."

"And I'll get the evidence back?"

"You'll get the evidence back. I swear."

Hearing the water cut off in the shower, she lowered her voice and said, "I'll be there. You just make sure I get what I deserve."

On the other end of the call, the man hung up and chuckled. To himself, he said, "Oh, you'll definitely get what you deserve. And more. You can bet your sweet little ass on that." Then he placed another call so everything would be ready when she arrived.

Chapter 14

Sunday morning, James woke up and reached across the bed. Not feeling a warm, pliant body, his eyes snapped open to a sight that was already foreign to him: Yazmine not by his side. The sheets on her side, yes, he was already thinking of it as her side, were undisturbed and cold. He cocked his head and listened, but he already knew he was in the house by himself.

Sitting up to check the time, he reached for his phone: 9:00am. They had both agreed to attend the Sunday service with his parents, so he sent her a quick text asking where she was. She didn't immediately respond, so he rolled out of bed and went to take a shower.

Reentering the bedroom, he checked his phone for her reply, but found nothing. Frowning now, he dialed her number and decided to leave a voicemail when she didn't answer. "Yo Yazzy, where you at? I guess you needed a night of calm after all the heat we been making. Well, maybe not heat, but warmth at least. Anyway, I hope you didn't forget about church. I'm gonna get dressed and head over to the big house. We'll probably leave in about 30 minutes. Meet us at the church if you have to. If you can't make it, it's cool, just let me know you're good." After a pause, he added, "Love you," before ending the call.

His parents belonged to one of those progressive churches that wanted its members to be casual and comfortable. He donned a pair of khakis, a white Ralph

Lauren button up, and some black Prada boots to fit that vibe. He decided against any jewelry or accessories, locked up the front, and walked through the back door towards his parent's house.

The sliding glass door was open and he entered to find his mother making him a plate. "I saw you coming," she stated as she loaded him down with eggs, bacon, and hash browns. Giving him a sideways look, she asked, "Where's Yazmine this morning?"

He slid over to her and hugged her from behind while planting a kiss on her check. He said, "I don't know where she's at. She got some kind of emergency call last night and I haven't heard from her since." Taking his plate, he took a step back and eyed his mother up and down. "And why are we dressed so spiffy this morning, Mrs. Jordan?"

She looked down at the short, black Valentino dress, and tall Louboutin sandals with her bronzed skin reddening. "Me and Sammy are going out to eat after the service." Looking up with a teasing smile, she added, "We've been together forever but we still need dates every now and then. You'll do good to remember that when you and Yazzy get older."

Sighing, James said, "Mom, don't start. Me and Yazzy are only friends. Plus, Alanah's only been gone a month. Don't you think it's too soon for me to move on?" Even to his own ears it sounded like he was searching for someone to convince him of that fact.

Leaning on the counter, Brianna studied her son before she responded. "You know, me and Sammy were just like you two when we were little. The same way you protected her, that's the same way he used to protect me. My cheekbones and eyes made it clear I was mixed with Asian blood, and the other kids would tease me and pick on me all the time. Until Sammy said enough was enough and claimed me as his own."

She came over and joined him at the table before she continued. "It's something about a bond that starts that early, it builds all the platform necessary to lay a solid foundation. When I saw how much you loved her as a child, I knew you would have the same thing I have with your father." Then she paused, like it pained her to continue.

Cutting his eye, he said, "Go ahead and say it. Not like I haven't heard it before."

"Alanah was a beautiful girl, and I loved her like she was my own daughter. But James, she just wasn't right for you."

"And I keep telling you…"

"I know, James! You loved her. She was perfect. She was kind, and patient, and smart. But, have you ever burned for her? Have you ever been turned inside out from just the thought of her?" After a pause, she said, "The problem was, you put her on a pedestal that she was destined to fall from. You thought that you were the lucky one for having her in your life. Son," she said, reaching over and grabbing his hand, "that's not what you want as the foundation for a forever. God is the only person you should ever worship!"

He sat silently, soaking up the knowledge and insight from this marvelous woman. "Now, Yazmine is your equal. She's always been your match. She's fire to your ice. High to you low. The anchor your ship needs when you encounter a storm. These last few years, you've been miserable without her in your life. Look at me, James."

His eyes connected with hers. "Look me in my eyes and tell me that your soul doesn't yearn for hers. Tell me that you don't feel a peace beyond understanding when she's near you. Deny the fact that she's owned your heart since you were 5-years-old and you saw her long pigtails and her sad hazel eyes. I know you loved Alanah, and it's alright to still love her. But, Yazmine is The One. Trust me, you can't see your face when she's around, but I can. All you have to do is open your heart to her. She's been ready, she's just waiting for you to catch up." Standing up, she kissed his check, then left him alone with his thoughts.

Soon after, his father entered the kitchen in a white Giorgio Armani suit with a royal blue dress shirt underneath. James laughed and said, "Where ya'll going to lunch, the French Riviera?"

His father struck a model's pose and said, "You just mad your brown ass can't wear something like this. Only us real African Mandingos can make this look good." When all James did was laugh again, Sammy said, "Bring your ass, boy! You gonna make us late for the service."

James rode in the back of Sammy's Range Rover, thinking about Alanah and Yazmine the whole way to church. His mother was right, his and Alanah's love had been strong, but he'd never burned for her. They had made out for three years strong before the episode with Yazmine, and not once had he lost control like he had in that shower. And it wasn't just sex. He hurt when he was away from

Alanah, but he couldn't exist without Yazmine. He knew people would look at him askew for being with Yazmine so soon after Alanah's passing, but it was time to be real with himself: It had been Yazzy all along.

Church was, well, church. There was some singing and reading and sitting and standing. Ultimately, he couldn't focus on the service. Brianna elbowed him numerous times to get him to put his phone away. But he couldn't dispel the notion that something was wrong. Even while at work, Yazmine would text with him back and forth. Her silence was making him edgy.

If he had known Yazmine would ghost him, he would have driven one of his cars. As it was, he ended up taking an UBER back to the house so his parents could go out and enjoy the rest of their day. As Sunday afternoon turned into Sunday night, he really started to worry. He became almost frantic with his need to find her. Sleep wasn't an option, but he didn't have a clue where to start his search. Finally arriving at his wits end, he called Sammy for advice.

"Boy, you getting lazy as hell. You can't walk over here if you want to talk?"

"Dad, you never walk over here. You either call or drive."

"That's because I'm the dad. I earned the right to do that. Now, what do you want?"

"Listen. I've called Yazmine about a hundred times. She's not responding to any of my text. You know she didn't show up for church. I think something happened to her. What do you think I should do?"

Sammy was quiet for about ten seconds. He asked, "And the last time you saw her was last night?"

"Yeah," said James. "She got a call about some kind of emergency and said she'd be back this morning."

"And she hasn't answered any of your calls or responded to any of your text?" asked Sammy.

"No! Nothing! What should I do?"

"With what you've told me, there's really only one thing you can do."

"What?" asked James desperately.

"Sit your simple ass down and give the girl a break! Since your accident, that girl has been glued to your side, trying her hardest to worm her way back into your good graces. She's probably trying to wrap up loose ends with one of her Sugar Daddies. Now that she has the golden goose sniffing around again, she has a couple chickens that need to be kicked to the side."

"Dad, I'm serious!"

"I'm serious too, James. Look, you know I've never been a fan of hers, and I do have sympathy for the things she's had to endure. But girls like her have only three things on their minds: money, money, and money. You didn't know her mother like me and Brianna did, but that's where she got her mind state from. I understand she's your friend, but don't get too attached. One of these days, she's gonna show her true self, and I don't want you getting hurt when it's revealed."

This was an age-old debate between father and son. Sammy had been ecstatic when Alanah had showed up and stolen his attention away from Yazmine. He saw Alanah as everything pure and good, and Yazzy as evil and full of deceit. His father could never explain to him why he felt that way, he would only say it was a feeling deep down in his gut.

Regardless of how his dad felt, if he wasn't gonna help him find Yazzy then he was wasting his time. "Alright Dad, thanks for your help."

"Hold on James," Sammy said, before he could hang up. "Let me call some people and I'll get back to you. I can have them check the local hospitals and other places she might be."

Breathing a sigh of relief, James said, "Thanks, Dad. I'll keep trying her and let you know if I hear anything." Sammy agreed with the plan and they both disconnected.

James wanted so bad to go ripping around the city looking for her. She could be laid out in a ditch somewhere waiting to be rescued. Or at her house having fallen ill. There were a million things that could be wrong and he was sitting in his mansion doing nothing about it. One thing was for certain, she still wasn't answering any of his calls or text.

Having a quick thought, he logged onto his social media ghost account to see if she had posted anything since yesterday. Nope! The last update was a selfie of them eating ice cream on his balcony about ten o'clock the previous night. And he wasn't the only one looking for her. The comments section was flooded with inquiries that Yazmine had yet to respond to. Everything he found was just making him more anxious. He started to pace in an effort to burn off some of the steam.

He was still pacing in the living room around one o'clock that morning when he heard his back door open and close. He raced to the kitchen, both anger and relief flooding his system as he thought it was Yazmine trying to sneak in. But when he entered the darkened room, he pulled up short because it wasn't Yazmine standing there, it was Sammy.

As James studied the look on his dad's face, his heart started to pound and his knees became weak. Sammy said, "Why don't we go in the living room and have a seat?"

"No," James said defiantly. "Just tell me what's going on."

"I think we should sit…"

"I don't want to sit!" James interrupted. "I want you to tell me what the hell is going on!"

"Alright," Sammy told his son. "I didn't want to tell you over the phone because I wanted to be here if you needed me. I had a friend run Yazmine's name and description through the log of all area hospitals. Presbyterian had a Jane Doe brought in around 4:30 Sunday morning. She'd been found unconscious on the top floor of a nearby parking deck. Upon arrival, the medical personnel took extensive photos of her numerous injuries and concluded that she'd also been sexually assaulted."

James backpedaled as if he could escape the words he was hearing. When his back hit the wall, he slid down to the floor, never taking his eyes off his father. "Is she alive?" he asked him.

Nodding, Sammy said, "She came to earlier this evening, but her ID, phone, keys, everything was stolen from the scene. Her car was up there and the police used her tag to eventually identify her. The problem is, she won't talk. She won't tell them who did it or why she was up there in the first place. All she does is stare up at... Wait, James... Wait!" But James was already up and running through the house.

His father gave chase, yelling for him to stop, but James exited the house, snatched the cover off of his Combat Wraith motorcycle, mounted it, turned the engine over, and zoomed off before Sammy could catch him. Only after he was halfway out of Jordan Estates did he pull over and put his helmet on. He knew Sammy would be running to the Big House so he could grab a car and come after him, so he wiped the tears from his face and blasted down empty road after empty road. Luckily, he didn't encounter one cop so he made it to the Charlotte hospital in under 20 minutes.

He entered the lobby almost frantic in his pace. Stopping at the nurses' station, he lied and said that Yazmine was his fiancé and he'd just gotten a call she was there. Oozing sympathy, the kind-eyed nurse gave him the room number and he was off and running again.

James had a pretty good idea of what he would find when he arrived at her door, but there was no preparation for the reality. As much as he wanted to launch himself in, scoop her up and transport her to safety, his feet wouldn't even let him enter the room. What he was seeing was incomprehensible. No human being could possibly be this barbaric toward members of its own species. But even as that thought entered his head, a picture of the responsible party floated across his mind.

He had little doubt who had committed this heinous act, but he had to get confirmation. And, knowing his dad, once he got here, he'd want to involve the police and the courts. Well, James of all people knew the courts were inconsistent at best, corrupt at worst. The presumed culprit was arrogant enough to have not hid his identity at all, but from past experiences, James knew Yazmine wouldn't want to press charges.

So, with time running short before retribution was out of his hands, he quickly made his way over to Yazmine's bedside. Looking down, there was nowhere to touch her that didn't have visible damage or was wrapped by a bandage. Just a glance told him one of each arm and leg was broken. Her head was covered and her long, dark trusses had been shown off. Her face was swollen and almost unrecognizable. He hated to disturb her obviously needed slumber, but he had to get answers before it was too late.

"Yazzy," he said softly. Her head moved slightly, but that was all the response he got. "Yazzy!" he said with more force. This time her right eye fluttered open, the left one was swollen shut, and she immediately focused on his face.

She was in tremendous pain. Her eye was glassy and he could see the IV drip working overtime to keep her comfortable. He wanted to curl up with her and cuddle until all the pain drifted away. That would have to wait. Right now, he needed some fast answers. After he finished doing his duty he'd come back and shower her with love.

He said, "I don't have a lot of time, tell me who did this." She opened her disfigured lips, but no sound came out. He glanced at the side table and saw a cup of water. He grabbed it, placed the straw between her lips, and let her sip before replacing the glass.

This time, when her mouth opened, her voice was weak, but the words were clear. "JJ, they cut off my hair." Tears leaked from her eyes and the hand that wasn't suspended in the air came up to rub at her bandaged head. "They cut off all my hair."

James knew Yazmine treated her hair like it was her pride and joy. She was always stroking it and twirling it. James remembered her getting a cut before her mother died and Yazzy had cried for days. After her mother passed, she had vowed to never cut her hair again in remembrance of her beloved Mom.

He didn't want to sound callous because he understood the impact of the act, but he needed her to answer his question. "Yazzy, I understand you're in emotional and physical pain right now, but I need you to tell me who did this!"

Still leaking tears, Yazmine shook her head and focused her eye on the opposite side of the room. "I don't want you to get hurt or in trouble. I'm alive and I'll heal and my hair will grow back. Just… Let it go."

He reached down and turned her head back to face him. The fear and anguish were evident all over her face, but he pasted a merciless mask over his own to accomplish his goal. Ominously, he said, "In 60 seconds I'm leaving this room. Right now, I have a list of a few people who I imagine did this. If you don't tell me which one, then I'm going after them all." Shrugging, he added, "The choice is yours, but somebody is gonna pay for this. I could care less if who I think did this is innocent or guilty, if you don't give me a name, I'll hunt each of them down to make sure I get the right one."

She stared up at him, not saying a word as he stared back with his heart in his throat. He let his eyes roam over her beaten and battered body before he clinched his jaw and turned to leave the room. He'd only taken a couple steps when her soft voice floated to his ears. "Why are you making such a big deal about this? You're acting as if you have to go avenge my virtue. It's not like it's the first time this has happened to me."

Spinning back around, he said, "But I promised you the last time would definitely be the last, didn't I? When that bastard put his hands on you two years ago, I told you that I would protect you. Well, look at you now. Yes, I kept tabs on you so that I could make sure you were ok. But when it came down to it, I let you down, just like I've done my whole life."

Holding her hand out to him, she said, "JJ, come here." He hesitated for a second but he walked over and gently took her hand. Beseechingly, she said, "When we were 5-years-old you told me that you would always be my protector. I believed you and you never let me down. It was only after I saw myself as unworthy of your protection that I actually got hurt. It was never you, it was my stupid fear that you would reject me once you found out what was being done. This isn't about you not protecting me, it's about my own stupidity once again."

The speech was touching, but James wasn't buying it. "Yazzy, look me in my eyes and tell me that this attack had nothing to do with me. If you can do that, I'll abandon my agenda, pull up a chair, and remain here with you." She opened her mouth to respond but then shook her head and turned away. "Look at me!" he demanded. When she turned back, he said, "Other than my mother, you're the most important woman in my life. I need to do this. Please, Yazzy, give me a name."

Finally, understanding seemed to dawn in her eyes. Either he was going after one person, or he was going after many. Bottom line, he was gonna make somebody pay. Softly, she whispered a name that caused pain to flash across his chest. All this was his fault. Now it was up to him to set things straight. He bent down and kissed her sweetly on her forehead. He said, "Don't tell anyone else. If it gets out that I knew it was him, I'll be the number one suspect." Kissing her once more, he said, "I love you, Yazzy."

"I love you too, JJ." Rubbing his face, she said, "Please be safe. I need you to come back to me." He promised he would and then walked out of the room.

He was halfway to the stairs when he heard a voice shout, "James! Where are you going?" Turning, he saw Sammy trotting up the hall towards him. James took off at maximum speed to derail his father's intervention. There wouldn't be any arrest or trials, but James would make sure justice was served. Even though the Knight family had lost a lot over the past month, by the end of the upcoming day, it was his goal to add to that list.

• •

Sitting outside the hospital, the man had decided to leave his white Durango in his garage for something a little less conspicuous. He'd had a busy day and from the looks of it, this night was far from over. But everything was working according to plan. Just a few more ducks to line up and he could go home and get some rest.

He'd actually been at the hospital for hours, so the last 15 minutes of activity was a welcome sight. First, James had arrived on his motorcycle. The boy had been in such a rush, the bike had almost toppled over when he hopped off. Probably, the only thing that kept him from laying the machine on the ground, was his hope that he'd need it to get to his next destination.

Then, Sammy had pulled up in a slate gray, 1969 Camaro that damn near shook the whole area with the roar of its engine. He was also in a rush, but he was far less reckless than his son. He locked and secured his vehicle, looked around the area like he could feel someone watching him, and then hurried into the hospital.

Within ten minutes, James was back outside, running full tilt for his bike. The man chuckled as he watched James roar off before Sammy could make it out of the building. When he did emerge, he realized he was too late and went back inside. It didn't take a genius to figure out that he was on his way to have a candid talk with Yazmine about his son's travel plans.

Well, there was nothing else he could do at the hospital, so he turned over the engine of his black Chrysler 300 and headed to the next scene of this little drama. Pulling out his phone, he had to alert the rest of the characters that their roles were coming up.

Alex answered with a simple, "Yeah."

"He's on the way. You know what to do. I'm about five minutes behind him, but I'll only expose myself if I see a need to."

"There won't be a need," said Alex. "If anything goes wrong, I'm gonna kill the bastard and dump his body where it'll never be found."

"Don't forget we have a deal," the man reminded him. "If you kill him before you get what I need, you're gonna end up in a world of hurt."

"Hey, you son of a bitch! Don't threaten me," yelled Alex. "I said I got it, so I got it. Don't forget, your fingerprints are all over this. If I were you, I'd be very careful about throwing threats around."

Driving down the road, the man chuckled again. "Just do your fucking job. The second you try to outsmart me, I'll wipe your whole family off the map. One phone call and all of you are dead. As far as any evidence you think you have, I know some people who will make that disappear right along with you. Now, I'm a man of my word. You get what I need out of James, and I'll make sure you're safe. You don't, and you might as well kill yourself and I might leave your family alone." Hanging up, the man threw the phone over to the passenger seat and continued on his way.

He had little confidence that Alex could achieve his goal, but his failure wouldn't affect the man one bit. What Alex didn't understand was that it was over for him either way. His life was forfeit the second he pulled into that lot in South Carolina. But, even with the death of Alex, the man still had one more person that needed to be taken care of, two if Alex could extract the information from James before he died. It was a lot of death but that's just how things had to go sometimes. No matter how it went, in a few days, the man would finally be in a position to fulfill his dream.

Chapter 15

James knew exactly what he needed to do. Although at times he could be quite reckless, at others he could be very calculating and effective. His victim had to be up waiting for him to show his face. If James believed the bastard was prepared for his arrival, then he needed to make some preparations of his own.

With it being July, the sun would come up not long after 6:00am. Looking at his watch, James could see that he had a little over three hours left to do what he needed to do. Right now, he was sitting down the street from his target, trying to ascertain what the trap set for him consisted of.

Directly after leaving the hospital, knowing his dad would be trying to interrogate Yazmine on his whereabouts, he had hightailed it back to his house. After changing into an all-black sweat suit, he gathered a variety of things he thought might come in handy for his mission. Then he loaded everything into the Aston Martin Vantage Coupe that he'd retrieved from Tim Earnhardt a couple days ago.

The trip from his house to his next destination hadn't taken long and James felt the time was right for him to make his move after studying the situation. Exiting the car, he loaded up all the things he'd need and slowly walked the block and a half to the target house. Everything was dark and still, but he wasn't fooled. There was no way that Alexander Knight Jr. had beaten and raped Yazzy, let her see his face, then wasn't expecting a visit from James.

He had been to the house a couple times when the Knights would have little parties and get togethers that the older couple didn't want any parts of. James was still convinced that AJ only allowed Alanah and Amia these parties at his house so that he had easy access to their friends. There had been rumors floating around for a while about his possible use of the date rape drug on the young girls, but there was never any evidence to support the allegations. James knew the man was capable of anything, and after what he'd just done to Yazzy, payback for his transgressions was on the horizon.

James never stopped scanning the area for threats as he eased himself out of the nearby bushes and pressed his back against the vinyl siding. From there, he worked his way to the back of the house so that he could use the wooden fence surrounding the backyard to hide from prying eyes. Still looking for the trap, he pulled a flat piece of metal out of his pack and scurried over to the backdoor.

Sliding the metal between the door lock and jamb, it took mere seconds to jimmy the door open. Taking one last cautious look to survey the area, he stepped inside and gently closed the door behind him.

He had the black toboggan to contain his dreads, and he also had on a black pair of leather gloves, what Yazzy used to call his fight clothes when you added in the sweat suit. But James wasn't here to fight this time. In the darkened interior of the kitchen, he pulled out a 9mm Glock with attached silencer that he'd picked up at a gun show last year. It was definitely illegal, but money could make the law look any way you wanted it to.

The house had three small bedrooms. Growing up, AJ stayed in the smallest, Alanah and Amia shared the middle room, and Alex and Amanda slept in the master. When AJ was forced out for his abuse and rebellious attitude, Alanah moved into the small room because it was the farthest from their parents sleeping quarters. Walking down the short hallway off the kitchen, he checked the smallest bedroom first.

Pushing the door open, all James discovered was an empty room. The room didn't have a closet, but it did contain a full-sized bathroom through a connecting door. He guessed that the previous owners had wanted to add a room they could rent out because whomever stayed in this room really didn't have to interact with the rest of the residents.

James stepped inside the room and a myriad of emotions and visions assaulted him. Alanah and her family had moved out of this house only months after James had started dating her, but they had shared a lot of first in this area. Their first kiss, first fight, and their first break up and make up. He could still remember their first ever shower together and the first time they'd slept in each other's arms. Rushing over to the bathroom, he quickly made sure it was empty, exiting the area before his emotions got the best of him.

He made his way back to the kitchen and pushed through to the other side where the living room and the hallway leading to the rest of the rooms was located. Thinking he would breeze through the living room and check the rest of the house quickly, he almost pulled the trigger in shock when the lamp clicked on as soon as he entered. The softly glowing light revealed AJ sitting on the couch directly in front of the big picture window. James smiled as he lined the barrel up with his target's forehead.

AJ didn't look the least bit worried as he leaned back with a smile of his own. "What took you so long? I've been sitting here for hours waiting for you."

"You probably didn't expect the gun though, did you?" asked James. "Probably thought we would duke it out and that would be that."

"No," AJ said, shaking his head. "I thought that this would finally push you over the edge. I did give you ample warning that I wasn't done with you."

As bad as James wanted to just shoot the man and exit the premises, something was telling him not to be so rash. The man's behavior was off. It was almost like he wanted James to kill him. "You want to try and talk your way out of this, or do you just want me to shoot and get it over with?"

AJ shrugged. "Do you have any idea the number of people who hate you? And how deep that hate runs? I don't know if it's because of something you did or if it's just who you are, but I've come to realize that not many people like you."

James gave a shrug of his own. "Mostly it's jealousy. The rest of it is the fact that I don't care what other people think. But we're not in this situation because people don't like me, we're here because you're a sick fuck and you need to die."

Smiling again, AJ said, "On the contrary, this whole thing is because of other people." Head cocked, he asked,

"What, you think I wanted to beat and rape Yazmine? I don't have any beef with her, other than the fact she's your slut and she seems to love you. But I wouldn't have touched her with a ten-foot pole if I wasn't ordered to."

James jerked from the confession. "Who the hell would order you to rape somebody? And what does her rape have to do with me?" James was confused and getting angry with the conversation. He hadn't come here for a chit-chat. For all he knew, AJ had called the cops and was just stalling until they showed up.

With resolve on his face, he lined the gun up on his target. "You know what? None of that matters. I'll talk to her to find out anything else I need to know. I came here to end you and that's exactly what I'm gonna do."

AJ seemed to look right at him, and asked, "Well, are you just gonna let this asshole shoot me, or do your job?" Too late, a footfall behind him revealed they were not alone. Something heavy landed on the back of his head and he went down, gun slipping from his grip.

He was lucid enough to roll to his back and look up to see AJ and Alex standing over him. AJ said, "I almost shit a brick when he pointed the gun at me. You would have waited any longer, he would have killed me."

Alex scoffed. "This chicken shit wasn't gonna shoot you. He only kills young girls and then uses his money to get away with it." Pulling out a long piece of rope, he added, "Now let's tie him up and get out of here. Get his keys so we can get rid of that car he parked up the road. And don't forget to pick up that gun and take it with us." They secured his hands and feet, hogtied him, then placed a blindfold across his eyes.

The next few minutes were a flurry of activity. James could hear them cleaning up the area and collecting items around the house. They thoroughly searched him and removed his pack, his shoes, gloves, watch, wallet, and everything else they could take without untying him. They wrapped his mouth closed with tape and finally hoisted him up and carried him outside. The two men seemed to have planned all this out perfectly as he was thrown in the back of a van, and within minutes, was whisked away from the scene.

He had to have been in some kind of work van because the back was completely empty. There was nothing to hold on to when he was jostled around from the turns and bumps. Whoever was driving seemed to be doing the speed limit, but took pains to go over every rut in the road they could find. By the time the van stopped about 30 minutes later, he was bleeding from several new spots because of the rough ride.

The driver got out and James heard a rollup door being opened. The driver got back in, drove forward about 30 yards, and turned the engine off. He got out again and James heard the door slam close.

About 15 minutes later, while he was still laying on the floor of the van, he heard the rollup door open again. The distinct sound of his Aston Martin Vantage drove in, then the door closed once again. All was quiet for about five minutes as James tried to get his breathing under control. All of a sudden, the voices of two men could be heard right next to the van.

Alex: "Alright, we secure him and then we go home so we can be there when the cops show up."

AJ: "But what about me? If the bitch talks, then they'll just lock my ass up."

Alex: "Didn't you give her the message? She knows the guy who set her up will still be able to get to her. She won't talk or her ass is going to jail."

AJ: "Okay, let's get this done and then we'll come back when the coast is clear."

Neither said another word as they snatched open the van's door and dragged him out to the dusty ground. They lifted him up and carried him about 20 feet before dropping him back down. They cut the rope that connected his hands to his feet and then snatched him up and roughly slammed him into a chair. Once they had him secured in his new position, they removed the blindfold so he could see their smiling faces in the darkness of the room.

AJ hauled back and punched him right in his unprotected stomach. James moaned as Alex pulled his son away and said, "Not yet, dumbass. It could be days before we can get back out here. A minor injury now and he could die while we're away."

"I don't understand why we have to keep him alive anyway. He was prepared to shoot me. Let me kill him and get it over with."

Angrily, Alex said, "It aint up to you to understand, you just need to do what you're told. Our benefactor needs some information from him." Looking at James, he said, "How long this goes on will be up to you. You don't have to die, but I'm gonna enjoy fucking you up while you rebel against what I need. We'll leave you alone for now, but we'll be back as soon as we can. You might get a little hungry and thirsty, you'll just have to stick it out until we return." Alex motioned his son to walk away and they both made their way over to the van.

Alex had the sense of mind to check the back of the van with a flashlight and then hurriedly cleaned the few blood stains he found. AJ ran over to the rollup door, opened it, and Alex drove the van out. AJ gave him one more sadistic smile before he let the big door slam close. Now, all was quiet as James sat looking around his huge prison cell.

He knew exactly where he was and it wasn't good news. He was in the farthest most hanger at the abandoned airport in Rockwell. No one ever came here because the buildings were ragged and anything worth stealing was long gone. Bottom line, he was in deep shit. All he could do now was fight his restraints and escape before his captors came back. Or maybe, after he was reported missing, Yazmine would alert the authorities to what she knew. Normally, she would die before breaking her word to him. This time he had to hope she went with her head and not her heart.

In the meantime, he would try to get free himself. They had left his car and he had more weapons in the hidden compartment in the back. One thing he definitely had to do the second he got free; pay the Knights a visit. And this time, don't talk, just shoot.

• •

Sammy was sitting in the hospital's cafeteria staring across the table at the dark chocolate, exotic eyes of his wife, Brianna. All his life those eyes could calm him or enflame him, depending on what mood they were in. Tonight, the beauty and intrigue barely registered because, all he could see in his mind's eye, was his hands wrapped around the neck of Yazmine Salazar.

His son had now been missing for 48 hours, and he was starting to think the worst. He knew James had been to the house because the motorcycle had been replaced in his driveway, and the Aston Martin was gone from his garage. To underscore the fact that James was about to do something stupid, he had left his phone at the house so he couldn't be tracked if an investigation arose.

Brianna reached across the table and grabbed his hand to bring him back to the conversation. "Sammy, I think it's time we go to the police. I mean, Yazmine isn't gonna tell us anything and he could be somewhere hurt, needing to be rescued."

Even though it was July and hot as hell outside, even at night, the inside of the hospital was freezing cold. Brianna was wearing a baggy pair of white sweat pants and a matching hoodie to combat the artic temperature. Sammy was in a similar outfit but his was all black.

Shaking his head at Brianna's suggestion, he said, "If the cops get involved, then we can no longer control the situation. After he just beat those two murder charges, the police won't be trying to save him, they'll be trying to catch him doing something illegal."

"Well, I'm not gonna keep sitting around not doing anything while my child could be out there in need of help."

"I tell you what, why don't you convince your little angel to drop the innocent act and tell us what's really going on. Then, I can go get our son and be done with this shit."

After James had evaded him early Monday morning, he'd ran back upstairs to question Yazmine on his destination. She swore she had no idea where he was going, and she claimed she'd given him no information on who attacked her because she didn't know herself. Sammy could tell she was lying but, short of torturing the girl, he couldn't get her to talk. An hour later, he followed behind James after his numerous calls went unanswered. He had searched his son's home, went and picked up Brianna, who had packed some of their clothes, and they have been at the hospital with Yazmine ever since.

Brianna frowned at him and asked, "Why do you hate her so much? I understand you're mad right now, I'm mad too. But you've always had a problem with her. Even when she was just a little girl."

Looking incredulous, he said, "Look at her! She's the spitting image of her mother! She talks like her, walks like her, and acts like her. That little act she's putting on now is what her mother was known for. Don't act like you forgot how she was."

"But that doesn't have anything to do with Yazmine! Her mother wasn't the nicest person to be around, but she just wanted to improve her station in life. You were rich from the day you were born, and you've been trying to make more your whole life. How much more drive do you think normal people have?"

"But most people don't resort to cheating and whoring and stealing and doing drugs! You think that was trying to improve her life? Anyways, all that caught up to her and it got her killed. Yazmine is a carbon copy of her. Just like her mother got two people killed, and our friend life in prison, Yazmine's bullshit has pulled James in for a similar fate."

Brianna sighed. "Sammy, that's not fair and you know it. What Cedric did was his own decision. You can't blame Sabrina for his demons."

Sabrina Salazar, Yazmine's mother, used to be in their circle of friends growing up. Cedric, Sabrina's boyfriend, was the 16-year-old boy who got life in prison for wrecking his opponent on purpose. Sammy always held the belief that, had Sabrina not cheated on Cedric, none of the turmoil after would have occurred.

When Sammy went public with his opinion, because he was so popular, it wrecked Sabrina's life. As school pariah, she dropped out, started using and selling drugs, and eventually had Yazmine a month after they had James.

When Yazmine was 11-years-old, Sabrina and two other guys tried to rob a drug dealer and she was shot and killed in the process. That was tragic for the young girl, but that was only the beginning of her nightmare.

Sammy, done with the conversation, stood up and said, "The doctor should be finished with her examination by now. Let's get back up there so we can take one more shot at her." Looking resigned, he said, "If she doesn't tell us anything this time, we'll contact the police. Having him in jail is better than not having him at all."

They discarded the meal, which they had purchased but had only picked over, automatically reached for each other's hand, and started the trek back up to Yazmine's room. Sammy squeezed Brianna's hand, which in turn made her smile while looking up into his face. This woman was his heart and soul. There had never been anyone else for him, and there never would be. The sun didn't brighten his day, her smile did. What he was about to do would test her love for him, but he needed her reactions to be authentic. With that in mind, they entered Yazmine's room where he would do any and everything to save the life of his son.

Brianna immediately crossed the room and asked Yazmine what the doctor had said. Sammy softly closed the door behind him and stood staring at the love of his life and the broken, young woman, converse. In a soft, but commanding voice, Sammy said, "Yazmine, tell me where my son is." Her left eye was still swollen shut, her two limbs were still suspended in the air, her body was still all kinds of messed up, but Sammy didn't care about any of that.

Yazmine first looked to Brianna before her eye swung over to him. "I've already told you, Mr. Jordan, I don't know where James went."

Sammy chuckled while taking a few steps closer to the bed. "You know, Yazmine, you're a lying little bitch, just like your mother used to be when she was alive." Yazmine gasped and Brianna opened her mouth to defend the girl.

Before she could talk, Sammy pointed at her and roar, "Shut up Brianna! Stay out of this!" The hurt that crossed her face almost brought him to his knees. He could only push on because he had to think about James and not himself.

Turning back to Yazmine, he said, "I knew your mother well growing up, and she was a lying, thieving, whoring, junky piece of shit, just like you're turning into. Because of her selfish and evil ways, I loss three friends; two to the grave, and one to prison. My wife asked me earlier why I've always showed hatred towards you? Well, this is it. I knew that one day my boy would get caught up in some of your shit and it would get him prison time or killed."

"But... but... but... Mr. Jordan, I... it's not... I don't know..." Yazmine stammered.

He talked over her. "For some reason, my son loves you. I guess a beautiful girl like you has tons of guys falling all over themselves trying to earn your favor. But that's not how it was with James. No! When he decided that he loved you and would be your protector, you were a dirty, worthless, smelly, little girl that no one else wanted. Not even your own parents cared about your wellbeing. But James did. I remember going to the school because, when James came home, he would eat like he was starving. I thought one of the other kids was taking his food. Then I found out that no one was taking his food, he was giving it to you so you could have something to eat at night."

Briefly, he let his eyes cut to Brianna. She was standing at the foot of the bed with silent tears cascading down her face. He could feel that she understood what he was doing, but she hated the thought of what it was doing to both

Sammy and Yazmine. He pushed his feelings to the side because he knew, at this point, emotions could lead to his son never being found.

To Yazmine, he said, "At 5-years-old, James was fighting for you, and he's been fighting ever since. At 18, he almost went to jail for you and, if it had been left up to you instead of a neighbor and a sympathetic cop, you would have allowed it to happen. Now he's out there again, fighting for your ungrateful, selfish ass. Only this time, something has gone wrong. He could be hurt, desperately clinging to life, and every second could be the difference between him coming home or us never finding him.

"So, I ask you, after all the fighting my son has done for you, will you fight for him? Will you fight for the boy who has loved you his whole life? Or, will you be like your mother and abandon the person you claim to love?"

Finding her voice, Yazmine said, "My mother loved me and she didn't abandon me. She was trying with everything inside of her to provide me a better life. And my claim of loving James is and has always been a reality. I would do anything for him to be home safe."

Sammy shrugged like the speech was nothing but words. He said, "Prove it."

He felt that he had pushed as hard as he could without outright threatening the girl. As it was, she was curled up around herself as much as her injuries and restrictions would allow. He could see that Brianna wanted to launch herself onto the bed and reassure Yazmine by wrapping her in her arms. He prayed that she could contain herself, because he thought he'd finally broken down the girl's walls.

After a couple minutes of silence, Yazmine said, "I'm sorry but James had made me promise not to tell anyone."

Brianna, sensing victory, but still being cautious, said, "I know you want to keep your word, but it's gone far beyond merely keeping a confidence. We need to save James if there is still a possibility to do so."

Yazmine exhaled audibly and said, "Okay, but I need to start at the beginning so you understand what you're up against. It's not really complicated, but it could be dangerous for all of us."

Sammy and Brianna crowded around the bed as Yazmine launched into her tale. When she finished, Sammy was stunned beyond belief. Yes, Yazmine had indeed gotten James mixed up in her bullshit, but she might not have been the only one. Sammy apologized to both women for his conduct, but he still felt the ends justified the means. With this new information, though, he didn't have time to hold any hands.

They talked and planned and came up with detailed steps that needed to be taken. They all agreed that the police would only be alerted as a last resort. Sammy, who was itching to be on his way, kissed his wife, and damn near sprinted out of the hospital.

It was 2:00am on Wednesday morning. His son had been gone for over 48 hours. Nothing would be off limits during his quest to find James. So, he made a few stops, got some gear, traded out his vehicle, and then hit the road. He had approximately four hours until the sun came up. By the end of the coming day, he would either have his son, safe and sound at home, or he would be dead. But one thing was certain in his mind; if he didn't find his son, alive and well, his body wouldn't be the only one growing cold at the morgue.

Chapter 16

So, this was to be his fate, thought James. His mouth was so dry he could feel his tongue starting to swell. Hunger made his stomach feel as if it was trying to turn itself inside out. Since he'd had to relieve himself while still secured to the chair, his own stench made him gag. His mind warred between anger and defeat. One second, he was fighting his ties with a ferocious hope, the next, he was slumped over, wishing for the relief of death.

The Knights had indeed been planning this for a while. The chair he was secured to was bolted into the floor with threaded, steel rods. The chair itself was metal with rebar reinforcements bracing the arms and legs. The ropes were tied expertly so that no movement was allowed. When he factored in the assault on Yazmine to get the ball rolling, and the ambush at the house, he was forced to admit that their plan had been brilliant.

He'd watched the sun rise and set twice, so he knew he'd been in the hanger for two days. In the distance, he could clearly see the sky brightening once again. Despair was making him weak as he thought their plan was just to leave him to rot. He had heard no sounds to indicate nearby people, so if they didn't come back, his life was over.

At one point, the thought crossed his mind that Yazmine had set him up. But to what end? Money? She had to know that he would give her anything she wanted. Payback? He had kicked her out of his life which led to one of the darkest and terror filled times of hers. Maybe, when he spurned her latest advances, she'd decided to make him pay for his past rejections. His mind was convoluted enough that anything sounded possible.

Then again, would she go through a beating and a rape just to set him up? Then, he thought about her hair being cut, and the foundation fell out of that direction of thought. James had only met Sabrina, Yazmine's mother, a few times. She'd been just as stunning as her daughter, but was an absolute horrible person. But Yazmine loved her, and he knew that Yazzy's dedication to her mother, regarding her hair, was deeply personal. The thoughts vanished like smoke and he chided himself for his mental accusations.

The hanger started to lighten somewhat with the approaching day and James felt as if this would be his last day on earth. Realistically, he knew he could survive for days with no food or water, but the pain lacing his body was almost unbearable. In an effort to escape the horrible feelings, he let his head slump forward in rest. He thought his nap would last only minutes, but when he jerked awake from the rollup door opening, the hanger was filled with sunlight.

He sat in unexplained elation as the black van inched its way in and AJ jumped out to close the door. James really had no reason to be happy about his captors' return. They could be here simply to shoot him and get rid of the evidence. But the thought of anything happening, other than him just sitting there dying of thirst, was reason to celebrate.

After AJ closed the door, he trotted behind the vehicle that Alex was driving. He pulled the van closer to James than the last time, only about ten feet away, and then turned it so that, looking forward, the van was all James could see. As AJ came closer, however, he immediately recoiled from the horrendous stench floating on the air.

"Oh my God!" he exclaimed. "We didn't think about this part."

Alex walked around the van smearing some kind of gel under his nose. "No, you didn't think about this part. I came prepared." When AJ reached for the tube, Alex jerked it back and said, "Use this as a learning experience," and pocketed the tube. While AJ stared evilly at his dad, it registered to James what the pair was wearing. It made him think dying of thirst might not be such a bad idea.

The duo had on white, plastic onesies that looked like what a scientist wears to a site contaminated with radiation. Black leather gloves and boots completed the image of two men about to put in some heavy-duty work. To add to the sinister look, Alex flicked open a switch blade, nodded to his son, then advanced towards James.

AJ turned around and pulled open the back door of the van while Alex made his way behind James. He tried to turn his head to watch the man's progress, but Alex mushed his head to force him back around. Heartbeat hammering in his chest, James could only wait to see what Alex would do to him. Feeling hands gripping his hair, he started sweating when he realized just how vulnerable he was.

Alex leaned down and whispered, "Any unnecessary noise and you die. Like I said the other day, you don't have to die, but you don't do what I tell you to do, death will be what you pray for." Then, he felt a pressure at the back of his head, and the tape was wretched from around his face.

James took one long deep breath and then moaned with pain. The added oxygen to his system seemed only to intensify the throbbing in his core. He fought to keep his inhales nice and short, and his exhales smooth and even. After a moment, Alex said, "AJ, what the hell is taking you so long?"

A second later, AJ appeared. "Just adding the final touches to the meal." He jumped down out of the van with a McDonalds bag in one hand and a bottle of water in the other. Looking at James, he sat the bottle down, opened the bag, gathered all the spit he could, and sprayed it into the bag. Folding the bag closed, he shook up the fries while grinning at James.

Setting the bag down, he picked up the water bottle and repeated the process. Afterwards, he said, "I know your throat's dry, I just wanted to add more lubrication to help you get it down easier."

Alex walked back around and snatched the bag and bottle from his son while shaking his head. "AJ," he said, "you really are a piece of shit. For someone who didn't want a part in this, you're sure starting to enjoy yourself." Looking over at James, he shrugged and brought the items over to him. He said, "This is all I got. If you don't want it, I completely understand, but it might be better if you just eat it anyway."

James knew he didn't really have a choice. While his mind was screaming at him to turn his head away in disgust, his stomach was growling for him to open his mouth. Feeling so low tears leaked from his eyes, he looked at Alex pleadingly and opened his mouth.

The whole time Alex fed him, AJ laughed at the spectacle. To James, the fries tasted like manna from heaven, and the water tasted like it was straight from the spring. Even though he knew what had been done, he sucked it up and took in the vital nutrients he needed to live. When all the food and water was gone, Alex walked over, grabbed AJ, and they walked away to have a discussion.

James watched the father\son combo have a conversation that started to deteriorate towards the end. AJ yelled, "What information?" before Alex gestured for him to stay calm and quiet down. After Alex finished explaining whatever he had planned, the two made their way back over to James.

AJ hung back as Alex stepped to within a few feet of James. A chill went through his body when he looked up into the man's eyes. The Alex that had just fed him and poured the water into his mouth was gone. In his place was a man who believed he had in front of him the person responsible for the death of his daughters. Without a word or warning, he launched the first punch straight at his nose.

There was nothing James could do as blow after blow landed on his face and head. He felt his skin splitting and swelling, the slick blood making some of the punches veer off target. The beating seemed to last for hours, and only paused when Alex stepped to the side for AJ to take over.

This must have been what the earlier discussion had been about, who was gonna do what and when. While Alex had focused on the head and face, AJ stepped up and started pulverizing his body. James could barely feel the fists striking his torso because his mind was in retreat mode. Instead of pain, all he could feel now was a slight pressure during impact. He wasn't even aware he had thrown up the water and fries until after the beating came to a halt.

Everything was a blur now. Both of his eyes were swollen to slits that made everything blend together into a watery backdrop. The only sounds that reached his ears were the thunderous beats of his own heart, and the tortured pants billowing from his lungs. If it hadn't been clear before, it became vividly transparent at this moment: James was going to die.

He had no idea why Alex had lied and said all he wanted was some information. They had come prepared for murder and that's exactly what they planned to do. There would be no question-and-answer session that ended with James going home to his family. Whatever time he had left would be filled with as much pain as the two men could inflict, and then the bottom of a hole where his body would lay forever.

Feelings of regret choked him. How could one stupid mistake on his part lead to so much heartache and pain? One family already devastated because of the loss of their girls. Now, his own mother and father would feel the sting of losing a child. No more hope of having a next generation, he could already hear his parents' wails of despair floating on the air. Deep down, James felt as if he deserved what he was getting. He just wished all the suffering would cease with his death.

Through the slits of his eyes, he noticed one of the blobs advancing on him again. His heartbeat and breathing was so erratic, he couldn't even hear the man's steps. He felt his head being pushed back and he could vaguely hear vibrations in his ears, but he couldn't for the life of him comprehend the words being spoken. A couple of well-placed smacks seemed to open his brain up to receiving some information.

"Hey! Hey! You still with us?" Somewhere in his mind it registered that Alex was the owner of the voice. "Don't die on me yet, you bastard. I told you I needed some information." James could hear and understand the words, but they sounded as if they were echoing down a long tunnel. In response, all James could do was moan and hope that was sufficient enough to starve off another beating.

The other blob materialized next to the other, and said, "The fucker can't even talk. Let's just kill him, clean this place up, and get the hell out of here."

Angrily, Alex said, "I keep telling your stupid ass that we don't have a choice. If I don't get the info, then we'll both end up dead. Plus, I'm curious as to what he has to say."

"Whatever," said AJ. "If you knew he would have to answer a bunch of questions, then you shouldn't have made it so he couldn't talk. There's no telling how long we'll be here now."

James felt a hand wrap around his neck. "Not a bunch of questions, AJ, just two. Two one-word answers, then we'll be done with this piece of shit." The hand tightened, causing his battered body to shake and convulse from lack of oxygen.

Abruptly, the hand was snatched away and James wheezed and coughed until he could breathe easy again. "Come on, Dad!" exclaimed AJ. "Ask whatever you need to ask and let's go."

James was smacked a few times and then the hand returned to his neck. "James? Nod your head if you can hear me," demanded Alex. James mustered up his strength and nodded his head. "Good, good. Can you talk?" he asked next.

James tried to say yes but it came out, "Yahh." Even that small sound sent a spike of pain from his throat to his brain.

Alex, with his hand still in place, said, "I don't want to hurt you anymore, all I want is for you to answer my questions. You cooperate, we leave, place an anonymous call as to where you are, and you can go home to your family. Do you understand?"

James worked his throat so he could express himself clearly. He said, "Lies!"

Alex squeezed for a second but then let his hand relax. "You killed my daughters, James. I trusted you with them and you returned them in pine boxes. Then, you pulled out your fancy lawyer and used your money and position to get away with it. You deserve this. You deserve to feel a sliver of the pain I feel with every breath I take. I don't have to kill you, and I won't, but only if you answer my questions."

James could feel the blood leaking down his throat. Without medical attention, he didn't think he would last much longer. He swallowed what he could to clear the passage, then said, "Ask."

To try and get James to tell the truth, Alex said, "I am asking this for someone else and I need you to be truthful. Obviously, the case was dismissed, so you don't have to worry about being prosecuted. I'm not recording this; I'll just relay the information you give me and we can all go home."

The man was lying, thought James. But, like it or not, he knew he had to play his game. On the slight chance the man was being truthful, James needed to hurry him along so he could possibly survive this. Once again, James said, "ASK!"

"On the night that Alanah and Amia died, were you racing at the time?"

"What the hell are you asking that for?" demanded AJ. "We already know he was racing. If there was any doubt, we wouldn't be here now!"

"Shut the hell up and let him answer the question!" To James, he said, "Just tell the truth, son. I need to hear you say yes or no."

Time was running out for James. Already, the voices seemed to be coming from farther away. He feared that if he passed out, he would never again regain consciousness. Only because he needed to finish this, he told the truth. "Yes."

The hand tightened a few degrees and Alex said, "I knew it, you stupid fuck. Why would you do that with them in the car? How could you say you love them and then risk their lives like that?"

AJ might have felt the answer was obvious, but Alex had still been holding onto his hope that it had truly been an accident. James shrugged mentally. It didn't matter anymore because he knew he wasn't gonna make it. Maybe it was best to give Alex the closure he needed before it was too late. Off of will alone, James whispered, "Sorry."

"Yeah, I bet you are!" screamed Alex. "You're sorry you got captured and strapped to this chair! You would have never told me the truth if you didn't think it would save your pathetic life!" The hand tightened a little more as the rage seemed to overtake the man's body.

Ironically, it was AJ that talked him down. "Dad! Stop choking him! Didn't you say if you killed him, we'd both die, also? You need to get a grip and ask your last question." Alex seemed to come out of a trance and he relaxed his hand once again.

James didn't even have the strength to cough this time. His body just jerked uncontrollably as it started to shut down. Close to panic, seeing his own life in jeopardy, AJ said, "We're losing him, Dad! You need to ask your question, now!"

Forcefully, Alex grabbed his face so James was looking right at him with his fading vision. He said, "James, make this right. Do it for Alanah and Amia and this family, which you have destroyed with your careless act. Just be honest and we can finally have closure."

James wanted to answer, but he feared the outburst had sapped the last of his energy. Once again, James whispered, "Ask!"

Alex said, "Just tell me the truth. Who was driving the car you were racing? Tell me who wrecked your car!"

James felt his body go stiff. Now that the question was voiced, he should have guessed that's what the question would be. He opened his mouth to give the man the name that he desperately needed to hear. But then Alanah's face flashed in his mind. She was giving him her lovely smile and those teal-colored eyes were holding him captive. She shook her head no, and then started to fade away.

Alex shook him slightly and said, "Come on, James! Just give me the name. Tell me and your nightmare is over."

As far as James could tell, it was already over. Alex was yelling right in his face, but James could barely hear him. His vision was faded to a pinpoint of light. He was fighting to draw every breath he took. But James did finally give him an answer. With a determination pulled from the very spirit his grandparents had used to not take the easy road and fight for what they believed in, James mustered all his will and said, "NO!" before his body went limp.

All his senses faded. The fight finally lost. But out of the darkness, a light started to solidify. He reached with all he was to hold the light in his sight, until he could make out two blond-headed, young women waving to him. He ran, arms pumping in his effort to join the two beautiful souls.

But, no matter how hard he ran, they kept drifting farther away.

Exhausted, he bent at the waist to rest. When he looked back up, the light had completely faded away. James walked on in darkness, only one thing driving his march: He had to catch up with that light, if only to explain how deeply sorry he was that he'd extinguished it in the first place.

• •

Alex continued to shake the boy. "James? James? Come on man, give me a name!" The stillness of death had claimed the body, but Alex could see he wasn't dead. He still breathed and, although weak, his pulse still pushed his blood through his veins. Standing up straight, he conceded that this round was over. They would have to come back another time to get the answer to that last question.

Turning to the side, he noticed how quiet and pale his son looked. He also understood the importance of extracting the name from James. They would both suffer the same fate if James didn't pull through to give them the information. But time was running out. So far, Sammy hadn't reported his son missing. That could change at any second. And because of the dismissed case, Alex would be the number one suspect.

AJ, looking sick, asked, "Is he dead?"

Alex shook his head. "No. He's close, but still breathing."

"Dad, I think we just need to kill him and clean this place up."

"I've already told you, we have to get a name first. If we don't, the person who set this up is going to kill us."

AJ said, "Not if we kill him first." Alex was already shaking his head, but AJ said, "Hear me out, Dad!" Alex gestured for him to talk. "This isn't gonna end with the death of James. Once we kill him, this guy will have other people he wants us to kill. The second we don't do what he asks, he'll either kill us or burn us. I don't want this asshole having that kind of power over me."

Alex thought about it and realized his son was right. The man would have power over both of them for the rest of their lives. But wanting to know the mystery man's name was starting to consume Alex. When it came down to it, even though James had stupidly raced with them in the car, the other guy had killed his daughters. He wanted to know who the guy was. He explained this to AJ, but he wasn't trying to hear it.

"Let's kill this asshole here and now, go end the idiot who planned this whole thing, and then go about our lives so no one will suspect us. James already said no. He's at death's door and he's still refusing to give up a name. We're just wasting time, and the more time we waste, the closer to prison we get."

Alex turned and stared at the slumped over body of James. It didn't matter if he gave them the name or not, he was gonna die. James wasn't stupid. Even though Alex tried to convince him he'd let him live, James knew it was over for him. Alex wanted that name. He would give it one more go, tomorrow, and then he would end this whole ordeal.

Turning back to AJ, he said, "You're right. You're out of it now. I want you to make yourself as visible as possible from now on and I'll handle this situation."

"But Pops…" AJ tried to complain.

"Don't fucking argue with me! I'm telling you, you're out. If anyone goes down for this, it'll be me. After I try one more time to get the name, I'll go and take care of the planner too. But I'm not taking you down with me. And that's final! Let's go!" he said while walking to the driver's side of the van.

When he got in, AJ was still standing there staring at James. "Dammit, AJ! I said let's go!" Finally, he turned and trotted next to the truck to open the hanger door when they arrived. Once they were out and on their way home, he looked over at his son.

AJ was scared, but he was also acting strange. He couldn't quite put his finger on it but something was definitely wrong with him. Maybe he was having second thoughts about all of this. Either way, Alex was gonna have to keep an eye on him in the future. Thinking that it might finally be the thing that broke his wife, but seeing no other alternative, Alex amended his plan to include the murder of his son if it became necessary.

Chapter 17

Detective Maxwell Hall was once again out doing rounds hours after his shift had ended. Even he knew that working this much was unhealthy, but so was sitting at home watching TV all night because he couldn't sleep. At least this way, he could do some good for the community he was hired to serve.

Wednesdays were always a slow time for this area. Even criminals seemed to experience the lethargy of hump day. While all the responsible citizens were collecting their energy to finish out the work week, the bad element was trying to stay out of sight while they planned their future weekend endeavors. All this left Max with nothing to do but drive around hoping that something would come up.

What he really hoped would happen was that he'd cross paths with a blacked-out Mustang Shelby. After James had somehow convinced the judge to dismiss the charges against him, catching the other driver was the only hope he had of achieving justice. But Max wouldn't commit the same mistake this time. There would be no booking or questioning or courtrooms, there would be a post-mortem investigation, and a closed case.

It wasn't like he'd never been involved in unsolved cases before, but this one was personal to him. This case embodied all that was wrong with the justice system. The rich got away with everything the system could safely allow them to, while the poor were turned into state sanctioned slaves. To be honest, he really didn't care about the fate of the downtrodden citizens, he just cared about knocking the rich off of their high horses. And yes, Max wanted to be rich himself, but he would never turn into an obnoxious snob like Sammy Jordan.

Just thinking the name put a damper on his already foul mood. He was getting sick and tired of the bastard always coming out on top. If he could think of some way to kill the man and keep suspicion away from himself, he would do it and retire a happy man. Max was aware it was foolish to hold onto a 25-year-old grudge, but his mind wouldn't let it go. Every time he closed his eyes, he relived one of the many humiliations Sammy had forced upon him. He knew he would never have peace until he could deliver the same type of feelings to his rival.

Sighing heavily, Max turned his car towards home, accepting defeat for tonight. He would keep investigating, keep searching for the other driver, until he had a suspect in his sights. While doing that, he would use his very formidable brain to think of more ways to bring Sammy Jordan to his knees.

Arriving at his one-story, two-bedroom home, he parked his unmarked in the driveway. He had a detached 2-car garage, but rarely had reason to drive either vehicle inside. Mostly, he worked, so for his day-to-day activities, he used the department's car. Maybe if he could achieve a couple of his most important goals, he could turn in the cruiser and pull out his own vehicles more often.

After a string of police car robberies a few years back, they were not allowed to leave any weapons in their cars.

Dutifully, he put his shotgun in a carrier, slung his rifle strap over his shoulder, and followed the path to his front door. Tonight, he was extremely thankful for the three acres surrounding his home. He just wanted to go in, have a drink, maybe catch a good movie, and end this day on a high note.

Entering his black as pitch living room, he dropped his hardware on the couch in route to the equally dark kitchen. Once there, he grabbed a chilled mug and bottle out of his freezer and slumped heavily at the table. He filled the cup halfway, took a few deep gulps, filled the cup back up, and then sipped leisurely as he leaned back and relaxed. There he sat for the next 15 minutes. He didn't get drunk, but by the time he stood up, things just didn't feel that important anymore.

He stored the alcohol in the freezer for later use, and made his way back to the living room. Turning right, he trudged down the hallway and made a left into the master bedroom. Pulling the gun out of his holster, he set it on the bedside stand and walked over to his closet. Once inside, he pushed some clothes out of the way to reveal the safe hidden in the back. He had a couple of things to check on before he could completely clock out for the night.

Inside the reinforced, theoretically indestructible safe, was enough evidence to put him away for a few lifetimes. Money, guns, drugs, documents, everything that a successful criminal needed to get rich and stay that way. The contents of the safe were dangerous and very explosive. But the evidence it contained on other people is what allowed him to sleep peacefully at night. Pulling out one of the phones lying on the top shelf, he returned to the bedroom to check how his numerous endeavors were doing.

He smiled at some of the messages, but grimaced at others. It was hard to find good help these days. The main problem was that most criminals were stupid. If a person wanted to be a doctor, they went to med school to learn the ins and outs. These idiots in the streets thought all they had to do was watch a few movies, put on a mask, and they were ready to outsmart the police. Being tough on crime isn't the reason why prisons are packed, stupid ass people committing the crimes was the cause. Shaking his head in disgust, he got up and tossed the phone back in the safe before slamming it shut and rearranging the clothes.

Max jumped in the shower, trying with little success to think of solutions to a few of his more pressing problems. He padded naked back into his bedroom, got dressed in shorts and t-shirts, never really reaching any concrete plans he could send to his minions. Shrugging, figuring he'd handle it tomorrow, he grabbed his regular phone and walked back to the living room to find a good movie.

He picked up the remote, stretched out on the couch, and started scrolling through what Netflix had to offer. Pausing, sensing something was wrong, he looked around the room wondering what was nagging him. Whatever it was had his instincts going into overdrive. He had just realized what it was when the voice said, "You move a muscle and this will end up being a very short visit."

The voice coming from behind him sent a chill racing down his spine. He didn't move as he mentally kicked himself for not realizing his gun case and rifle were missing from the couch. He heard no footsteps on the carpeted floor, but he definitely felt the gun barrel mashed up against the top of his head. He rolled his eyes up and stared into the demonic eyes of his longtime enemy, Samuel Jordan Jr.

Sammy smiled and said, "I've been waiting for you to come home all day. I need to warn you; I don't have the time or the patience to deal with your shit. So, tell me where my son is, and I'll leave you to continue your sad and lonely existence."

With a confused look, Max asked, "James? You talking about James? How the hell would I know where your son's at?" Sammy eyed him for a minute, shrugged, and shot him in the foot. "AHHH!" he yelled, sitting up and grabbing the injured area. "What the fuck, Sammy? I'm a cop! Oh God!"

Still calm, Sammy said, "That can be the only injury you get tonight, but that's up to you. Tell me where James is or I shoot you again."

"What the hell are you talking about, Sammy? I don't know where your son is!" he screamed. The next, near silent, shot blew his shin to smithereens. "Ahhh! Ahhh!" he exclaimed, now rolling around on the floor. "Why are you doing this? I swear I don't know anything about James!"

"She talked, Max," he said in a neutral tone. "Yazmine told us everything. About how you caught her transporting drugs out of the club in Charlotte, and how you held on to the evidence to blackmail her. She told us how you forced her to wear a wire when she visited James in the hospital. Even explained the new deal, and its perverted terms, when she couldn't get James to talk about the case. But the kicker is, you're the one who called her and told her to come to the parking deck where Alexander Knight Jr. raped her after beating her up.

"Way too much of a coincidence," he continued. "If that isn't enough to convince you, the idiot you sent also ran his mouth. While he was brutalizing that young woman, he told her that this was a setup to get James to an undisclosed location. Since I peg you as the mastermind, you must know where that location is. So, I'm going to keep shooting you until you tell me what I want to know, or you die."

When Max continued to roll around on the floor moaning, Sammy brought the gun up once again. "Alright! Alright! I'll talk, just.... give me a second."

"I'll do you one better," said Sammy. "I'll give you three seconds and then I'll start aiming at vital parts. One... Two..."

"He's at the abandoned airport in Rockwell!" Max proclaimed. "I got a text saying that he's alive but in pretty bad shape. Alex and AJ said they were leaving him alone until tomorrow night when they'll question him again."

"Question him about what?"

"I just wanted to know who the other driver was. I didn't tell them to hurt the boy, I only wanted to find the man who hit me on my head. All the violence was them trying to get some get back for Alanah and Amia."

Sammy studied the man for a minute, then said, "Get up." When he hesitated, Sammy pointed the gun at his chest and Max sprung up off the floor. Sammy said, "Down the hall. Let's go."

Max hopped down the hall on one leg, grimacing and hissing the whole way. Halfway, Sammy said, "To your room." Once they entered, Sammy ordered him to freeze while he went and collected the handgun off the end table. Then he pointed to the closet and said, "Open the safe."

"Safe? I don't have a safe," Max said. In response, Sammy flicked the gun up and shot the detective in his left elbow. "Goddd! Come on man! Ahhh!" He fell back on the bed, but when he looked up, Sammy was aiming at the other arm. "OKAY! Okay! Wait a second! Just… Wait!" he said, with his hand up in defense.

Stone faced, Sammy said, "Move! Now!"

Max got up and staggered into the closet with Sammy pressing the gun to the side of his head. Growing weak from the blood loss, he pushed the clothes out of the way and entered the digital code to the lock. When the door clicked open, Sammy grabbed him by the neck and threw him to the floor. With his gun aimed at his mid-section, Sammy said, "Move and you die," before turning to peer into the safe.

On first sight, it was plain to see that Detective Maxwell Hall was a full-fledged criminal. Money, drugs, guns with the serial numbers filed off. There were also several bags lined up with the word "Evidence" scrawled across them in bright red letters. Sammy turned back towards Max and said, "You want to live, stay exactly as you are. I don't need to keep you alive, but I really don't need to kill you either. I'm taking everything in this safe, then I'm gonna tie you up and go get my son. If he's not where you said he's supposed to be, I swear I'll come back and kill you."

"He's there, Sammy! I swear it! I never told them to hurt him. I just wanted the name of the other driver."

"Whatever. I don't care about what you wanted." Pulling out a duffle bag from his waist line, he opened it and started filling up the bag with the contents of the safe. He had no idea what was important to who, so he was gonna take it all and sift through everything later. Once finished, he shouldered the bag and directed Max to crawl back into the bedroom.

Max felt himself fading as the blood loss was getting more severe. He needed the hospital desperately. He said, "You got what you came for. I can't even report this how it happened because all that evidence can be tracked back to me. We can get past this, Sammy. Just go get your son, let me call an ambulance, and our paths will never cross again."

Sammy looked down on him as he lay sprawled next to his bed. Sammy sighed and said, "You don't need an ambulance, Max."

"Sammy, I really do. I'm fading fast man. I need help. Just go now so I can make the call."

Bringing the gun up level with Max's chest, Sammy said, "You misunderstood. You don't need an ambulance because I have no intentions of letting you live."

"Wait! Wait, Sammy!" Gathering his breath, Max said, "I'm still a cop. Right now, I can work this so it ends here.

If you kill me, you'll have the whole department on your ass."

Sammy's smile took all the fight out of Max. It spoke of a long ago decided outcome that he had no power to alter. Sammy said, "Fuck you. I tried to teach you back in the day to leave what is mine alone. You didn't listen then and you won't listen in the future. 25 years you've held onto this grudge. Well, it ends tonight."

"No! Don't…" The gun was silent, but the three bullets entering his chest were the loudest sounds he'd ever heard. He was on fire, then everything went cold. He couldn't breathe, and the only sound he heard was a loud ringing in his ears. He wasn't feeling any pain, but he almost wished for it. The numb feeling overtaking his senses alerted him to how close the end truly was.

Sammy didn't even stay to see his last breaths. He walked through the house spraying a type of acid that was designed to destroy any forensic evidence left behind. After that was done, he eased out the back door and, sticking to the shadows, made his way back to his car over two miles away.

He made one stop to stash the evidence where only he could retrieve it, then he set off to get his son. Both of the Knight men would die tonight, also. Everyone who had a hand in this would pay the ultimate price. Sammy had never considered himself a killer, but for his family, he would take on the devil in hell. But, as he zoomed down the highway, it was God that he called upon. He didn't care what punishment he had coming for his sins, all he asked God to do was to please protect his son until he could get there and take over the job himself.

• •

Alex has good instincts, so when his gut tells him something is wrong, he never ignores it. While Amanda slept beside him, the feeling of impending doom had kept him wide awake. So, he'd gotten up and prowled around the house, going from window to window, expecting at any moment to see uniformed officers surrounding his home. If the police weren't what was setting off alarm bells in his mind, he wondered what else it could be.

The last message he'd gotten from Detective Hall had said to take his time and make sure he got the name. The cop had admonished him for beating the boy before he'd secured the identity of the unsub, but told him all was good. James hadn't been reported missing, so they had some time to play with. Thinking of Det. Hall or James didn't cause his hackles to raise, so he was still feeling wired when he sat down in his recliner.

In the darkened room, he replayed everything that transpired over the last few days. Even though the whole situation was extraordinary, everything was pretty much going as planned. But, something didn't sit right with him and he needed to figure out what it was. He would be leaving AJ to go back out tomorrow night... Something about AJ... It was floating around in his mind but he couldn't grasp the thought.

Alex felt his son had come a long way since the days of his rebellious youth. Maybe it had been a mistake to include him in something like this. He had gone from an unwilling participant, who had to be threatened to do his part, to a

259

joyous member of the team. Then, as soon as Alex started questioning James, AJ had become adamant that they abandon that plan and kill James instead. Even suggested going after the cop also.

He got that tingle deep in his gut that told him he was on the right track, but he still couldn't connect the dots. Standing up, he knew the only way to reach any type of conclusion was to go to the source. He retrieved his clothes, dressed out in the living room, and exited his home. Starting his truck was sure to wake his wife, so he set off walking the block and a half to AJ's house.

As expected, the structure was dark when he arrived. Both of them had been on edge for weeks, sleep was something they both needed at this point. He walked up to the door and rang the bell. After 30 seconds of hearing no movement, he rang the bell again. Still nothing.

He pulled out his phone and dialed his son. Vaguely, he could hear the ringing of the device from deep inside the home. Pressing the bell over and over after the call went unanswered, that feeling of dreed filled his core once again.

Alex hadn't anticipated his son not answering the door, so he hadn't brought his keys. He had pictures of his son, with bloody wrist floating in the tub, running through his mind. Launching his weight at the door, he was preparing himself to find his last remaining child dead by his own hand. After crashing into the door twice more, he burst inside and quickly searched the rooms for his son.

Slit wrist, a gunshot wound to the head, poison, pills, or even hanging wouldn't have shocked him at this point. He understood that something had malfunctioned inside of his son. But when he arrived at the last room, nothing could have prepared him for what he found. Not knowing how to deal with the discovery, he quickly fled out of the house and ran full speed back to his own.

Chapter 18

The thunderous roar of the engine seemed to shake the whole building, as well as James' soul. He actually smiled at the predictability of the whole situation. Of course, when the hanger door had rolled up this time, no black van had been in sight. But the Ford Mustang GT500, belonging to The Black Sheep, had rumbled in loudly to announce its presence.

The man himself exited the vehicle, closed the hanger door, jumped back in, and roared his way over to James. Since it had to be somewhere close to midnight, the whole area was pitch black. The Mustang had its high beams pointed right at his face when it rolled to a stop about six feet away. The Black Sheep revved the engine menacingly, then cut the car off, throwing them into darkness.

Getting out of the car, James could barely see the man as he strolled to the hood and leaned back against it. James didn't know what to expect. Would the man shoot him? Beat him to death like he'd attempted to do to him? Or was he there to talk? Seeing as James was hungry, thirsty, and just plain sick of all this bullshit, he decided to cut to the chase.

"What took you so long? I thought you would have doubled back as soon as you and your father left. I knew you couldn't let me tell him the truth."

The Black Sheep, AKA Alexander Knight Jr, said, "Had to let myself be seen around town, so when your dead body turns up, people will remember seeing me doing normal things." He pulled a cellphone out of his pocket, turned on the flashlight, and leaned it on the bumper so they could see each other. This wasn't the phone he normally saw AJ with.

Since the beating was hours old, the swelling had gone down some around his eyes. He saw that AJ was dressed almost identical to how he'd been the night he'd whipped his ass at The Strip. All black clothes, black gloves, black toboggan. He was leaning back, looking smug and superior, so James assumed he wanted to talk before he turned him into the dead body he'd mentioned earlier.

James said, "Since it seems you want to talk, explain to me why you just couldn't take your loss like a man? You ended up killing two innocent girls, who happened to be your sisters, over a stupid street race."

AJ studied him for a beat before answering. "You can't understand because you've never lived how I had to live. You call them my sisters like that means something to me. Fuck them!" he screamed. "I never cared for them and I don't care they're dead. All they've ever been were two little bitches that were set on ruining my life."

"How could two girls who loved and worshipped you be trying to ruin your life?" asked James.

"Like I said, you wouldn't understand. You're The Golden Boy. Everyone loves you. Well, I had that love, until Alanah showed up. After that, my parents ignored me and focused on their new little angel. When Amia was born, it got worse. They could do no wrong and everything I did was wrong. I've hated them all my life. When I hit your car, I wasn't purposely trying to kill any of you, but I didn't care if you all died."

James could only stare at the jealous, hateful, evil little boy standing in front of him. He really was a sociopath. He was able to kill his own sisters and have no remorse because he was incapable of the emotion. James concluded that he really was about to die, but the realization brought clarity to something he needed to do.

"Listen AJ, you want to kill me, that's fine. I'm really not afraid of death. But let me tell you a story so the killing will end with me."

AJ picked up the phone and looked at the time before setting it back down and saying, "Alright, I have a few minutes to spare. Make it quick though, I still have to transport your body."

James chose to ignore the cold way AJ talked about murdering him so he could at least try to save a life that mattered to him. "Two years ago, a couple of weeks before our high school graduation ceremony was to take place, Yazmine disappeared. I wasn't talking to her then, but I kept up with how she was because I still loved her."

"Yeah, I bet you did. After the other night, I think I love her too." His smile was cold, but James gritted his teeth and went on with the story.

"Anyway, I asked around, but ultimately, I figured she just wanted to be left alone. So, graduation day came and she was nowhere to be found. Right after I crossed the stage, I got in my car and drove over to the house she shared with her dad. No one was home, but a neighbor told me that she was in the hospital in pretty bad shape.

"I rushed over to Northeast Medical Center and there she was, beat up, raped and not telling anyone who did it to her. She wasn't really receptive of me at first, I hadn't spoken to her in a year. After a while, she started to understand that I was only there to help her. But, no matter how many detectives and doctors tried to get her to talk, she never said a word about the assailant.

"A week later I showed up and I passed her father on the way in as he was leaving. He looked upset, but who wouldn't after their daughter had almost been murdered. When I got to her room, she was inconsolable. I begged and begged for her to tell me what was wrong. Finally, she relented and told me it was her father who had done that to her. She said he'd been raping her since her mother died when she was 11-years-old. She said he only beat her because she tried to fight him and he got mad.

"She pleaded with me not to go, but I made my way to her house and found her dad loading up his car with everything that would fit. I beat him to within an inch of his life while all their neighbors stood and watched. I warned him that if he showed his face in the 704 area again, I would finish him off on sight. Even though the police came and I was arrested, her dad chose to disappear instead of pursuing charges."

"If this is your way of threatening me, I don't think you're fully aware of the circumstances," said AJ, pulling out a gun. "This won't be a fight, it'll be me putting a couple bullets in your head, then hiding the body."

James shook his head. "You miss the whole point of the story. I just want you to understand that you can leave her be after this. She doesn't trust the police and will never report you to them. After you kill me, I'm asking you to leave her alone because she's not a threat to you."

AJ chuckled. "I'm not sure if you understand what a threat is, James. North Carolina has no statute of limitations on violent felonies. That means, 20 years from now, the stupid bitch could have a change of heart, and tell the law everything. But, you can rest assured that I won't kill her. Not because of your pathetic story, but because someone else has been assigned that task. It's out of my hands," he said with a shrug. "She will die before the week is out."

James said, "I don't understand. Who else would want to hurt her?"

"James," AJ said with exasperation, "You're a fool. You think a call from me could have gotten Yazmine to a parking deck in the middle of the night? I got a call just like she did. That crooked ass cop is who got both of us there. He's the one who has to kill Yazmine to keep his name out of all this shit."

"Crooked cop?" James asked in confusion.

"Yeah, the one with the hard-on for your family. That fucking Maxwell Hall."

The revelation made his stomach fall to his feet. Det. Hall? Dirty? He knew the detective hated his dad for some old, high school beef, but the situation was dire enough for him to setup Yazmine, and by extension, James? Since AJ was gonna shoot him, he had no reason to lie, but what he revealed was still hard to believe.

"But, hey," continued AJ, getting up from his perch, "at least you two won't be separated long." Looking speculative, he said, "I wonder how that's going to work. You'll be reunited with my two bitch sisters, and the whore, Yazmine. I'm sure all of your pure souls will end up in heaven. Which one of them will you spend eternity with?" AJ stepped farther into the light and pointed the gun at his head.

James was terrified, but there was nothing else he could do. He wasn't gonna beg this murdering scum, so he stared directly into the eyes of his fateful executioner. AJ nodded and smiled like he respected the choice James was making. The gunshot was loud, and it accomplished two things: 1) James flinched and cried out in surprise. 2) The smile on AJ's face disappeared as he stumbled and looked down at the red stain spreading on his shirt.

Gathering himself, AJ brought the gun back to his original target, not willing to die without taking James with him. The second shot was just as loud and shocking, but this one resulted in AJ being launched off his feet with a hole in his head.

James turned his head as the footsteps echoed up from the darkness to his right. A couple of faces flashed in his head on who it could be, but the man who stepped into the light had to be an angel sent from God. No way was he one of the faces he'd guessed. Either way, the situation wasn't over. The man with the gun firmly held in his grasp turned his head towards James, looked back at the dead man on the ground, then brought the gun up one more time.

All James could do was yell, "NOOO!" as the gun barrel found its target. The blast didn't come but the gun didn't waver. James wondered if God could perform one more miracle to solve the new situation he found himself in.

• •

"Why wouldn't you want me to pull this trigger?" the gunman asked James.

Feeling drained from all the emotional highs and lows, James said, "No more death. I won't pretend to know what you're feeling, but no one else needs to die."

Tears cascaded down the man's face as his eyes bounced from James to the body of AJ. "Look what I've done. I'm a complete and utter failure. My two daughters were killed by my only son, then my son was killed by me. There's no coming back from this. All I need to do is pull this trigger one more time and both of our pain will end."

Alexander Knight Sr. cried tears of defeat as he faced off with James, gun pointed at his own head. James didn't understand why he was trying to talk him out of killing himself. Maybe it was because he was remembering the man who used to greet him with a hug every time he showed up to the Knight home. Or, he was just tired of seeing dead bodies. Either way, James felt something deep in his soul telling him to fight for this man's life.

"Listen to me, Mr. Knight. You must have heard everything AJ said for you to shoot him like that. So, you know this was not on you. Your son just had a troubled soul, but he's resting now. I want you to think about Alanah and Amia and how much they loved you. Remember how they used to smother you with kisses while you faked like you were trying to get away? They need as many people living in their memory as possible. Other people loved them, but there is no love like a father's love towards his daughters."

The gun slid down an inch, but Alex still looked as if his heart was broken. James needed him to switch his thought from the dead to the living. "Think about your wife. She's probably at home right this second sleeping peacefully in the knowledge that you'll be by her side when she wakes up. You've been married to her for 23 years. When she finds out that all her children are gone, she's gonna need you to be there for her. To be her rock that she can lean on."

Alex closed his eyes and roared with his pain, but the gun slid down to his side. With one hand covering his face, he wept in anguish for his decimated family. After a few minutes, he gathered himself, put the gun up, pulled out a knife, and walked over to James. They stared at each other for a few moments until James said, "No one will ever know what happened tonight. You cut me loose and get out of here and I'll take care of all this mess. Just go home and be next to your wife when she wakes up."

Making a decision, Alex walked around behind James and squatted down just as James yelled, "No, Dad! Wait!" Standing ten feet over to the side, Sammy had his gun pointed right at Alex's head.

"Get the fuck away from my son or I'll blow your fucking head off, you piece of shit!" Out the corner of his eye, James saw Alex stand up and heard the knife hit the concrete floor. "Put your hands up and get out here in the open!" Sammy demanded.

As Alex did what Sammy told him to do, James continued to explain the new developments. "It's over with, Dad. Alex just saved my life and was about to cut me loose."

"Be quiet, James. Let me handle this." To Alex, he said, "Get on your knees."

"Dad, just listen for a second," James implored him. "AJ was the one who wrecked my car and killed Alanah and Amia. Earlier today, Alex questioned me about who the other driver was. AJ, attempting to keep his secret, came back tonight and tried to kill me. Look to your right and you'll see Alex killed his own son to protect me."

Sammy glanced over at the figure that could barely be seen in the peripheral of the light. His head jerked back around and he asked Alex, "You killed AJ?" When Alex nodded, James expected the gun to be lowered. Instead, he firmed his grip and said, "Naw, you're just cleaning house. You knew AJ was the weak link, you just made sure he wouldn't be here to crack under the pressure."

"Dad, don't do this. It's over. Look at all he's lost. He's been like family to us, and when you're dealing with family, you have to forgive. Look at me, Dad!" When Sammy turned his head to focus on James, he said, "The one who hurt Yazmine is dead. The man who killed Alanah and Amia is dead. Alex responded out of desperation, thinking that I was at fault in his daughters' deaths. Look at you now! I'm still alive but you're ready to kill to protect me. How can you expect any less from a father who loves his children?"

Sammy shook his head. "They're other things you might not know."

"What? Like this was Det. Hall's plan all along? And the fact that me sitting here has more to do with his beef with you than his quest for justice? I know a lot more than you think. I also know that Alex needs to be getting home so he can comfort Amanda when she wakes up. And, we have our own women who are no doubt worried about us and need to know we're ok."

Slowly, Sammy turned back to Alex. "So, you want to just let him go and then we have to worry about him coming after us in the future?" he asked James.

Alex, having been quiet all this time, said, "You don't have to worry about me ever again. All I have is gone. All that I am is gone. I just want to make sure my wife will be okay because she'll take all this very hard. I'm sorry, Sammy. What I did is inexcusable. But I promise that I'm not a threat to you or your family. And I won't blame you if you don't believe that and pull the trigger anyway."

Everything was quiet as Sammy decided which course of action to take. James could plainly see the inner struggle all over his father's face. The tension was high and, not wanting to disrupt the process, James remained silent, hoping that his sometimes-irrational dad would make the right choice.

The gun didn't lower, but Sammy jerked his head at Alex and said, "Get the hell out of here."

For a man who had recently been about to kill himself, he sagged with relief over Sammy's words. He looked at James and said, "I'm so sorry, and thank you for all your help." Then he got to his feet and ran for one of the side doors.

Sammy watched him leave, the gun tracking his progress, until the door slammed shut behind him. He then rushed over to James, picked up the knife that Alex had abandoned, and cut away his binds. James sagged to the floor from the pain of the blood rushing to his tangled limbs. Sammy rubbed his son's hands and feet trying to speed the process so they could leave.

When he could finally stand, he told his dad, "We have to burn this whole place to get rid of the evidence. Then we have to get Yazmine out of that hospital because Det. Hall is supposed to be killing her to keep her silent."

"Well, you don't have to worry about that last part. Det. Hall is dead. After he told me where I could find you, I got the evidence Yazmine needed from him and then killed the fucker."

"Evidence? What evidence would Yazmine need from him?"

Sammy sighed and said, "I'll let her explain that to you. Just know, in my opinion, she did everything she could to not complete the task she was given." When James still looked confused, he said, "Just... let it go. She was terrified and desperate and did what she thought she had to do to save herself. But, it's really nothing. Let's go on with this burning so we can get back to our family."

James put his shoes on and then rushed over to his Aston Martin, opened the front door, and popped the trunk. Accessing one of the side panels inside, he removed several gas cans containing high-octane fuel. Handing one to Sammy, they went around splashing the walls and floor with the super-flammable gas.

After James moved his car to the outside, Sammy looked over at him and said, "I'm parked around the back. We'll go home and clean up, then we'll go to the hospital. You need to get checked out yourself. You look like shit. Remember, we don't ever talk about this. People will assume and speculate, but we can't give evidence on ourselves. All the girls need to know is that you're safe." Holding his hand out, he asked, "Deal?"

James shook the hand and said, "Deal."

With AJ's body and car still on the inside, along with all the evidence the other occupants could have left behind, James bent down and touched his lighter to the gas trail. Sammy patted his shoulder and then took off to retrieve his own car. Within moments, the gas did its job and turned the hanger into an inferno. Glad that the whole ordeal was behind him, James climbed into his car, pulling off from the scene without a backwards glance.

Epilogue

Yazmine looked up from the wheelchair and exclaimed, "Oh my God! What did you do?"

James had just walked into Yazmine's hospital room four weeks after the fire at the hanger. It was 10:00am and he was there to pick her up and finally take her home. In response to her question, his hand smoothed over his close-cut hair and a smile spread across his face.

"I told you, we're in this together from now on. Whatever you go through, I'll always be right by your side." He walked over and leaned down, kissing her soft lips before rubbing on her equally low haircut.

Her hands came up to bracket his face as she said, "I really do love you, JJ," before kissing him again.

He said, "And I love you, too," before standing up and looking around the room. "You sure you got everything?" At her assurance, he placed her bag over his shoulder and then started the long trek down to the parking lot.

As Yazmine shared some heartfelt goodbyes with the nursing staff, James reflected on the last month. Amanda, predictably, had a massive breakdown after hearing of her son's death. There had been some talk as to whether the Mustang had been the one police had been searching for, but the fire destroyed any evidence that could have linked it to the wreck.

When the body of Detective Hall was discovered in his home, next to a safe containing traces of heroin and cocaine, the police began to close ranks. They quietly questioned Alex, Sammy, and James, but really, they just wanted the whole investigation to end.

True to their word, neither James nor Sammy said a word of what happened in that hanger, so not even Yazmine and Brianna knew the whole story. They probably assumed Sammy killed both men but, they were so happy James and Sammy made it back safe, they didn't care about the details.

James was pulled back into the present by one of the nurses saying, "I love the new haircut, James. You two make such a beautiful couple."

He smiled at the middle-aged white woman and said, "Thanks, and I appreciate how wonderful you've all been. Don't forget that all of you are invited to the cookout this weekend. Even if you just stop by for a few minutes, it would be an honor to have you."

Sammy was throwing a family and friends get together in two days to celebrate the recovery of Yazmine, who was shocked by the gesture. All the nurses promised they would drop by as James waved and sent a clandestine wink before wheeling Yazzy down the corridor.

Thanks to a team of very skilled surgeons, all Yazmine's wounds were healing up nicely. Her arm was almost as good as new, and her leg was good enough that all she needed was a walking boot. Once they reached the elevator, Yazmine looked up at him and asked, "How are Alex and Amanda holding up?"

James smiled because Alex was actually doing good. "I think it helped that Sammy let him come back to the shop. Considering all they've been through, both he and Amanda are doing pretty good." It had taken Sammy a couple weeks to thaw towards Alex, but with consistent pressure from James, he had finally relented and forgave Alex for what he had done. He wasn't sure the men would ever be good friends again, but they were cordial and trying to coexist.

Arriving on the first floor, James wheeled her out and asked, "How long have you been off of your medication?"

Confused, she looked up and said, "About four days. Why?"

He smiled and said, "You'll see." Her look said that she thought he was losing his mind, but she shrugged and turned back forward. Only when she saw what was parked in front of the door did she understand his question.

She inhaled sharply and squealed, causing everyone around them to recoil in surprise. Jumping up, she hobbled the rest of the way out the door, still squealing and saying, "Oh my God! Oh my God!" over and over again.

She lumbered over to the creamy-purple McLaren 570S and snatched the driver's side door open. After a quick glance at the interior, which he'd had redone so 'YAZZY' was spelled out all over the place, she spun around and asked, "You did this for me!" He walked closer and nodded, barely getting his hands up to catch her when she launched herself into his arms. "Thank you! Thank you!" she said, smothering him with kisses.

He hugged her tight as he laughed at her enthusiasm. "Alright! Damn girl, you gonna drive the thing or what?" The nurses, who had known about the gift and made their way down to see the reaction, watched on with tears in their eyes. Finally, Yazmine released him and dove into the driver's seat.

The nurses hooped and hollered as James jumped into the passenger seat and Yazzy roared off from the curb. James glanced over with a smile, but it quickly faded when he saw the tears coursing down her face. Pulling up to the exit, she dropped her head into her hands and bawled like a baby.

"Hey! What's wrong, baby?" he asked, pulling her over so he could wrap her in his arms. A horn beeped behind them, but he waved the car to go around as he continued to hold his girl. "Tell me what's wrong! Did I do something? I'm sorry, Yazmine!"

She shook her head and said, "I'm just so happy." Leaning back and wiping her eyes, she said, "I hate that my happiness came at the expense of so much death and pain, but I'm so happy that you're back in my life. I missed you so much, JJ." He reached over and pulled her in for another hug as she said, "The car is nice, but you know, all I've ever wanted was you."

"Yazzy," he said, kissing her softly. "You got me. You've always had me. I was just too stupid to open my eyes and see the blessing God had given me."

Looking sad, she said, "I still have to tell you what led to this situation with AJ and…"

"No, you don't." When she started to say more, he leaned in and captured her mouth in a soul searing kiss. Pulling back, he said, "None of that matters. You did whatever you had to do and it led to us sitting here right now. So, whatever it was, I'm extremely thankful you did it." She searched his eyes and, finding nothing but honesty and love, she smiled and leaned forward for another lingering kiss.

By now, several cars were lined up blowing their horns in annoyance. They separated and laughed as Yazmine returned her focus back to the road. She asked, "So, where are we off to?"

He simply said, "Home."

She smiled and said, "Silly, I mean my home or your home?"

He looked at her seriously and said, "Our home, Yazmine. Wherever you want it to be, go to our home."

She reached over and rubbed his freshly cut hair. She said, "I love you, James Jordan."

He said, "And I love you, Yazmine Salazar. Always have and always will."

Smiling broadly, she exited the parking lot and made a left, turning in the direction that would take them home, to the Jordan family estate.

ABOUT THE AUTHOR

Leon A. Burch was born in Philadelphia, PA and now resides in North Carolina. He attended Temple University. L. A. Burch started writing in 2022 and his first book was released in 2024.

To contact L.A. Burch with questions or comments please feel free to reach out to him at authorlaburch@gmail.com.

Author's Message

Just wanted to give a quick message on loyalty. It seems to be a lost art in a world where everyone is out for self. But it is a quality that is desperately needed for society as a whole, and for personal relationships in particular. I just want people to think of the person that's always been there for them. Who had their back even when they were dead wrong. The person who helped you when you had nothing. When you finally get to a place where you can return the favor, don't hesitate. Don't be the guy who always accepts help from others but never return the favor. In other words, be loyal to the people who are loyal to you!!!

COMING SOON

www.ingramcontent.com/pod-product-compliance
Lightning Source LLC
Chambersburg PA
CBHW050713180626
46814CB00002B/424